JEROME
& his women

Also by Joan O'Hagan

Incline and Fall: The Death of Geoffrey Stretton

Death and a Madonna

Against the Grain

A Roman Death

JEROME & his women

JOAN O'HAGAN

BLACK
QUILL

PRESS

To Jim

First published 2015
by Black Quill Press, Sydney
info@blackquillpress.com

National Library of Australia Cataloguing-in-Publication entry:
Creator: O'Hagan, Joan, author.
Title: Jerome and his women / Joan O'Hagan.
ISBN: 9780646943701 (paperback)
Notes: Includes bibliographical references.
Subjects: Historical fiction.
Rome--History--Empire, 30 B.C.-476 A.D.--Fiction.
Dewey Number: A823.3

ISBN 978-0-646-94370-1

Cover design by Amelia Walker
Back cover painting by Dominic West

Printed and bound in Australia

CONTENTS

FOREWORD

A NOVELIST TAKES US INTO WORLDS other than our own—be it the Hampshire villages of Jane Austen or the byways of Germany or London with the spies and counterspies of John le Carré. A novelist introduces us to new people—the respectable, middle-class girls of the Bennet family, the shadowy Smiley and his seedy colleagues. Such novelists draw their inspiration from people they know, but almost always put a disclaimer that all such characters are imaginary and any resemblance to actual people, living or dead, is purely coincidental.

Not so Joan O'Hagan. Here, most protagonists are 'real' people, long dead but once very lively indeed, although the world they inhabited is further removed from ours than Austen's eighteenth-century England or le Carré's mid-twentieth century Europe. The fourth century AD was a time of political turmoil as the Western Roman Empire faced waves of barbarian invasion, but it was even more a time of intellectual ferment and strife. Three centuries before, in a minor province of the Empire, an itinerant religious preacher had attracted quite a following, but had also incurred the hostility of the authorities and had ultimately been put to death. Yet his ideas had continued to win followers until, by Jerome's time, the Christians numbered hundreds of thousands and included the Emperor himself. However, for the previous six hundred years the educated classes had been schooled in the philosophies of Plato, Aristotle and a swarm of commentators and opponents, modifying or disputing these ideas with considerable learning, subtlety and skill. It was going to take more than the fervour of a Jewish preacher and his uncouth followers to persuade them to accept the new religion.

This is the world into which Joan O'Hagan plunges us. We are less accustomed, nowadays, to widespread religious commitment and theological argument leading to violence, though it happened in Europe, and continues today in the Middle East and other regions. In Jerome's day this was the normal climate as Christian thinkers attempted to define exactly what it was that they believed. Jerome was a major participant in these arguments, and his beliefs constitute one main theme of this book.

In particular, Jerome taught that celibacy was the ideal lifestyle to which Christians should aspire. He urged the young to espouse lifelong virginity, and those who had married and been widowed to refrain from remarriage and to commit to celibacy for the rest of their lives. That is hardly likely to be a popular idea in any age or society, and certainly not in Ancient Rome where noble families could boast of Julius Caesar, the Scipios and Catos and the like amongst their forebears and collaterals, and expected subsequent generations to add to the records.

The surprising thing is not that Jerome was unpopular but rather that he had such a following. Of course, he was a highly regarded scholar whose intellect and command of Latin, Greek, Hebrew and Syriac led Damasus I, the Bishop of Rome, to commission him to produce a definitive Latin version of the Bible out of the melange of versions existing in bits and pieces in various languages up to that time. A standard, approved Latin text would do much to unify a Church in danger of splintering. This production, the Vulgate Bible, is the monument by which Jerome is best remembered today, but it is not the central topic of this novel. Instead, it is how a man with no taste for compliments and a fine command of invective won so many friends and followers amongst the upper-class ladies of Rome. They supported him financially, they encouraged him in his inevitable bouts of despondency, and when at last he ran out of defenders and had to abandon Rome altogether, it was these high-born women who established a monastery in the Holy Land where he could live in peace and pursue his scholarly labours.

So while Jerome is a central character, the women in his circle are at least equally important to the story: Paula, his main patroness; Marcella, who speaks plainly to him in his depressions; Blesilla, whose latent asceticism contributes to her premature death; and a wider circle who see in this socially awkward man someone of unexpected vulnerability as well as moral strength.

Thus this is more than a historical novel bringing alive to us an unfamiliar time and society. It is essentially a story about human hearts and minds facing challenges of a kind that, in time, confront us all.

Richard Johnson
Emeritus Professor of Classics
Australian National University

PREFACE

THE EVENTS IN THIS BOOK take place in Ancient Rome at the end of the fourth century, between the years 382 and 385 AD — a relatively short, but critical, timespan which marked a crossroads in the history of Western civilisation. It was crunch time for the Roman Empire, long racked by internal riots and external threats, particularly from the Germanic tribes to the north. Christianity had developed from a splinter group of Judaisim in Roman-occupied Jerusalem into a widespread movement with its own beliefs and rituals which brought it into direct confrontation with the existing social order.

The old gods, with their power to unify their subjects, were being replaced by a new and very different God — one available to all, women too, independent of status. While many of the older generation remained faithful to the pagan gods, others from all walks of life were increasingly drawn to Christianity and, in worshipping a new God, weakened their allegiance to the Empire. In short, if you worshipped Christ, you could not also worship the Emperor. For the Roman Empire, therefore, the political ramifications of the spread of Christianity were dire. Persecution — that time-honoured recipe of governments the world over to opposition — hadn't worked either, as the conversion of the Emperor Constantine himself to Christianity in 312 AD had demonstrated.

Was the spread of Christianity the straw that broke the back of the Roman Empire? Many — most famously, the historian Edward Gibbon — argue that it was; at the very least, most agree that it played a critical role in its eventual collapse. But without recourse to a single authoritative text, would Christian leaders have secured their religion's supremacy in the West? Probably not. It was Damasus I who, in commissioning Jerome to translate the Bible into a single definitive Latin version, accessible to all, who bequeathed to Christianity the perfect means by which to spread its influence and consolidate its authority. In so doing, he firmly established Rome as the centre of Christianity. It was a political masterstroke, the inspiration of which can elude us in our modern era of digital communication.

This book is, therefore, amongst other things, a tribute to that master statesman Damasus I, as well as one of history's greatest, albeit most controversial, scholars, Saint Jerome. If we cannot fully embrace all the conclusions he drew, we must yet acknowledge Jerome's scholarship as well as his sheer energy and passion. It is also a tribute to certain women of Late Antiquity who, rich as they were, were often scholars in their own right and risked everything they had to adopt the ascetic life — an ideal almost unimaginable in today's age of celebrated secularity, individuality and hedonism. First and foremost among these women is, of course, Paula.

The main characters are all historical figures — from Damasus, Jerome and Paula down to Toxotius, Hymetius and Praetextata. Those people who figure significantly are expanded upon in the glossary of names at the end of the book. Some lesser characters are my creations, primarily Aetius and Bassus, whom I felt could well have existed. In an effort to recreate the spirit of this distant age, I have tried to bring them all to life imaginatively, drawing on knowledge of the times where possible, and reasonable inference where it was not.

I have also tried to convey a sense of the heady excitement attached to the theological debates of the day, and the rigorous scholarship underpinning them. As in Ancient Greece, the skills of rhetoric and argument were highly regarded, and matters such as the freedom of the soul and the nature of free will were debated at length and could divide men as easily as bringing them together. (I use the term 'men' here deliberately; in the male-dominated world of fourth-century Rome, that certain women, such as Blesilla and Marcella, were able to leave an impression on history at all is remarkable.)

Central to the whole story is the relationship between Jerome and Paula, a much-speculated subject even in their day. Intimacy there undoubtedly was, but whether it was intellectual and spiritual, or something more, I leave it to the reader to make up his or her own mind. Regardless, the accomplishments and legacy of these ancient people deserve our attention.

Joan O'Hagan
Sydney, January 2014

'What Jerome is ignorant of, no man has ever known.'

Saint Augustine of Hippo

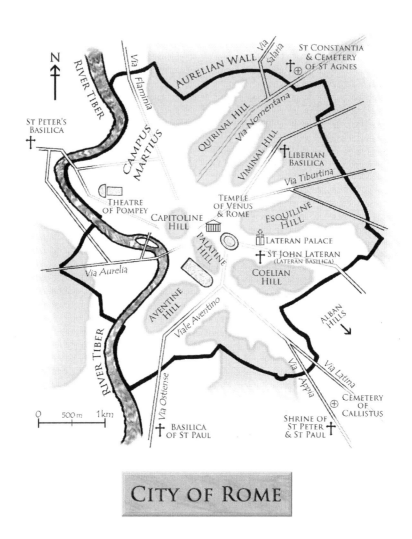

N

RIVER TIBER

Via Flaminia

AURELIAN WALL

Via Salaria

ST CONSTANTIA & CEMETERY OF ST AGNES

ST PETER'S BASILICA

CAMPUS MARTIUS

QUIRINAL HILL

Via Nomentana

VIMINAL HILL

LIBERIAN BASILICA

Via Tiburtina

THEATRE OF POMPEY

TEMPLE OF VENUS & ROME

CAPITOLINE HILL

ESQUILINE HILL

PALATINE HILL

LATERAN PALACE

ST JOHN LATERAN (LATERAN BASILICA)

Via Aurelia

COELIAN HILL

AVENTINE HILL

Viale Aventino

ALBAN HILLS

RIVER TIBER

Via Ostiense

Via Appia

Via Latina

CEMETERY OF CALLISTUS

0   500 m   1km

BASILICA OF ST PAUL

SHRINE OF ST PETER & ST PAUL

CITY OF ROME

NOTE TO THE READER:

AD (Anno Domini, in the year of Our Lord) is used for the convenience of the reader, but was not used in Jerome's time.

PART ONE

THE
COMMISSION

1

'Virgins,' said Damasus, the Roman Pontiff, to Jerome. 'Let us never forget our virgins.'

The old Pontiff moved to an easier position on his cushions and rested his eyes on the view from the window of the Lateran gardens and the gleaming countryside beyond. In this year 382 AD, he was nearing eighty but the hard rock of his personality still dominated any group. He was confident of being the most important figure in all the Roman Empire.

He continued. 'Our dear Bishop Ambrose of Milan has written a fine piece on them in a recent tract. They are "like gardens heavy with the scent of flowers", he says, "like shrines filled with solemn worship." Beautiful images, don't you think?'

'Your Holiness, they are.'

'I myself have written one or two things on virginity, but time lacks, Jerome. In Rome we're short of writings on the fundamentals of our faith.'

'We have never had an Origen, Your Holiness.'

'Ah, the man from Alexandria, one of our most distinguished theologians. Still a great force over there, you tell me?' Damasus waved a hand to embrace the whole of the Roman world right up to the shores of Palestine.

'A giant, Your Holiness.'

'Well, I liked that piece of his you translated for me, about human and divine nature being woven together in the virgin birth of Jesus. That was well said.'

Damasus's eyes glittered. 'We kneel before the vision of Mary conceiving through the Holy Spirit, unstained by virile seed, leaving Christ's flesh free of the stain of the sexual act.'

He added with emphasis: 'The perpetual virginity of Mary is what our congregations should forever have in their minds.'

He pondered before continuing. 'And our Roman virgins and widows bring it home to them. They have an important role. Alone in their bedrooms, turning their backs on marriage, on childbirth, on the demands of their great families — to serve God. Their influence goes far ...'

Damasus gazed at the horizon, and Jerome involuntarily turned to glimpse the gleam of silver tableware in the Pontiff's private dining-room, resting on a gold-embroidered tablecloth.

'Their contribution to our Church is inestimable,' Damasus concluded.

The message did not fall on deaf ears. In Jerome, the words instantly conjured up visions of silken altar cloths and golden veils; of legacies, endowments and gifts; and of immense and valuable properties stretching from end to end of the Roman Empire.

Jerome gazed with satisfaction at the man whom he had at first seen only from afar in synod meetings, a stately figure escorted by obsequious clergy down the marble corridors of the Lateran Palace. Damasus's face was still that of a strong man, and shrewdness glinted in the faded eyes. Despite an occasional quaver, his voice remained authoritative.

'It's only a month or so since you reached Rome from Constantinople. Not long enough to have met our important families, but I shall see that you do. Their ladies are almost all with us and it's largely through them that their menfolk are being converted. And about time, too. More than fifty years have gone by since the Emperor Constantine gave the lead and became one of us.'

Damasus twisted the ring on his hand that so many had knelt to kiss, and regarded the man before him. Haggard as Jerome's face was from long days and nights of study and prayer it had, he reflected, an intensity and dark handsomeness that would appeal to women.

'You'll find that a number of these devout and wealthy ladies are highly educated and eager to study the Scriptures,' he continued. 'I want you to help them in any way you can. They know of your reputation and will welcome you. One is the Lady Paula, who is in my thoughts today. Her husband has died — one of those nobles still committed to the old gods.'

Damasus pondered the rapt face in front of him. Then abruptly he changed course. 'I've read your notes on Apollinaris. Now there's a fanatic! Supports our Nicene Creed, but he goes too far. To deny that Christ had a human mind ...' He paused for a long moment. 'I've heard you attended his lectures over in Antioch.'

'I did, Your Holiness,' Jerome admitted. 'His lectures were brilliant. Such unerring logic!'

'Well, it won't do, Jerome. I was the one who saw the dangers of his views. The Roman Council I called a few years back, as well as the Second Ecumenical Council last year, have condemned Apollinaris's teaching. Brilliant he may be. *Only he's wrong*. Never forget that the test of any creed's orthodoxy is endorsement by the direct successor of Saint Peter — by me.'

Damasus's tone was hard and final. The corners of his mouth turned down, and he added, 'I want you to draft a formula of belief both in Latin and Greek which his followers will have to sign before they can be admitted to communion. To deal with a Greek theologian you need to think in Greek, as you have no trouble in doing. Our Latin fails us continually when we translate such things from Greek, as the whole world knows by now.'

Again Damasus paused before saying deliberately, 'You have studied under a number of different men, some whose views are suspect if not downright heretical. I'd like to be sure that none of these heretical ideas have rubbed off onto *you*.'

Jerome responded with passion. 'Your Holiness, I assure you that as I follow no leader but Christ, so I ask guidance of none but Your Blessedness, of the Church of Peter. My letters from the desert surely make that clear, those letters that begged for guidance when the seamless vest of the Lord was being torn to shreds by the feuds of the East!'

'Indeed. Well, we've no place here for any but the strictly orthodox,' Damasus said sternly. In silence, he looked fixedly at Jerome for so long that Jerome grew uneasy.

Finally, he said, 'For the man worthy of it, I have a commission. Such a commission that all else pales beside it.' He hesitated. 'It would test even you.'

His eyes took in the expectancy of the other man. 'The Bible,' Damasus stated slowly and impressively. 'I need a man who knows not only Greek but Hebrew. I want a revision of the existing Latin translations to produce a single authentic version. Our Church must have one, universally accepted, Bible. We both know the bewildering variety of Latin translations of the Greek version of the Old Testament. It's essential for my man to go back to the original Hebrew. Not something anyone here can do.'

Damasus looked into the gardens again, and back. Finally he ended Jerome's suspense. 'I want you to begin with the Gospels. Your Latin will have to correct all the errors that have crept into existing translations.'

Jerome clasped his hands together. 'Humbly I accept ... cognisant of my poor gifts ... with fear and trembling ... unworthy of this great honour ...'

Damasus watched him curiously. He knew Jerome's reputation as a hugely self-confident writer, as notorious for his ferocious polemic as he was admired for his learning and stylish Latin.

'The work will be heavy and long,' he warned. 'You will get opposition and criticism from all sides — sheer prejudice from many. You must take that in your stride. You'll need help, so I'm assigning you a young man named Aetius, one of the Lateran clergy. Although lowly in rank, he has a good education and is clever. It's true that one of my deacons says that Aetius unsettles some people. However, I've spoken to the young man myself.'

Damasus paused. In fact, the deacon had added, 'What's more, the fellow's a devil. He has an uncanny power for mischief.' But Damasus didn't care for the deacon in question and had thought little of his judgment in such a matter.

'Aetius will call on you when he finishes his present work,' Damasus said, indicating that their meeting was over.

'An authoritative version, Jerome,' he added, as Jerome stood up. 'A version to last down the centuries and unite our Church. It is fitting that it be done in Rome and on the initiative of the successor to Saint Peter.'

The Pontiff's eyes rested on a marble tablet, handsomely inscribed, and fixed to the wall. It was a Catalogue of Roman Bishops which he himself had edited, and updated, nearly thirty years before when he was deacon to Pope Liberius. It was a continual pleasure to Damasus to see his own name on a list which began with Saint Peter as first Bishop of Rome 'under the rule of Tiberius, when Christ was crucified and after His ascension'. The list would outlast rolls of Roman Emperors and Consuls, giving expression to the natural leadership of the Bishops of Rome, ruling in the place of God.

2

Paula, so dear to Damasus, had been at the head of the cortege of her husband, Julius Festus Toxotius, as that late autumn day in 379 AD it wound down the Via Appia towards his final resting place. She remembered clearly the grand parade of noble Roman families, glad to attend one of their own with due ceremony and high dignity and to let the populace see them do it. Down the long avenue marched the lofty green cypresses, the surrounding countryside ripe with the colours of early summer, to the villa of the Julii Festi.

Some of the onlookers remembered the magnificence of the games that Toxotious had given as Praetor, and gossiped about the circumstances of his death.

'Toxotius had an attack down in Campania, I heard,' muttered a distant relative to his brother. 'Out riding, wasn't he?'

'Yes. A fine mare!' The brother was momentarily convulsed.

'What do you mean?'

'Flavia. He died in her arms.'

'How old was he?'

'Fifty-six. Let it be a warning to you.'

'Does his wife know?'

'Bound to. These things always do come out.'

'I know that Paula is a very devout Christian, but you don't see her around much now. Apparently she's showing signs of extreme tendencies ...'

Behind the bier, Paula walked with her children, tense with concentration. She thought of Flavia, that high-born widow who had so captivated Toxotius. Slave women—and there had been many—were one thing. Flavia, with her laughter and vigorous mind, who could hold her own in a roomful of men, was quite another. Slim and red-haired with a caustic wit and arrogant eyes, Flavia wore her clothes — gorgeous clothes — with aristocratic indifference: she was a law unto herself. Paula wondered momentarily if Flavia suffered on this day.

They were at the family tomb now — large, circular, more than thirty feet across and faced with travertine. Inside, a great central pillar already accommodated the sarcophagi of six Julii Festi in its niches. Toxotius's lay ready on the inner wall. Under the light from the flaming torches, ecstatic marble Maenads carved in exquisite high relief cavorted in the cortege of Dionysus. The bearers raised Toxotius's silk-clad body from the bier and placed it inside his sarcophagus. Attendants handed roses to Paula and her children. Wine was sprinkled, then oil. Finally, they scattered the roses over him until his form was barely visible through the carpet of bright red petals.

Toxotius had left Rome fifteen days previously for Campania, as he had done so many times before. This time he had been putting a new horse through its paces in preparation for the hunting season; all the men in his family were keen huntsmen. The domed roof of the tomb was brilliant with mosaic scenes of the chase. When Paula's brother-in-law, Hymetius, had got back to Rome he had given her details of Toxotius's riding accident. The body, however, had shown no sign of the injury which had occurred — or so Paula was told — as he fell from the horse at full gallop.

Her suspicions aroused, she had questioned a slave.

'Had Toxotius's hunting spears been returned?' she asked.

The man had not understood. 'What would Toxotius have been doing with hunting spears?' he said.

'Where did you bring him back from?'

'From Sabaudia, my lady.'

She had said no more. Sabaudia was not noted as a hunting area, but it was where Flavia had a seaside villa.

Paula stood immobile, her hands filled with flowers, staring at the still handsome face of her husband, now covered with gypsum plaster. The great orator Praetextatus was already intoning a eulogy.

Those squeezed inside the tomb fell silent as the tall and elegant old man spoke of Toxotius's career. As Vicar of Asia, Toxotius had, he said, gained a reputation for fairmindedness, diligence and personal courage in defending Ephesus against looting brigands in the surrounding hills. What a soldier he might have made in that long distant age when Roman patricians had taken the field at the head of Roman armies.

Praetextatus paused. 'And Toxotius remained true to the gods of our fathers, who had always protected this city and its citizens ...'

The air in the chamber grew stuffy and heavy with incense. Paula kept her eyes lowered, aware that these people knew that Toxotius had not been the sort to insist that his wife worship his gods. He had been tolerant of her God — only a little concerned about her charitable activities, in case they should threaten the accumulated wealth of generations of her family and his.

'But while we pay tribute to Toxotius's civic virtues, let us not forget his higher qualities,' the sonorous voice rolled on. 'We may be sure that Toxotius looked upon his earthly life as but a point in the infinitude of the universe — the sphere of the mortal and transient, and that he was ever ready to listen for the eternal harmonies of the heavens. He honoured the gods, he followed the divine light which presides over prophecy and healing, over generation and destruction, to which men have given the name of Sol or Apollo or Jupiter ...'

'God have mercy!' Paula whispered to herself. 'He's *lecturing* us!'

Praetextatus's listeners were growing restive. Among the cluster outside the door, one young man muttered, 'The old fellow's launched now ... Forgotten where he is!'

Paula hardly listened. Her eyes were fixed on Toxotius's

whitened face, which she would never see again. Dear God, she thought, is that all that is left of him who for twenty-one years I called husband? She moaned. Ah, if only she could have persuaded him to convert to Christianity, be baptised, her sadness now would have been one set in peace.

Blesilla, her eldest daughter, pressed her hand, murmuring, 'Mamma ...' several times with such love and compassion that Paula broke down. Her sobs caused her young daughter, Paolina, to slip fainting to the floor. As she was carried out of the tomb through a hushed crowd, Praetextatus looked around in startled fashion, coughed and embarked on a conventional peroration for the dead aristocrat.

***

After the funeral, the men of Julius Festus Toxotius's family had returned to Rome, leaving Paula and her children to the women of the house for a few days, out in their villa.

'It all went off very well. Fine oration, wasn't it?' Hymetius, the brother of the dead man, addressed a cousin as they sat one evening in a ground floor room in Paula's mansion on the Aventine Hill.

Cornelius was silent for a moment. 'Did you think of Toxotius as religious?' he enquired.

'He would attend the Mithraeum, out in Ephesus.'

'Really? I didn't know that.'

'Well, a man needs some kind of release from the pressures Toxotius was under,' rejoined Hymetius. 'He had so much on his shoulders: speeding up collection of arrears of taxes, judging appeals in the local courts ... I visited him in Ephesus once. He was advising on the rebuilding of a temple at the time, and you wouldn't believe how hectic it was. '

'I can imagine.' Cornelius spoke feelingly. He himself was well content with a life of seclusion on a luxurious Sicilian estate.

'Toxotius had an instinct for such matters, of course,' continued Hymetius. 'Not afraid to take action, either. Look how he tackled those bandits. In person, once or twice. They were threatening Ephesus at the time. The army commander was ineffectual—Toxotius took over some fifty soldiers himself and made for the mountains. Caught the bandits in a surprise attack on their camp in the foothills and slaughtered the lot—a brilliant operation! I saw what the Prefect wrote about it to the Emperor. A glowing report if ever there was one!'

Toxotius might have gone far under the Emperor Julian. Quaestor in the Imperial Palace? Even Praetorian Prefect ... Both men fell silent, gripped by a vision of the glory that might have been. The death of the Emperor Julian—killed, it was rumoured, by a Christian in the thick of the battle that he himself had taken to the Persians, in the footsteps of Alexander—had smashed the dreams of high office of many a Roman senator. The devout Christian who had taken Julian's place—the Emperor Valentinian, son of an Illyrian peasant—professed no love for the Roman nobility.

'As for me ...' Hymetius sighed and his cousin knew he was thinking back to the time he was charged with embezzlement of public funds while governing Africa in '71, thanks to one of Valentinian's officials who had shared his master's special abhorrence for the Roman nobility. It had almost cost Hymetius his head, and did cost much of his fortune.

'Fine statue the African provincials put up of you later on though,' Cornelius said soothingly as he got to his feet. 'I'd like to have another look at Toxotius's Greek things.'

He led the way to a long gallery adorned with marble and bronze statuary, and paused in front of a skilfully carved head of Apollo. 'This is the prize, don't you think?'

'There's a story about that head,' said Hymetius. 'That's all that's left of a very fine statue, thanks to the Christians. While Toxotius was in Ephesus, all the temples were being restored and the Christians were out to make trouble. The day the Apollo was carried up a ramp into his temple, a violent brawl broke out when some Christians began jeering at the workmen. They lost their tempers and began throwing stones — you know the sort of thing. Toxotius happened to be nearby and brought in the guards, just in time to see a man swing a hammer at the body, then aim at the head. By some miracle the head wasn't damaged, and my brother brought it back with him. Lovely piece, isn't it?'

'I bet he came down hard on the culprits!'

'Oh yes. Those who didn't manage to escape were arrested and … disappeared forever that night. People said he was too severe on them — but he was confronted by abuse of all that the Emperor held sacred.'

'Paula must have been upset.'

'She probably never knew. But they wouldn't have forgotten Toxotius in Ephesus.'

'Oh, he was made of stern stuff, alright. No wonder he was bitter at missing out on a promotion.'

They paused in front of a sinuous statue of Aphrodite, carved in a luminous cream marble.

'He lived it up back here, of course,' Hymetius smiled as he ran his fingers down the goddess's shapely arm. 'A natural host. Those banquets at his place down the coast, tables groaning with delicacies and sumptuous dishes served on gold and silver platters!'

'Rumour had it that those platters were on occasion hurled into the sea afterwards,' chuckled Cornelius. 'Is that right?'

'Oh yes!' Hymetius laughed. 'Toxotius liked to cut a fine figure. But he'd had a net hidden underneath the surface, you know …'

'Paula must have doted on these displays,' said the other drily.

'Very wisely, she went along with all the entertaining.'

'Plenty of golden platters likely to be thrown away now,' Cornelius noted. 'And no net underneath to catch them, either.'

'Eh? Oh yes, I see what you mean.'

'I hope Paula keeps her head. Her gifts to Damasus have already been considerable. Imagine the scandal if she should follow in Antonia Melania's footsteps, selling everything up and travelling around the East on a donkey. A woman of education, and culture, too! Rich as Croesus. Shocking for the family!'

'Paula's very quiet, nowadays,' said Hymetius uneasily. 'She can't have much enjoyed the Flavia business.'

'Your brother didn't neglect his family or estates, though,' Cornelius pointed out. 'Pity his only son is still so young. He waited so long for a son ...'

'Toxotius was the best of husbands and an excellent father.' Hymetius chose his words with care, settling on an image of Toxotius that would, if repeated often enough by future generations of Jullii, effectively expunge the unfortunate circumstances surrounding his death.

'Oh indeed,' agreed Cornelius. 'Paula—'

'Paula,' interrupted Hymetius, 'must be absolutely shattered.'

'Despite everything,' added his cousin.

3

And shattered Paula had been, so suddenly deprived of all the strength and restless energy that had been Toxotius's. For he had been her life since, as a girl of fifteen, she had been given to him in marriage—cement of an alliance between the Julii Festi and her own clan of the Cornelii Scipiones. At the time, Toxotius had seemed all a young girl might desire—that tall, robust man in his late thirties, with his commanding presence, thick brown hair and hazel eyes.

'Little Paula?' she had overheard her father say to Toxotius once. 'A serious child. Remarkable memory. It's a pleasure to hear her recite her Virgil. Homer too—in Greek, you know. She follows her mother, naturally, in her—ah, observances,' he had added—a tame description of the passionate religious conviction that the devout lady had passed on to her little daughter. From an early age Paula had been schooled to disregard the traditional Roman gods and goddesses of her father's family and was nourished instead on the mystery and grandeur of Christ.

Toxotius had, Paula recalled, returned that day from a visit with his brother Hymetius to the Black Sea where the family had property. He had arrived with all the glamour of foreign travel upon him and with the news that Emperor Julian had appointed him Vicar of Asia for the coming year. That had been the second year of the Emperor Julian's brief reign—and his short-lived attempt to reinstate the old gods.

It's all a long time ago now, Paula reflected, and I can only know with my mind how in love I was … She sighed. After their marriage, Toxotius had given her such lovely gifts, taken pride in her education, had been so very generous to her. The little silver flask on her bedside table that he had brought her back from the market in Smyrna with the picture of a Christian saint and some oil from his shrine was still one of her most treasured possessions.

'If I'm to have a Christian wife, I must learn to please her,' he had said, and she had thrilled at the warmth in his smile.

For a time she had entertained wild visions of Toxotius undergoing baptism. But only briefly. She soon came to recognise in him a certain scepticism about things religious, though he respected traditional observances. Christianity might be one of the ways one reached God, he would say, and Paula might worship as she pleased.

But she, in turn, must be tolerant of others — a trait, he pointed out, for which Christians were little noted. He himself, he always maintained, could never accept a god who had taken on human flesh and come so late into the world. It was hardly a matter to be settled by argument, and certainly not with a man so overwhelmingly alive. And their talks would end in kisses, modest promise of passionate nights to come.

She had been excited at the prospect of accompanying him to Asia Minor. When, however, by the end of July of the year 362 AD, she knew that she was with child, he had said kindly, a distant look in his eyes, 'I think you'd do better to stay here, my dear. Travelling isn't the thing for you just now.'

'But there's nothing wrong with me, Toxotius,' she had objected. 'I'm just having a baby!'

He was adamant. 'You can come later if all goes well, Paula. And bring me my son.'

He had left in September, without her. She had felt acutely disappointed and lonely. But she settled down to life as mistress of a villa on the Aventine Hill, chafing at the attentions of Toxotius's womenfolk. Praetextata, the pretty, meddlesome wife of Toxotius's brother Hymetius, was particularly solicitous after the death, from a sudden fever, of Paula's mother. A new vigour was investing the Julii Festi ladies now that their men, after the long reigns of Christian Emperors, were especially favoured at the court of the new Emperor Julian.

There had been no son: only Blesilla, born after a long and difficult labour. And I never did get to Ephesus, Paula lamented. Toxotius's duties and perpetual travelling ensured that the time was somehow never ripe.

Drawn inexorably into her husband's family circle — or trapped, as she called it privately — she found comfort in the rituals of worship. She attended mass, prayed regularly, and kept her fast days. She also began to see a good deal of Marcella, an older woman widowed some years previously who, despite the secluded life she led in her palace — also on the Aventine Hill — wielded surprising influence among Roman high society.

***

That Marcella was a forceful woman Paula could tell from the very first day that she had encountered her, holding forth amidst a cluster of senatorial ladies in her salon. She watched Marcella's strongly delineated features, the lofty set of her head, and her dark eyes.

'Origen.' Marcella had dropped the eclectic name into the ladies' midst, as though offering up a priceless jewel.

And she had, in the short space or an hour or so, lifted a curtain on discussions and activities enticing to a quick-witted young woman, and the very antidote to the stifling attentions of the Julii Festi ladies.

'Consider Origen's words in this passage from his *First Principles*.' Possessed of a formidable memory, Marcella quoted, effortlessly: '"The soul, falling away from the good, encounters and falls prey to evil. If not guided back, it is killed by its folly and transformed into a brute by its wickedness."' Marcella fell silent. 'Well, ladies, what do you think of that? Where, in Holy Scripture, could Origen have found that?'

Her fine eyes searched the faces around her but the ladies, conspicuously, said no word.

'Ah, you are silent,' Marcella continued. 'And rightly so.'

The ladies brightened visibly.

'Plato,' said a sharp-faced young woman, 'claimed somewhere that philosophical souls can be changed into bees and nightingales.'

'We are not concerned with Plato,' said Marcella witheringly.

'There is that psalm,' ventured Paula, 'that talks of the man who has riches without understanding perishing like the insensate beasts ...'

Marcella beamed at her. 'Just so! But if Origen had been thinking of Psalm 49, then he misunderstood its true meaning. What Origen says here is quite against Christian truth, whatever the philosophers may say about the movement of souls. Men may live like beasts—indeed, history is full of them, Scripture too. But only in life, not in death: that is what the psalm means. The human soul is created in the image of God and is destined to rule over the animals. The human soul, inasmuch as it is rational, cannot be transformed into an animal.'

Marcella paused, triumphant. 'Ladies, Origen is here guilty of heresy.'

There was a murmuring.

'I refer such matters to the bishop,' Marcella said. 'Now, in your reading of the great theologians, always be on your guard against heresy—intentional or not. Study your Scriptures with purpose, ladies.'

After the gathering had broken up, Marcella turned to Paula. 'Our work is very demanding, you know, but I hope we will see more of you. Your mind is quick and your knowledge of the Scriptures striking. And you know Greek.'

'Thank you!' Paula said. Her heart leaped. It had been a long time since anyone had made her feel that warm glow inside, since they had told her that she was intelligent, as her tutor had, or her father. She was filled with awe for a woman who had, she knew, read some tens of thousands of lines of Origen and who, furthermore, had examined and questioned them.

Marcella looked into Paula's eyes and held them. 'Why don't you spend some time with us when you can?'

Which was just what Paula had done.

***

On Toxotius's return, after two years' absence, Paula had been in a delirium of happiness, though it was, she immediately saw, an older, harder man who swung himself down on the wharf at Ostia to greet her. That night she begged his pardon for having given him a daughter instead of the son he had so passionately desired.

'We'll make a son this night,' he breathed.

They lived in a whirl of social activity. Toxotius was often absent, closeted with friends, when at their insistence the saga of his strong vicariate in Asia was told and retold. But he was still unfailingly kind and considerate of her, when he was there.

Disillusionment had come swiftly. At a banquet in their villa in Rome only weeks after his return, Toxotius had disappeared with other enthusiastic revellers. Toxotius's mother smiled indulgently to Paula, and the ladies retired to their own quarters. When, towards dawn, Paula went in search of him, she found him asleep naked in the arms of one of her own slave girls.

Jealousy, gnawing at her confidence and pride, had finally given way to resignation. She came to understand him, recognised something of what drove him, even in his whoring. She sensed the savage satisfaction he derived from enforcing his authority out in Asia Minor born of his instinct for life and for danger. Now he seemed to have outgrown the narrow limits of Roman life, his energies finding their outlet only in hunting of wild boar and deer, plaguing the overseers on his estates, and — she shuddered — his sexual escapades.

Even so, he had always been protective of her, even more so after his relationship with Flavia began. For her part, she had attended and given banquets and receptions, frequented other society ladies, and had borne — with increasing terror of the protracted agonies of labour — three more children, though still not the son that her husband craved. And more and more she found, with Marcella, her refuge.

***

To her intimacy with Marcella, Toxotius had raised hardly an objection beyond the occasional remark, such as:

'Marcella does lead a strange sort of life, tucked away on the Aventine.'

'Strange?' Paula had been unreceptive.

'All those women …' he frowned. 'What do they do?'

'Study Holy Scripture. Is that so strange?'

'I've heard they don't eat,' he said uneasily. 'I wouldn't like *you* to go without food! After all, you are in the world in a very real sense, Paula.'

It was the year 374 AD, and Paula was heavily pregnant with her fifth child. She was silent.

'Too much religion is unhealthy,' pronounced Toxotius.

She stiffened. 'But it's alright for someone to spend his whole time editing Sallust, like your friend Nicomachus does?'

'Livy, not Sallust. But what's that got to do with it? Surely you women aren't editing your Holy Scripture!' Toxotius was startled into a snort of mirth.

'We try to grasp its inner meaning. Better than doing a new edition of a dreary old historian like Sallust!'

'*Not* Sallust. Livy.'

'Oh, Livy, then!' Paula burst into tears of frustration.

'There now, calm down.' Alarmed, he took her in his arms.

'You mustn't excite yourself.'

Sinking onto his chest, she cried herself out while he held her. He had always taken pride in his secure family life. He had given Paula everything she wanted, yet her family hardly seemed enough for her these days, despite her loyalty to him and the children. But that loyalty had always been unswerving and would remain so. He couldn't foresee any problem there.

'This is a lovely room for you to sit and study in,' he commented expediently, as she quietened. 'I was quite right to insist on your taking it over, with its view over your herb garden—look at that thyme, aniseed ... and is that cinnamon? I can't see from here ...'

His words trailed off, his attention evaporated. He was preparing to leave Rome for undivulged business. He was going to Flavia, of course. He was captivated by Flavia, not only bodily, but by her mind, her rich insolence and wayward caprices. So different from the steady and reliable woman that Paula had become.

Their family life *was* a solid one, he told himself later, as his carriage rattled down the Via Appia, and a son would complete it.

***

'So I've everything I could wish for, have I, Praetextata?' mused Paula, a few days later.

'You have four lovely daughters and probably a son as well soon, and a husband like Toxotius, so devoted to you all—'

'Who's almost never at home,' Paula cut in.

'Most women would count that as a blessing,' Praetextata suggested.

They were strolling through Toxotius's long gallery with its statuary on either side, on their way out to the garden.

'How well the Apollo looks here,' Praetextata exclaimed. 'He quite dominates the rest.'

'That statue was broken in a riot in Ephesus,' Paula said. 'I heard what happened. Not from Toxotius, though—from one of his slaves. Did you know the man carving Toxotius's sarcophagus comes from Ephesus? He was there at the time, and saw it all.' She waited a moment, and added: 'His young brother was executed with the others. He was just a boy.'

Praetextata said nothing.

'Secretly, at night, with two others,' Paula continued. 'Their families asked for the bodies back so that they could be given a Christian burial. It was my husband who refused them even that.'

'Yes, well, we had the whole story from Toxotius, of course—' Praetextata began.

'*I* didn't.' Paula's tone was icy.

She walked out into the garden as though escaping something, dragged down by the weight of the child within her. Praetextata followed her, breathing in the heavy scent of the magnolias.

'Consider, my dear, what you possess! This mansion with so many rooms, your own baths, and a library! Not to mention your country estates …'

'Oh, as to money, of course we have it in abundance,' said Paula. She did not add that most of it was hers.

'Well, complain you have too much if you like. Everybody talks about the number of poor people crowding your door. You're a soft touch, they say!' Praetextata's cheeks grew flushed, and she added spitefully, 'It's easy to be a philosopher with the riches you have!'

Watching her depart, Paula breathed a sigh of relief. Worthy woman as she was, who had bravely borne the confiscation of much of her husband's fortune years before, Praetextata tried her patience to the limit.

Paula retreated to Marcella's house, where she could breathe a different air. There, the women wore no silken garments, no bracelets or long earrings, no chalk powder on their cheeks or false hairpieces held in place by jewelled pins. Instead, they brought with them simply what they could summon up of intelligence and goodness.

Pushing open the door of the little salon, Paula heard Marcella's low and clear voice: '"Christ bestowed this on us also, that we should possess upon earth, in the state of virginity, a picture of the holiness of the angels."

'The words of the great theologian Athanasius, ladies! It was studying his *Life of Antony* as a girl that inspired *me* to try and live like the monks and virgins of the Nile Valley. Some of us —' Marcella's eyes dwelt fondly on little Eustochium, who sat listening intently, a faint colour in her cheeks, 'seem blessed by God from birth to picture that holiness of the angels.'

Paula was hardly conscious of the ladies in the salon, intent as she was on a train of thoughts all her own. Her eyes gleamed as she thought of the manuscripts, the learned commentaries, and the statements of doctrine that flooded in from the East, and of Marcella reading them all, sifting, criticising and explaining; in short, applying to the texts her formidable intellect and powers of analysis — all of which reflected a life dedicated to Christ.

I could go further than Marcella, thought Paula, if my life were my own.

***

'Athanasius,' said Marcella later to Paula, as they were sitting in her salon, 'was champion of our faith, and the very soul of orthodoxy. Did you know that he was exiled five times for his defence of Christ's divinity?'

'Oh, yes! Seventeen years in all!' Paula's imagination was fired by the image of Athanasius's extended period of suffering. 'To be banished for your convictions … That would prove your commitment beyond doubt!'

Marcella raised an eyebrow. 'We, too, can fight for our beliefs,' she said.

'But wouldn't fighting for our beliefs mean interpreting the Holy Scripture independently of men? And didn't Paul say that women should be subject to men?'

'He said women shouldn't teach, as well!' Marcella pointed out. 'It is arguable, however, that he was referring to speaking in a public space in which he would have seen the risk of a woman usurping the man's authority. We, on the other hand, concentrate on the inner journey of our own souls.' She smiled. 'Anyway, I am sure he didn't mean women like us, my dear.'

There was a silence, as each contemplated Paul's words.

'I could renounce everything too, Marcella.' Paula leaned forwards. 'I would gladly give up my rich clothing, my dinner parties, my private estates — and travel to the desert, further and further to the remotest of tombs …'

Her eyes were bright as she pictured the night-long vigils, the prayers, of men and women seeking to burn out of their bodies all lust and greed, conquering their private wills to attain a higher form of liberation.

'If our souls are free, as Origen says, we can choose the life we want to live: to endlessly contemplate the divine mysteries, or lose ourselves in petty domesticity … Freedom is the greatest gift of God, but I look around and see everyone misusing it, some barely even conscious of it.'

She paused. 'Contemplation isn't something you can do in a crowd.'

Marcella smiled. 'You don't have to lock yourself up in a fort for twenty years like Saint Antony, either!' she countered. 'Where lies the greater challenge? Living amongst people or removing oneself from their midst?' She shook her head. 'The hardest thing on earth is to put up with people around you.'

'I'm not so sure …' Paula puzzled. 'I keep wanting something more.'

'Really? The Gospel teaches us to love and serve others. We may live in Rome, not in holes in the Egyptian desert, but I never took another man after my husband died. I help the poor and needy, I study with my women, I fast and study Holy Scripture.'

'Don't you ever feel it's not enough?'

'There's more than one path to God,' said Marcella. 'We're not all made to be desert monks. I live partly in the world for my mother and my family's sake.' Pointedly, she regarded Paula's swollen belly. 'You must consider your children. Does Paul not tell us that it is our duty to train our children in piety and religion? That it is through bearing children that we can earn salvation?'

'Of course,' said Paula, sinking back into her chair, suddenly exhausted. 'My children.'

***

The pains began before dawn next morning, prematurely. Her labour was long and nightmarish, despite the gentle massage and warmth of the cloths soaked in heated olive oil that her women laid across her stomach. Attended only by her midwives—for she had not sent word to Toxotius, still absent from Rome, nor any of his relatives—and gripping the armrests of her elaborate birthing stool, Paula was delivered, at last, of a son.

4

Alone with her children in her villa on the Via Appia the day after her husband's funeral, Paula thus relived the past, warding off all intrusion from the outside world.

Over five years since the day I gave birth to my boy — and almost died, she thought. She and Toxotius had never slept together again, at her own request. He had readily agreed; Flavia had crowded out all other needs.

From a downstairs window, Paula gazed down at her son, ostentatiously putting his pony through its paces in a nearby field. He is angry, she thought. Angry at his father being taken from him. But always surrounded by his cousins, his tutor, his friends, he never looks to me. He was always his father's anyway, not mine.

Little Toxotius had grown up with all the advantages a wealthy father could bestow, including — it had been silently acknowledged by all — his father's gods. Only the eldest girl, Blesilla, had enjoyed almost equal place in her father's affections. His favourite daughter was, people observed, cast in the same mould as her father, with his hazel eyes, his thick, wavy hair and luxuriant physique — but with her mother's quickness of mind.

I've been leading a double life, reflected Paula. At the undisputed centre of her family, and loving them all, she jealously brooded on the rupture with her husband even while clinging to him and to the shelter of marriage. Yet at her very core, she realised, was an increasing longing to shake off the world altogether, to turn inwards towards an ideal denied her in the clutter and clamour of family life and high society.

***

Back in her mansion on the Aventine Hill, Paula paced her marble floors and looked with fresh eyes on her surrounds. She passed through the slaves' quarters below, where the women spun their wool, mended, cooked and cleaned, intent on lower domestic politics, eyes watchful, tongues wagging; and through the old nurseries — schoolrooms now — where her younger girls were taught their Virgil by a eunuch tutor. She continued through the long gallery leading out to the splendid gardens, past rooms where exquisite statuary from all over the Greek world gleamed with the high sheen of marble, gold or bronze — gods and fauns, nymphs and goddesses, all reclining gracefully or erotically clinched, in every manifestation of frankly sensuous delight. At the centre of them all, the head of Apollo gazed at her — mocking her, she felt.

Restlessly, she climbed upstairs and entered the cool of her bedroom, where the semi-closed shutters and glass windows kept the heat and noise from the outside world at bay. Even in the shadowy light, her mirrored reflection revealed a figure which, in her thirty-second year, was still shapely; features still beautiful in their refinement; and abundant hair piled fashionably high over the forehead that Toxotius had once called so aristocratic. She was desirable as well as wealthy; in short, an attractive proposition.

Remarriage? She shuddered. More than one man I know will try it. To be locked into the concerns of another man, my body used once more to join family to family, wealth to wealth …

Remarriage now, when she was flooded with such love as no husband could warrant or give, and that, unexpended, she felt might suffocate her? She shook her head. Such passion as she felt now could only be turned toward Christ.

But how to explain to people like Praetextata and Hymetius that the old life was no longer enough for her? Especially now, when they were trying to be kindness and tact itself? Hymetius was invaluable in the way he guided her in handling the complex administration and taxation of her estates; she could not have had a better adviser. But if only the relatives hadn't gone to such lengths to comfort her, and if only that comfort had not included such heavy eating!

As she said, later, to Marcella: 'I never want to see another rich sauce again, or mullet or woodcock ...'

'I've never seen the need to cram oneself with food,' agreed Marcella. 'Certainly no one ever worshipped God more effectively with an overfull stomach.'

'It's not only the eating!' exclaimed Paula. 'It's the dressing and talking and acquiring *more* of everything, all to impress — and I'm sick of it!'

***

Over the years that followed, resolutely Paula began — in secret at first, then openly — to sell off some of her inheritance. First she sold a small property near Volaterra. She promised the proceeds to Damasus to build a chapel in the newly restored Basilica of St Paul out on the road to Ostia. Then she began to sell some of Toxotius's statues. One by one. But not the Apollo. She had made up her mind to sell the statue but, when the moment came, found that she was helpless.

'Why, Toxotius, even dead you master me!' cried Paula. 'I can't *touch* the wretched head!'

***

'You can't get near her these days,' complained Praetextata to her husband, as they looked over their new mosaic depicting a hunting scene on the floor of their villa. 'I found Paula praying on her knees this morning in an oratory I've never set eyes on before! Mind you, even when Toxotious was alive she busied herself in feeding the poor — though he used to dismiss it as pandering to the lazy. But she's worse now — spends half her time on it! And she has two old bishops still staying with her, one from Cyprus and the other from Antioch.'

'You must know that there was to be a big church council here earlier in the summer. They invited the Eastern bishops, but only those two turned up. They're finding it comfortable to stay on.' Hymetius laughed contemptuously. 'It's a power struggle: East against West, bishop against bishop, doctrine against doctrine. Terrible animosities, all these bishops croaking like crows and ready to slit each other's throats. And they call that religion!'

'One thing is obvious, Hymetius. Damasus is after Paula's money. She's retreating more and more from her family and friends, selling off her properties quite recklessly, in my opinion. If it continues, who knows where it may lead? Why, she might even leave her children unprovided for.'

'What a terrible thing to do to Toxotius now he's dead. He was always so fond of his children and so tolerant of Paula.'

'That's just what I've been telling her, Hymetius. And what does she say? "Oh yes, Toxotius was very kind — and very cruel." And not another word.'

Praetextata would have been even more concerned had she been aware of the turn that Paula's life was to take following her encounter with a Dalmatian monk recently arrived from Constantinople.

***

Called by her majordomo, Paula entered her reception room where a tall, spare man stood on the loggia, gazing out across the luxuriant gardens. He swung round at her approach, and bowed. As he straightened up, she noticed that his eyes were inflamed.

'My lady Paula.' His voice was deep and compelling. 'My name is Jerome. I have come to prepare the ground with the bishops before they meet His Holiness tomorrow. They don't know any Latin — and Damasus, that stalwart Roman, doesn't always choose to know even a little Greek.' He smiled.

'Did they bring you over as interpreter?' Paula enquired.

A flicker of annoyance passed over his face. 'I have been able to assist with the language, in addition to my regular duties, yes,' he said.

'And what work is that?'

'Framing new formulae of belief and dealing with His Holiness's private correspondence.'

'Valuable work indeed,' she said hastily.

'Of the greatest importance,' he agreed.

'Please let me offer you some refreshment while you wait for the bishops. They are at prayer just now.'

He bowed again. 'Thank you, no. I am on my way to the Senator Pammachius. I will, however, leave some notes that I prepared for the bishops with you, my lady, if you permit.'

'Of course.'

He paused. 'Pammachius and I studied together in Rome years ago.'

'I see.' She saw that it pleased him to tell her this. 'Haven't you been in retreat in the Syrian desert?'

'Yes,' he said simply.

'Oh, how I envy you!' she exclaimed. Only as she uttered the words did she realise how deeply she meant them. 'You see, I've read about Antony,' she explained. 'About his great battles in the desert to master his body and how, after twenty years, his body could overcome every privation because his soul had attained purity.'

Paula's pale face glowed. She looked striking in her severe but elegant black gown, and he noticed her absence of ornament, her luxuriant hair free of restraining jewel or ribbon.

'Yet you … who had this same chance,' she continued, then cut herself short as he made an impatient gesture and, muttering something indistinct, wiped his eyes.

'Oh, what's the matter?' she cried.

'It's my eyes, always my eyes,' he spluttered. 'I'm reading and translating far into the night. At His Holiness's bidding, you understand. I cannot – nor do I wish to – stop.'

'Then you must bathe your eyes immediately!' Paula clapped her hands and a eunuch rushed off, returning a moment later with a bowl, sponge and bottle.

And so, in the elegant salon that had witnessed some of the grandest gatherings of Roman nobility, a modest little scene took place as the lady of the house herself directed the application of her lotion to the eyes of a humble priest.

'It works!' Jerome stood up presently. His eyes were fully open now and clearer.

'You must take the lotion with you then.'

'Your ladyship is too good!'

'You'll have to use it regularly,' she warned.

'My lady, do you realise what you've done for me? My eyes are my whole wealth.' He gestured to the loggia. 'Suddenly, it's a beautiful day for me!'

'Not as beautiful as all that,' she laughed, as together they walked over to the stone balustrade.

The sun had lightened but not lifted the thick vapours that hung in the valley below, and a tired, marshy air welled up from the river.

Jerome turned to Paula. 'I saw you yesterday morning in the Liberian Basilica, my lady, and afterwards, giving out alms in the street below. I have heard much of you and of your goodness to the poor.'

She coloured, and he was moved to respond in the language that came so readily to him: 'As the sun's purity struggles with the fog, so do you shine, here on the Aventine Hill, high above the vice in the valley below. Goodness like yours fights a lonely battle, my lady, in the Rome of today. Why, our very Church is torn from within.'

'One needs to escape, like Antony,' she said. 'But then, you did.'

'I *thought* I would escape,' he corrected her bitterly. 'I hardly expected that the very search for God would engender ambition, rivalry and every sort of animosity in those around me.'

She felt the full force of his emotion as if it were a physical impact.

'I would still like to try,' she murmured.

'Ah, you … yes, you might succeed!'

And that was the second marvel of the morning, that a man who, she was to learn, was as proud and touchy as any on earth, had talked so frankly and uninhibitedly to a virtually unknown woman.

5

'So you envy me my time in the desert, do you?' said Jerome, turning to glance at his rich senatorial friend Pammachius.

It was the day after his meeting with Paula, and the two men were making their way amongst the crowds of the faithful towards the shrine of the apostle Paul on the Via Ostiense, outside the walls of Rome. This was only a halfway point in the long procession which took place every year on the twenty-ninth of June in celebration of the martyrdom of the saints Peter and Paul. It had begun at dawn at Saint Peter's Basilica on the Vatican Hill, and would end at dusk at the joint shrine of Peter and Paul at the third milestone on the Via Appia.

'Life at Chalcis was tough,' Jerome continued. 'The sun was scorching, the food spare, not to mention the endless copying out of manuscripts … I buried myself in my own studies, and began learning Hebrew — that's how I got through it. But enough of that now.'

Damasus was celebrating mass outside Paul's shrine. His words hung in the sweet country air over the gathering — people had come from the country and the city, from every class and from the farthest limits of the Empire.

'Come and look inside,' Pammachius said, stopping in front of the shrine. 'The whole building is to come down. Damasus wants to build Paul a huge new basilica. He's only waiting for permission from the civic authorities to build over the road.'

No one knew precisely where it was that Paul had been beheaded, with the Emperor Nero looking on, whether here or at the Salvian Springs, more than three hundred years ago. But Paul's remains, wrapped in linen and spices, had been buried by a Roman lady, Lucina, in her vineyard on this very spot and were now inside that bronze sarcophagus. Of course, many others were buried as well in the old funerary hall with its stacks of graves, scrawled over by families who held banquets to commemorate their dead.

A group of kneeling women were wedged close to the open grating of the confession, the better to breathe in the odour of sanctity. Repeatedly bowing low down, they prayed, 'Holy Paul, ease the passage of my beloved husband – or daughter – or son – into Heaven. Grant him – or her – a bountiful reception on high. Intercede in Heaven for us who still labour here below ...'

Foreheads touched stone, and rose, like wind rippling the surface of a field of corn. As the wailing subsided, a new chorus would begin. If there was one thing the Roman people loved, it was a martyr they could call their own: Damasus understood this perfectly.

Jerome and Pammachius glanced into the shrine, and then headed for the shade of a country wall where, well away from the clerical party, Pammachius's slaves awaited with plates of dates, fruits and other refreshments.

'It's about time we had a proper basilica,' said Pammachius, 'now that Saint Paul is all the rage with our Roman intellectuals. You've probably seen one or two commentaries on Paul's letters that have been written here lately.'

He gazed at Jerome while talking, for the two hadn't met since their student days in Rome some sixteen years before. The old impetuosity was still there in Jerome's leaner, bronzed face.

'Commentaries?' Jerome waved a long-fingered hand. 'I believe I've seen one,' he said indifferently. 'Damasus sometimes asks my opinion of such things – when I'm not expounding the Bible for him myself.'

'Do you really?'

A hint of a smile played around Jerome's lips. 'His Holiness has no Greek, you know, let alone Hebrew.'

'Well, who the devil knows Hebrew?'

Jerome's eyes held Pammachius's for a long moment.

'What!' he exclaimed. 'You're not telling me you've learned Hebrew!'

'It was a worthy enough … solace,' Jerome said testily. 'Although I did miss conversing with men of my own intellectual calibre in the desert.'

'Maybe, but did you accomplish what you had set out to do there?'

A boy-slave of Pammachius's offered them cups of sweet wine, and they drank.

'When I went to the desert,' Jerome began deliberately, 'I had resolved to conquer self-will, to return body and soul to the uncorrupted state of Adam.'

As Jerome recounted his experiences clearly and with rising passion, Pammachius smiled his appreciation. His old friend had lost none of his eloquence.

'To work for the union of my body and soul, that union which God expressed for us in the Incarnation of Christ …'

People around them had begun to draw closer and listen, though they did not all understand. But the little meal had finished and Pammachius rose. 'Keep talking,' he urged Jerome, 'but let's move off with the rest. It's a long way to the Via Appia.' He gestured in the direction of Damasus. 'I hope the old man makes it. He's pushing eighty, though still strong.'

'Stronger than some of his senior clergy,' muttered Jerome. 'Stronger than the Deacon Riparius, or Gaudentius. What paunches! And Anemius reeks of drink. If they paid Christ the same attention they give to filling their bellies they'd be pious indeed.'

'I dare say you're right,' Pammachius placated him. He waved, and the crowd scattered. A hawker of relics picked up his baskets and darted away. 'Tell me about the Syrian desert.'

People always made way for Pammachius, whose erect figure and imperious look signalled his noble rank. Yet Jerome detected an air of dissatisfaction in his questions, and in his eyes a yearning.

'Oh, it was a struggle alright—against the heat, against hunger, against sex, a struggle even to stay alive,' Jerome said dramatically. 'How often, in those scorching sands and rough caves did thoughts of Rome's pleasures come to haunt me, and how I despised myself for my weakness! Parched and emaciated, with sackcloth for clothing, cold water and unheated food for my only sustenance, I cast myself at the feet of Jesus, for five long years taming my mind along with my body by devoting myself to fasting, prayer and manual labour.'

Pammachius's eyes rested on Jerome's slender, unmarked hands. 'You did well to find the time to compose your brilliant letters,' he observed.

'I had a few fragile links with the outside world,' Jerome allowed. 'Thanks be to God for my correspondence. As a Latin speaker amongst so many Greeks and Syrians, my manuscripts meant much …'

'But what about the others you met? There must have been someone amongst the hermits with whom you could identify?'

Jerome shook his head. 'I hadn't bargained on having to struggle with them. You wouldn't believe how jealous some of those monks were. As if the solitary life were a race which they had the right to win! They were eaten away with envy of my education.' He shuddered. 'I did all I could to keep myself apart.'

'You had a few visitors, surely? Your patron and generous supporter, Evagrius, for instance.'

'The priest of Antioch? Oh, they hated me for that too. But don't we all try to reach God in our different ways? Was I to renounce *thinking*? Isn't meditation itself in part an intellectual process?'

'Still got your appetite for debate, eh?' Pammachius smiled. 'Tell me instead about your Hebrew studies. Anyone to help you there, apart from your Jewish convert?'

Jerome laughed. 'Are you joking? Some didn't know any language except that gibberish Syriac. Others went to terrible extremes, living like beasts, grubbing for nuts and berries. I heard of one who copulated with a donkey ...'

Pammachius's eyebrows rose as his friend went on to talk of madmen, drunk on Christ, living in filth and shackled in chains. Deftly, he steered the conversation back onto issues of doctrine.

'Oh, you can argue that the whole East is a hotbed of religious controversy!' Jerome expostulated. 'What a fool I was to think the desert would be any different. Just as the church of Antioch was racked by a dispute over who would become bishop, so too were the monks of Chalcis divided by argument. I was forced to take sides, but whatever I said was wrong.' Violently, he kicked aside a pebble. 'Never praise the piety of the illiterate to me! It was those monks who drove me out finally, back to Antioch—'

'That must have been rewarding,' put in Pammachius.

Jerome took a deep breath. 'Yes, I was content, studying the Scriptures, beginning to write myself ...'

'Then, I heard, you went to Constantinople and studied under the great Gregory of Nazianzus. The places you've been to and the people you've met—how I envy you!'

'True, from my position I just about managed to touch the skirts of some of the great, as you might say. More importantly, I started to translate the Greek saints into our Latin. And I wrote my first exegesis of Isaiah. Damasus says he has never read anything better.'

'You'll soon be famous!'

'But you, my friend, are known to all Rome, are you not?'

'Only for the money I give,' observed Pammachius.

'For the great amount of money, I might add! The portico we walked in this morning coming from Saint Peter's — that's mine. And the narthex for the basilica which is being planned — my money will pay for it.'

'Having no money, but only my wits with which to serve God ...' began Jerome.

'You've been ordained,' Pammachius reminded him.

'That was Paulinus's idea — there's no arguing with the Bishop of Antioch, is there? But I'm not really the pastoral type.'

'I don't think you are either. But now that Damasus is making a great thing of being heir of Saint Peter, all that learning of yours and your powers of expression will be in great demand.'

'Yes,' said Jerome, with evident pride. 'He keeps me busy all hours of the day and night. Not only with Church records, but drafting letters and translating works on theology.'

'Something tells me,' said Pammachius, who had seen Jerome's eyes blaze with excitement, 'that you've found your niche at last, my friend!'

'Perhaps I have.' Jerome looked as though he might say more, but only added, 'Have you found yours?'

'Ah, well,' Pammachius looked troubled. 'Perhaps if Paolina ...' He changed the subject abruptly. 'You've heard from Rufinus?'

'Of course. It's been a year now he's been with Melania in Jerusalem heading up that monastery of hers. They say that it is going to become a magnet for pilgrims.'

'Who would have thought, at school, that he'd become so important?' Pammachius looked closely at Jerome. 'What was your phrase? "A man with the stride of a tortoise?"'

Jerome laughed. 'Did I say that?'

'Oh come, you always gave him the sharp edge of your tongue.'

'To be a companion to the holy Melania must be like living at the centre of a tornado.'

'Wealth is power. She saved those monks of Nitria from persecution and disguised herself as a man so she could minister to them. Did you hear what she said to the Governor, when she revealed her identity? "I am the daughter of the Roman Consul Antonius Marcellinus, and the wife of the Roman Prefect Valerius Maximus. I am Christ's slave."'

'I heard about that. The judge apologised and let her go, insisting that she be accorded all the respect she demanded. He even let her take the monks to Palestine without interference. Dramatic, eh!'

'But genuine,' Pammachius mused. 'There are ladies here who are trying to live in their houses as if they were in some sort of desert! My own cousin Marcella, for one. She's anxious to talk with you, by the way.'

'She has already. She called me to her palace on the Aventine the other day. She's more impressive than half the monks in Chalcis!'

'There's Paolina's mother, Paula, as well …'

'Yes,' said Jerome, his voice softening. 'I had the privilege of meeting her yesterday.'

6

The following morning, Jerome was strolling in the portico of Pompey's Theatre, close by his own lodgings in the building that housed the Church archives. He hadn't accomplished anything this day on account of his eyes. Paula's lotion had eased, but could not cure, his eye strain. Ah, his cursed eyes, failing him just at this point, when exhilaration throbbed in his veins at Damasus's commission. At least his new assistant, Aetius, was due later in the day.

He gazed through the colonnade at the magnificent white stone of the theatre itself, and the fountains and statues of the garden beyond, silhouetted against the vivid blue sky. Dedicated in 55 BC by Pompey the Great and site of the assassination of Julius Caesar eleven years later, the theatre and its surrounding complex was still, undeniably, a major attraction, and perfectly suited to satisfy the Roman appetite for spectacle. It was swarming with tourists and pilgrims — attracted largely, Jerome admitted, by its magnificent temple dedicated to the Roman goddess of love, Venus Victrix — although Pompey, he knew, had only built it to get around the law on the construction of theatres.

Christ, however, had triumphed over Venus and the other pagan gods and goddesses. True, certain Roman nobles clung to their past, and in underground places paid homage to foreigners from the East, to Mithras and Isis or, worse still, submitted to that bloody baptism of initiation to the Roman mother goddess Cybele. Jerome shuddered: what sort of barbaric ritual of purification involved the blood of sacrificial bulls showering down over the initiates?

Shouts from a nearby gladiatorial school reminded Jerome that even the senators gave games, public displays of slaughter which passed as sport. Senators, of course, were something of a tourist attraction themselves, when they appeared at public ceremonies in their striped tunics and purple-edged togas, presiding over the games in the most sought-after seats.

Jerome had not been to the races for years. Indeed, it seemed a lifetime since he had sweated with excitement in the arena beside Pammachius, who used to get complimentary tickets for his student friends. Yet now he seemed to be giving up all such entertainment, though he still fulfilled his public duties. Jerome recalled how eagerly Pammachius had questioned him about his travels, and wondered whether his friend was tiring of his senatorial role.

Pammachius had surprised him by turning up early that morning, announcing: 'Let me show you how Damasus is changing the face of Rome!'

He had taken him to what had been the great hall of a public bath which was being transformed into a church. In the apse, craftsmen were at work on a fresco depicting Christ seated among the apostles, with Peter and Paul at either end.

'The apostles are wearing the toga,' Jerome had commented, in some amusement.

'Yes, the Church is really Roman now,' Pammachius had replied with satisfaction. 'We are more than ever the heart of the world.'

Well, it was certainly the heart of Jerome's world, this city that had formed and educated him from the moment that he had arrived as a young man fresh from Dalmatia. His parents had always had ambitions for their clever son, and years of classical study in Rome under the most prestigious of teachers had filled his retentive mind and honed his wits to razor sharpness. It was here, too, that he had begun to compile his precious library — the one possession to which he clung and had, somehow, managed to keep intact throughout his travels. But Rome wasn't the East, with the intellectual ferment of its big cities such as Constantinople and Antioch and Caesarea, each rife with controversy, hot-beds of debate. That Ecumenical Council in Constantinople last year! Jerome shook his head. What a stormy affair it had been, each bishop accusing the others of heresy…

And was heresy really defeated now, with the banning of that arch heretic Arius, whose doctrine that Christ had been created by the Father and was thus subordinate to Him had had the East seething with hatred for some sixty years? Had it really ended that dissension, during which the keenest minds of the East had argued over the nature of the Trinity, and in particular the Holy Spirit, with passionate subtlety? Yet none of these 'heretics' had been wicked men, each only fiercely in-sistent that he alone understood the true nature of God. Even though, in future, he himself would doubtless be called on to inveigh against one or other of them as a devil of the deepest dye! For—and Jerome's fine lips twisted wryly and his stride involuntarily lengthened—his pen belonged to Damasus now, and his creed was the Nicene Creed of Damasus.

Jerome strode on, unconscious of the appreciative glances of many passers-by who responded instinctively to his vitality and nonchalant self-possession.

I read Origen for the first time in the East, he pondered. Now there was a man who spent his life searching out the deepest meaning of the sacred texts, and pushed the implications to their furthermost boundaries, not afraid to contemplate the to-tal freedom of the soul …

His thoughts were interrupted by the passage through the portico of a flashily dressed young matron followed by a trail of eunuchs, and at her sides a gaggle of men ogling her. Just try telling her that she was only a thought in the mind of God, this material world a mere fleeting moment in the eternal life of the soul; that she was given this earthly chance by her Maker to re-deem herself, painfully, so she might turn back to Him!

Jerome glowered at her half-bare breasts, then turned away

and headed back towards his office. Passing one of His Holiness's new churches, his thoughts reverted to Damasus.

The Romans should be grateful to him for pouring out money on so many new buildings, Jerome reflected. Could he be making up for the troubles he had when elected to his 'throne' in '66? Even after all these years, people haven't forgotten the rioting between Damasus's supporters and those of Ursinus and, worse, the slaughter in the Basilica of Sicinius before the city prefects banished Ursinus and restored order. Ah, the bitterness of those old lines I heard just the other day:

> *'Close on two hundred 'neath the sod,*
> *We'll not forget the price they paid*
> *Ambition made this man of God*
> *Forget the Word, prefer the blade.'*

And someone had added:

> *'But now he's firm on Peter's Chair.*
> *And tickles wealthy ladies' ears*
> *With heavenly visions, golden prayer*
> *And costly words to calm their fears.'*

Well, he considered, I can hardly question Damasus about it; he probably had had enough of Ursinus's continued intriguing and plotting even if it could no longer damage him. Pammachius asked yesterday if I had found my 'niche'. Rather, I would say, the greatest commission of my life! It could be the making of me, a scholar from Dalmatia, with no place on earth to call my own now that our family properties there have been ravaged by the Goths. I shall meet Damasus's challenge. With God's help, nothing will stop me!

***

The afternoon heat was sweltering as Jerome picked his way down the stone steps of Pompey's Theatre, from the top tier on which he had enjoyed a faint breeze, and hurried back to his apartment to receive his new scribe.

Aetius arrived out of breath, and perspiring. Jerome stood up to greet a tall, slender man of olive complexion, whose green eyes were tinged, he noticed, with yellow. Undeniably handsome, though his mouth was perhaps too full-lipped. He drained his jug of wine and water that Jerome gave him, and smiled as he wiped his face. He was young. Or was he? Probably nearing thirty, Jerome decided. Aetius bowed as he replaced his cup, his loose gown revealing a glimpse of skin that glistened like polished marble. How the girls must itch to caress it!

'We'd better settle down to work at once,' Jerome said abruptly. 'There's a mountain of it. There will be letters to be dictated each day, passages to be copied — and I must make time to translate Origen's homilies, too. I wish to introduce His Holiness to his writings.'

Jerome searched among the rolls and sheets of paper stacked on his desk. 'Here's a rough timetable. It won't leave you much free time.'

The young man glanced at it, and said, 'This isn't a timetable.' His lips curled in amusement.

Jerome snatched up another sheet. 'My eyes again!' Biting back an oath, he quoted: '"He has sent upon me the anger of His indignation, a visitation by evil angels." Ah, but I would serve God and Damasus better if He hadn't put this affliction in my way.'

'Trials of the soul, like gold in the fire,' said Aetius grandly. 'That's what the psalm is telling us.'

Jerome laughed aloud, reaching out as though to throw an arm around Aetius's shoulders.

'You'll be my eyes.' He passed a weary hand over his forehead. 'Bad sight in a scholar: what is God's purpose?'

Aetius made a deprecatory gesture. 'A discipline?' he suggested. 'Like all evils, to lead us to humility.'

'I shall be humble indeed, if I am to get through all my work without eyes to see with!'

Jerome mopped at his eyes with a cloth dipped in water. 'Why am I talking like this?' he demanded suddenly. 'Why am I, the most committed of Christians, questioning the ways of God! Are you a demon, Aetius, working your evil magic on me?'

Peering at his papers, Jerome missed the flash of exultation that passed over the other's face. But Aetius's voice was light as he remarked: 'Surely your wisdom makes you immune from magic, sir. Reason makes you impregnable.'

'Perhaps, but no man is so strong that he can't be tempted by the Devil. I can only pray to God for strength and guidance.'

With that, the two men settled down to work.

***

Hours later, after Aetius had left, Jerome remained seated for some time, musing. Despite his fatigue, he relished the weeks and months ahead. To go back to the fountainhead of Holy Scripture, cut out the falsities of existing translations, create an elegant yet limpid Latin version that would last through the ages. But the difficulties! Take the Book of Job, for instance. Part-prose, part-poetry, its present Latin translations debased, mutilated, with hundreds of lines missing. Ah, the exquisite challenge of rendering in Latin the exact words of the original Hebrew to make the meaning of the text transparent while preserving its feel! There was an indirectness, though, a slipperiness, in the whole book, even in the Hebrew as the Greek orators themselves noticed: it was like trying to hold onto a little eel, the more you squeezed it the sooner it escaped.

And later, his own commentaries would dissect the Scriptures for the mighty spiritual truths they embodied —

always bearing in mind Origen's various shades of meaning —
and expose the very soul within those sacred texts!

Mindful of his strained eyes, Jerome resisted the urge to resume work by the flickering light of the oil lamp. He stood up
and stretched; he felt that he could almost purr with satisfaction,
like an Egyptian cat, complacent and clever. Restlessly, he paced
up and down his cramped quarters, then wandered out onto the
balcony and watched a golden dusk set upon the old city. It must
be time for *cena*, the evening meal.

He was very hungry, he realised, as walked into the adjoining room where his slave-boy had set out soup and bread
and wine. He ate and drank more copiously than usual. Afterwards, Aetius invaded his thoughts. Now there was a mind as
quick and educated as he might ever find in an assistant. And
he had almost flung his arm around him.

In one blinding instant Jerome was transported back almost
twenty years to when he was still a student here in Rome. He
was in the arms of Chloe, the slave girl who had catered almost
nightly to his needs. Her skin, too, had been fine and creamy,
and her features as yet untouched by the coarseness that would
come with brothel life. Her Latin had been broken, except where
it was designed to inflame and hasten a man, so they had talked
little, but that hadn't mattered.

Such memories might surface as erotic dreams, but Jerome
had suppressed them with a measure of success ever since God
had called him. If they returned to plague him tonight, then Aetius must be the cause, thought it was hardly his fault. Jerome
knelt down and prayed but still the images assailed him.

'Dear God,' he moaned. 'On this night I am not worthy even
to pray to You. I am like a diseased sheep strayed from the
flock. Seek me out, show me Your mercy, forgive me!'

That night, however, he slept long and deep, blessedly free
of dreams. Next morning, his mood was clear. The night before had simply been an uncharacteristic lapse, his willpower

faltering into lewd memories. But with a merciful God, there was eternal hope.

'A sign, Lord, give me a sign,' he breathed.

An early morning breeze at the open doors swept a pile of manuscripts from the table. Just in time, he rescued a sheet from being carried off the balcony. As he retrieved it, he saw a quotation from Saint Paul's Epistle to the Romans:

'For I know that nothing good dwells in me, that is, in my flesh ... I see in my members another law at war with the law in my mind ... Wretched man that I am! Who will deliver me from this body of death?'

The paper fluttered away in the draught from the inner door which opened to admit Aetius, glowing with the freshness of the morning. Dextrously, he gathered up all the papers and offered them to Jerome, the quotation from Saint Paul on top.

Jerome breathed more easily. Surely this was a sign from God, a reassurance from Him?

'I am late, sir,' Aetius was saying. 'I was held up by a long procession. Even the senators were there.'

'Oh, and what was that for?'

'For the inauguration of a new city prefect.'

Jerome clicked his tongue impatiently. 'Couldn't you have cut across it?'

'Cut across it, sir!' Aetius looked shocked. 'All the great families, sir — the Fabii, Ceionii, Symmachi ... so many distinguished men! Even the Anicii, and the great Petronius Probus himself, were there.'

Aetius's eyes shone, as he thought of the proud way those noble senators moved, filling space so confidently. Cut past those men, who walked the earth as if they owned it? And much of it they did own.

He added, 'I saw the man who, some say, will marry one of the daughters of the Lady Paula,' Aetius added. 'One of the Furian clan, that is.'

'What of it?'

'The Lady Paula must rejoice that her daughter will marry a man so rich in everything — all the Christian virtues, too.'

The irony was unmistakeable but Jerome, anxious to begin work, let it pass.

7

Down on the Bay of Naples, Petronius Probus, head of the powerful Anicii family, was host to a great many guests. It was the summer of 382 AD, and the heady combination of plentiful food, sweet wines and the humid air affected everyone. Probus himself reclined on silken cushions in an arbour, dreaming private dreams and barely listening to the leading councillor of the city of Capua who stood before him.

'Your Eminence has the very prince of villas,' the councillor declared. 'First, for its situation on the promontory overlooking Puteoli and Naples, the lakes and islands; then, for the grace of its buildings, and the gardens descending to the sea, with their pines, and profusion of flowers and fountains ...'

Probus wondered when the man would arrive at his request. He was patron of Capua, and clients had plagued him for days for favours and advice. And this evening, after the previous day's pleasurable excesses at his estate in Baiae, he felt all of his fifty-six years.

'Wealth used with such artistry, such splendour ...'

The councillor had paused for breath, but Probus, about to cut him short, was a fraction too late; he was off again. 'This marble in your steps, for instance ...'

Was the fellow after a ministry post in Milan or had he got wind of likely crop failures in Africa and saw an opportunity to buy grain before prices rose? Probus had been appointed for the second time Praetorian Prefect of Italy and Africa for the following year, so there was practically no limit to his powers of patronage. It was amusing to guess what the man from Capua wanted.

What he wanted, it emerged a little later, was stable boys. Frontier prices for slaves were more moderate and boys easier to come by. At least, Probus reflected, slaves from Illyricum were easier to transport than wild beasts from Africa, which another leading Capuan had wanted for the games he planned to give the following year.

Always supposing that we're all still here and the Goths haven't overrun us. Probus, half-asleep, had a sudden premonition; the words had formed in his brain in an instant. Ah, that terrible defeat just four years ago when the greater part of the army of the Eastern Roman Empire had been slaughtered at Adrianople, together with the Emperor Valens, still sent shivers through the heart. Who would have thought that our legions could be vulnerable to mere cavalry? Those barbarians had plundered and burned rich villas throughout the Balkan provinces. Precariously pacified, they might break loose at any moment. What was there to oppose them — except other barbarians just as savage and potentially just as dangerous? Where would it end? Down here in Italy itself? God forbid! Probus crossed himself hastily.

'Write to my head of staff about your stable boys,' he dismissed the councillor. He noted with satisfaction how the persistent little man, clearly a little drunk on Probus's excellent Falernian wine as much as his own sense of self-importance, quickly bowed and left.

'Petty concerns!' Probus muttered. 'These provincials, immersed in their trivial affairs, leaving to those who hold duty sacred — great men like myself — the never-ending task of administering the Empire!' He spat in disgust and a slave hurried to wipe up the spittle.

There are just rewards, of course, Probus consoled himself. This villa, for one.

He watched the golden burnish of the sea as dusk stole on, a glorious backdrop to the terrace and lush gardens below, over which his aristocratic guests swarmed like bees over honey. Refreshed by his afternoon siesta, he felt ready for the evening entertainment. Tonight it would be dancers!

The soft chatter and laughter of the ladies floated up from the terrace. Amongst them, he noticed, were two young women — Juliana, one of his own distant relatives, soon to be married; and Blesilla, the daughter of Paula, vivacious and beautiful at eighteen. At least, Blesilla had been there a moment ago. Where? ... Probus dozed off.

***

He awoke to find one of his nephews, Aemilius Bassus, standing in front of him. On the young man's shoulder was perched a magnificent parrot he had brought back with him from Alexandria the week before.

'Do I disturb you, sir?'

'What?' Probus groped his way back to reality. Bassus had fleshed out in the years he'd spent away studying. Probus remembered him as an overactive boy, as clever as he was headstrong; one who naturally led. Now he was an adult with an air of consequence, and held himself regally. He was looking at him intently, and Probus recalled why.

'As your father's overseas,' he said, 'I've looked into the matter myself. 'I would have to advise him against your marrying the girl. You're out of touch after all these years away. Since her father died, the mother Paula's gone all ascetic and is bent on throwing her money away on the Church and the poor. Anyway' — Probus looked hard at the young man — 'it seems that Blesilla's family has arranged for her to be given to one of the Furii.'

Probus broke off at the rebellious look on Bassus's face. 'I hope you haven't said anything to the girl?'

Bassus shook his head.

'There's another reason.' Probus's expression was stern. 'I've arranged an excellent post for you in Milan in the office of the Imperial Quaestor. In a couple of years you'll be able to afford to marry well up there.' He paused. 'From what I've heard of your self-indulgence, a rich bride would be doubly advisable.'

51

***

Blesilla had wandered away, leaving the women to their veiled conversations and merciless gossip. The elder Anicii ladies were also arrogantly religious. Blesilla was only here, she knew, because her mother Paula had felt that she could entrust her to the Anicii clan while she herself was increasingly taken up with her charitable works. But Blesilla had been angered to overhear her hostess talking — she was sure — about her mother.

'Religious devotion can be taken to extremes for a woman of birth.'

'You, Anicia, cultivate a more responsible Christian observance in your house,' rejoined another. 'Worship infused by the intellect!'

And so the chatter had gone on, punctuated by laughter, of fashion, intrigue and, Blesilla thought she overheard, of a religious poem composed by none other than Anicia Proba's aunt.

***

Down on the lower terrace, Blesilla leaned on the stone balustrade, looking down on the sea, smooth as a sheet of sapphire, then up at the now familiar face of this man who, since his appearance in Baiae a week earlier had monopolised her time. Despite his correct demeanour, he was still, to her, the rascal of a boy with whom she'd played as a child in the long summers down in Campania. She found herself talking to him with much of the old ease, only conscious now of her attractiveness to him, and of her quickening pulse whenever he appeared.

'Soon I'll be leaving for Milan,' he said. 'My uncle just informed me of a position that's come up — a great opportunity!'

She could see that he was excited. 'I wish you weren't going,' she said impulsively.

His grey eyes twinkled. 'I've got a month or so here first.'

He was so close that she could feel the warmth of his breath on her face. Blesilla began talking quickly about the journey that the ladies had just made to the baths for their various ailments, and the medicinal properties of the water from the sulphur springs underground ... Roughly, Bassus pulled her to him, and she fell silent.

***

The risks they ran in the weeks that followed terrified Blesilla, willing accomplice though she was. They were both aware that in the rigid, unforgiving society Bassus risked his neck in seducing this high-born girl, fiancée of another man; and Blesilla, social disgrace and humiliation.

A month later they made their separate farewells to their unsuspecting hosts and departed Baiae, Blesilla wrapped up in her private passion, and Bassus relieved that one more reckless adventure had concluded successfully, leaving him free to concentrate on his new career.

***

'This Jerome,' said Blesilla to her sister Rufina, the day after Blesilla's return to Rome. 'Who is he?'

They sat with little Toxotius in Blesilla's bedroom while her maid Clea and one other slave brushed Blesilla's rich copper hair. Occasionally Rufina threw a nut through the ivory fretwork of a cage containing a resplendent green and yellow parrot with a red beak, and a neck encircled by a fine black marking.

Rufina talked at length of how their mother was planning to help Jerome with his research, together with Marcella and her group.

'But why should he lecture Mamma?' Blesilla asked.

'He's giving readings to Mamma and the other ladies, not lecturing them. He gets carried away, she said … he's captivating all the ladies!'

'Jerome,' piped up little Toxotius, 'writes to Mamma every day. I know because his secretary Aetius – the cleric – brings the letters.'

'*Hello darling!*' screamed the parrot suddenly.

Rufina started. 'I will never get used to the way he screeches like that. In Greek, sometimes, too! How nice of Bassus to send you the parrot, Toxotius.'

'He didn't,' said the child. 'He gave it to Blesilla.'

In the silence, Blesilla felt their eyes trained on her. Nervously, she peered at her reflection in a bronze mirror.

'Bassus,' mused Rufina. 'Such an ugly little wretch as a boy!'

Blesilla said nothing.

'Not good-looking exactly,' Rufina reflected. 'But attractive.'

'*Bassus!*' screamed the parrot. '*Bassus!*'

A slave entered, and said to Blesilla, 'Aetius is outside with a message from the Lady Paula. She wants you to attend Jerome's lecture.'

'Why not go?' said Rufina, as Blesilla made no reply. 'Especially as I can't – I've got my Greek lesson.' She yawned. 'It's harder than Latin …' She added plaintively, 'Baiae must have been nice. It was so hot here over the summer. Bassus –'

'Oh!' exclaimed Blesilla, 'Leave him out of it!' She slapped down the mirror.

'Well,' said Rufina, 'Baiae doesn't seem to have done you much good, Blesilla. You've come back in such a temper.'

***

Outside in the corridor, Aetius chatted with the maid Clea, released now from attendance on her mistress.

'So you were down in Baiae with the Lady Blesilla?' he enquired.

Clea nodded.

'I have seen the fun and games of the nobility bathing,' whispered Aetius.

Clea stared at his impudence. 'The Lady Blesilla stayed with a pious Christian family,' she snapped. 'This family always used to go south for the summer until master died.'

'A pleasure-loving lady, Blesilla, so I've heard,' prompted Aetius.

'The Lady Blesilla had a chest ailment. The doctor advised sea air and the mineral baths.'

'The Lady Paula must have suffered to think of the temptations her daughter faced. Of course, she had you to look after her.'

Clea paled as Aetius watched her.

'You would never be swayed from your duty, would you?' he asked. 'That's a lovely bracelet you're wearing. Rarely must a slave receive such a gift. Your service to your mistress must have been exceptional.'

The door opened and Blesilla walked in, her hair now curled and glistening with ribbons and gems. Aetius inclined his head, clasping his hands respectfully to his breast. Blesilla's silk gown swished as she walked. Behind her, a slave carried the parrot in its ivory cage.

'You can tell my mother I shall come to the lecture,' Blesilla told him coldly, 'even though I'm still tired from my journey.'

She turned on her heel.

'*Tell her! Tell her! Tell her!*' screeched the parrot as, twisting its emerald head through the bars of the cage, it bit the hand of the slave.

***

When Blesilla reached the gathering, Jerome had already begun his address.

'I looked on the burning desert, but it was nothing compared to the temptations that were burning my soul,' he was declaring, throwing his voice to full effect. Through the window of Paula's resplendent salon, the rays of late afternoon sun slanted on his face, taut from his self-imposed struggle. His dark eyes, under curving eyebrows and wide forehead, inexorably drew his listeners into his own highly charged world.

'... and in that vast solitude, my bare bones hardly holding together, my mind drifted and I saw crowds of girls dancing before my eyes. My face was pale, my body ice-cold with fasting, yet my mind burned with desire, and the fires of lust lashed my flesh as good as dead. I would rush from my cell, fling myself — metaphorically speaking — at the feet of Jesus, and water those feet with my tears.'

His audience of twenty or so ladies committed to Christ shuddered their appreciation. Cut off by choice from fashionable gatherings, from dinners and receptions, from performances of itinerant masters of rhetoric, it was long since they had been treated to such a dazzling display. Hot as it was in the salon, the ladies, leaning towards the man in their midst, might have been outside on a winter night, warming themselves at his fire. They barely noticed Blesilla slip in and arrange her skirts deliberately about her as she took her seat, aware that with her youth, silken clothes and jewels she was a challenge to them all.

Blesilla's gaze took in Marcella, distinguished in simple black, surrounded by her protégées. She recognised Asella, who fasted to extremes and had hardly said a word since the age of ten — and she must be in her fifties now. It was said that she had prayed until her holy knees were hard as a camel's. Beside her, Lea, who could have had a hundred or more satins or brocades, dressed in sackcloth and spent her nights in prayer. On the other side was her younger sister Eustochium who, inclined to plumpness, was one of the few to have gained in attractiveness from her spiritual exertions, at which she was already adept. She smiled at Blesilla, and Blesilla thought how very like their mother she looked.

And there, at the very front, was Paula, whom Blesilla admired beyond everyone, immobile in her concentration, staring at Jerome as though she lived for this moment. It occurred to

Blesilla that her mother had a vein of true splendour. She was capable of a passionate and total commitment to what she believed in, of rising above criticism and throwing off earthly ties. Paula, with her deepening religious fervour, was slipping away from her — perhaps, thought Blesilla, had slipped away, and was a mother only in her strictures on the holy life.

'I fixed my eyes on Heaven,' Jerome said in throbbing tones, 'and I felt myself amongst the angelic hosts.'

From Paula's rapt attention, thought Blesilla, he might have flown up to those limitless heights to look on the Kingdom and come back expressly to show her the way. Anger rose in her at the spectacle. Oh, he was a distinguished scholar, talking excitingly, bringing the whiff of the desert into this sumptuous room. But why, then, did he not remain there?

There was a pause. Someone sighed. Blesilla shifted in her chair and Jerome was distracted, momentarily, by the creak.

'But you left,' Blesilla challenged him. 'Why?'

His voice was quiet as he answered, 'I had the will to stay, but my fellow men drove me away. The Arian frenzy had spread everywhere. The Church of Antioch was divided and each faction wanted me for its own. Every day the monks demanded a declaration of my faith. Like wild beasts, they hounded me for heresy of which I was never guilty.'

He threw his arms wide, and his voice rose again: 'How could I allow myself to be dragged down by such disputes? The only dignity remaining to me was to stand apart — or leave. Duty therefore brought me to Rome, and to this home, where I find as true a dedication to Christ amongst you learned daughters of senators as ever I met in the desert.'

A murmur of gratitude rippled through the gathering.

Marcella broke in: 'We have been reading Saint Paul, and are wondering about his words to the Corinthians on virginity. He says that it is good for the present distress that a man remain a virgin. Can you explain to us what he meant by "distress"?'

'He was referring to the plight of man when the lusts of the flesh weigh heavy on his soul,' Jerome declared. 'Although some maintain that he is, more prosaically, referring to the famines which caused regular devastation at the time …

'On the other hand, Origen, with whom I know you are all acquainted, would answer that he meant more — marriage itself, which makes man a social animal and binds him like a vice to the things of this world.

'Do not, Origen says, think that just as the belly is made for food and food for the belly, that the body is in the same way made for intercourse. If you wish to understand the apostle's reasoning, then listen. The body is a temple to the Lord, and the soul a priest serving before the Holy Spirit that dwells in you.'

Blesilla shrank within herself as Jerome talked on, developing the relationship between the flesh and the Holy Spirit. She didn't feel at ease in the company of these virgins and chaste widows, and was hardly prepared for their living commitment to Christ. And these women hadn't even noticed her or, if they had, had simply dismissed her. It seemed to her that they inhabited another, infinitely deeper, world. Under cover of the questions that followed, Blesilla stole out.

PART TWO

INTRIGUE IN HIGH PLACES

8

Some time later, Jerome escorted Aetius to Pammachius's home on the Coelian Hill. It was mid-afternoon, and a breeze was beginning to stir the canopy of pine trees. Paolina, now married to Pammachius and in her seventh month of pregnancy, was ailing; and Aetius, it was known, had a gift for medicine.

Lying on cushions in her room, she brightened at the sight of Aetius. He bowed low before he took Paolina's pulse and listened to her lament her nausea, dizziness and food cravings.

'None of the doctors has done me any good,' Paolina sighed. 'I'm so tired, and my serving women watch me all the time. I'm never alone … I dream … I dream of miscarrying.'

'In the third stage of pregnancy,' said Aetius, 'the diet should be light and nourishing.' He recommended eating boiled eggs and porridge, and having her stomach massaged with a variety of ground leaves, rose oil and the cleanest of olive oils. 'I suggest also a little wine as a sedative before sleeping. It will relax you and give you strength.'

'I believe you're right,' said Paolina gratefully.

***

Shortly afterwards, Pammachius, that fine figure of a Roman gentleman who in his youth had excelled at wrestling and athletics, conducted Jerome through his oratory, recently built.

'My retreat from the world,' he explained, with a glance towards his wife. 'Paolina never stops complaining. Perhaps your young assistant will do her some good. Now let me show you the rest of my renovations.'

It was in the nymphaeum that Aetius finally joined them, in front of a fresco of the current favourite myth of Peleus and Thetis done by a master hand. Staring at it, he raised his hands in mysterious gesture, part-obeisance, part-rejection.

'The Lady Paolina?' enquired Pammachius.

'Rest, a careful diet, and certain sedatives that I have prescribed her,' replied Aetius, his eyes still on the fresco. 'Sweet-water baths will help too.'

'It's what she's already been told,' Pammachius frowned.

Aetius was no longer listening. He had fallen to his knees and his lips moved in prayer. Then, straightening up, he slid his hand slowly over the fresco.

'I've had a vision,' he muttered.

'By Hercules!' exclaimed Pammachius.

'Leave him be,' Jerome advised. 'He had a dream last night which has troubled him ever since.'

Aetius leaned against the wall, his face showing red in the setting sun.

'This morning we were in the catacombs,' said Jerome. 'Ever since worshipping at the holy resting places of the martyrs, he has been strangely excited.'

Aetius suddenly sank down and put his face to the ground. The other two men instinctively backed away as Aetius slithered his way across the stone floor towards the centre of the nymphaeum.

'Look!' cried Pammachius. 'He's gone mad!'

Standing up, Aetius struck his chest and muttered: 'Martyrs have their abode here. I was shown the position in my dream. You will find them beneath this floor, which must be raised.'

'It's true that two martyrs lived next door,' Pammachius agreed. 'But not here, in my house.'

'No, it was here.'

'Who were they and how did they die?' he asked slyly.

'John and Paul ...' Aetius was sweating now. 'And they were beheaded.'

'I never heard that they were buried here!' Pammachius

looked sceptical. 'In a private dwelling, inside the city walls?'

Aetius was adamant. 'They were buried in their own house. In secret. There can be no doubt.'

'I'd have to have the floor taken up to find out—and my nymphaeum has only just been built!' Nevertheless, Pammachius was not unmoved. 'I'll see what can be done. You can't be more precise, I suppose?'

Aetius bowed his head, waving a hand towards the fresco. Composed now, he spoke clearly and with self-assurance. 'Underneath there. On three successive nights I have seen the sea nymph Thetis arising from the waves, with the Nereids around her. I wondered why these creatures of legend should appear to me, a man of the Church. Now I understand. In the catacombs I breathed the scent of sanctity. I breathe that same fragrance of holiness now.'

Pammachius and Jerome, aware of the divine power of dreams, could not help but be impressed by such certainty. Jerome and Aetius left soon afterwards, assured that Pammachius would consider taking up the floor.

***

The workmen began the next day at dawn. By noon they had uncovered two skeletons, the heads severed, with stains of what was reputed to be dried blood: the brothers John and Paul, two soldiers martyred under the Emperor Julian over twenty years earlier for refusing to give up their faith. Of their identities there could be no doubt, for the hands of each were piously crossed over a small metal disc bearing his name.

As soon the news reached Damasus, he had himself carried to Pammachius's home to see the relics, and ordered that they be put on immediate public display. News of the martyrs' bones spread more quickly by word of mouth than if it had been carried by than the Imperial messengers. Throngs gathered outside Pammachius's home, the curious and the fervent, the maimed and the sick among them, praying that the two martyrs might intervene with God on their behalf. Soon, it was rumoured, relics might be on offer, if a certain member of Pammachius's household staff were approached with an appropriate gift. Damasus was thunderously hailed as the finder of the bones of the martyrs.

After they had made their prayers, Pammachius had a lengthy discussion with Damasus's representatives concerning the church which Pammachius was already planning to build over the site where the martyrs' bodies had lain. This would entail destruction of part of his own home, since the nymphaeum covered those vital remains of the house of John and Paul. The cost would be great, but money there was in plenty — Pammachius's money — at the Church's disposal.

***

In the excitement, Paolina had been all but forgotten. Pammachius found her tucked away in her bedroom, sulkily sipping from a silver cup, but she knew better than to complain. She had learned by now that she ranked well below any religious matter that had taken her husband's interest.

'I'm glad to see you've got some colour,' he commented, after they had discussed the bones. 'What's this you're taking?'

'A little wine and water does me good, Aetius said.' She set down the cup and began struggling out of bed. 'Now for the relics. I've been longing to see them!'

'It's out of the question, Paolina. You know you must lie in bed for eight days. Would you endanger the health of our child? Anyway, you're much better off here. It's developing into a dangerous situation outside. The few men I've got can't manage the crowds; more men are being sent from the Lateran to help out.'

After he had hurried off, Paolina fretted and drank another cup of wine and water to calm herself. For good measure, she then took a cup of wine without the water. Then another. And finally succumbed to sleep.

***

Early the next day, Jerome, who had seen the bones only briefly but shuddered at the thought of the boisterous crowd jostling outside Pammachius's portals, presented himself at Paula's mansion. He had more urgent business to attend with Blesilla, whom he found on the loggia.

'A word only.' Jerome began his onslaught with uncharacteristic understatement. 'Your mother has given me leave to talk with you.'

Blesilla showed no enthusiasm. She refused to be moved by the intensity of that voice that compelled so many. She tilted her head to indicate that she listened, but inwardly she was frantic. In his eyes, wasn't a girl's intact body her most precious possession? To make matters worse, the monthly curse of women was for her now overdue by more than a week.

'You are educated, the daughter of nobles, of a Christian mother and a distinguished father. I know you are highly intelligent. I have heard that even as a child you shone at your father's social gatherings.'

'I didn't "shine",' she said. 'We children used to play outside in summer, down in Campania. It was only that I could recite any amount of Virgil, and this used to impress the adults.'

Her father, she recalled, had been proud of her memory. Outside, Bassus would chase her until he captured her, and they would fall to the ground, shrieking with laughter until, one day, their games were observed by the adults ...

'You are a human being,' Jerome was saying. 'But your body, this flesh and blood, in its purity is a wondrous gift which, if you choose to keep intact, could be made into a temple of God, as Origen puts it—an offering dearer to Him than any vessel of gold or silver ...'

'By not marrying, you mean? If we all did that, the human race would come to an end,' she fenced.

'Never fear,' he said with grim humour. 'Only those of great quality can rise to the challenge.'

He waved his hand at the crowd milling round in the court-yard below waiting for Paula's daily handouts. 'Look at them! What are they capable of? But *you*, upon whom God has bestowed so many natural talents—how much you could accomplish if you freed yourself from the shackles of the marital bond and devoted yourself instead to His glory!'

He voice rose, and he stepped closer. 'My child, forsake your coloured necklaces, your elaborate curls, the rouge that covers your cheeks, the belladonna at your eyes! Your face so white with chalk you look like an idol! What are you trying to achieve; whom are you trying to impress? Is the natural beauty with which God endowed you not enough? Consider the humble Eustochium, content with simple clothing, a veil for her head, decked out with no ornament, defiled by no make-up.'

He paused. 'Will you allow your little sister to outstrip you in the eyes of God?'

Blesilla looked at him mutinously. 'My marriage is all arranged,' she murmured. 'My family has taken charge of that.'

Jerome ignored her remark.

'What does marriage offer a woman?' he continued. 'A prison! You'll be the servant of your husband. You'll be humiliated, a captive in your own home. Think of it—nine months of sickness, the delivery, with the blood, dangers and pain—and then afterwards, the crying of infants, the cares of managing a household, the giving in to your husband's desires, the jealousy when you find out about your rivals in his affection … the complete, utter lack of freedom. All stemming from a lack of vision, a short-sightedness, an unwillingness to rise above the demands of the body!'

She was silenced now, staring at him with horror.

'The end of marriage is death,' he rapped out. 'The prize for virginity is eternal life. Oh, don't get me wrong, marriage has its place — after all, it gives us virgins — but never forget that it is the result of the Fall, and that virginity, when chosen freely, confers a higher honour. The beauty of this world is but a pale shadow of the spiritual world. And yet you seek sensual gratification — fine clothing, rich food, and the pleasures of the marriage bed!'

She gasped and reddened.

'My child,' he beseeched her, 'seek Christ instead! Married love-making will never approach the blazing embrace of Christ in the spirit. I implore you, keep your body for Christ!'

'I can't.' She could hardly force the words out. 'It's too late.'

'It's never too late! You can break your engagement.'

A door banged. A maid hurried out and whispered urgently to a eunuch. He bowed, and said in his high-pitched voice:

'She's come from the Lady Paolina. She's been taken ill!'

Blesilla sprung up. 'The baby!' she cried.

'Ah, my lady, there will be no baby,' the maid sobbed. 'She *would* see the bones. She would go! She crept down to the nymphaeum before anyone was awake, by the light of a tiny lamp. The floor was taken up, all the tiles piled up just as the workmen left it yesterday, and she fell into the excavations. They heard her terrible screams — she went on, crazy-like, for hours. And the pains began at once. They say she can't live …'

Jerome fell to his knees in prayer, and the maid retreated respectfully. To Blesilla, though, he was a figure of doom. Hadn't he said it? 'The end of marriage was death.'

***

What the maid didn't tell them, but what Pammachius was hearing from the physician at the same time, was no less alarming.

'She would never have gone, her women say, never have defied you, my lord, if she hadn't been ...'

'Hadn't been what? Speak up, fool!' Pammachius snapped as the slave faltered.

'Perhaps she was taken by a wild impulse, as women in her condition often are —'

'Are you saying that my wife is irrational? What nonsense! For a woman, Paolina's as sane as they come!'

'Well—I mean—the fact is, my lord, she wasn't in possession of her senses.'

'Spit it out, man! What are you saying?'

'She had been taking wine.'

'You mean that she was *drunk*?'

'Very much so, my lord! Oh, my lord, never before in her life ...'

***

With the loss of her baby, Paolina suffered severe haemorrhage and her life was despaired of. The family gathered around her where, pale as one of the petunias in her own garden, she lay on her ample chair, supported by cushions, while the physicians and midwives laboured. Maids pressed hot compresses against her sides; others applied cloths soaked in warm olive oil over her stomach. The room reeked of strong smelling herbs, designed to trigger her senses and keep death at bay.

Then, on the third day, she rallied, sustained perhaps by the prayers offered up by the entire household, or by the tiny bag of bone fragments from the skeletons of John and Paul which her husband had hung around her neck.

***

Only days afterwards, some graceful verses celebrating the memory of the martyrs John and Paul had appeared and were circulated around the city. In the verses it was suggested, again, that the discovery had in fact been made by His Holiness himself.

'Of course,' Aetius remarked to the Deacon Innocentius, 'it was I who found John and Paul, not Damasus.'

'Really?' Innocentius levelled. 'The crowd took up the cry from the moment Damasus appeared in Pammachius's portico that day. No one could have convinced them otherwise. What does it matter who finds them?' He shot Aetius a sideways glance. 'After all, Damasus did appear in your dream pointing the way to the site of the bones, I believe?'

'It is so.' Aetius was cornered, and he knew it.

'His Holiness is very old,' smiled Innocentius. 'And remember that a vision such as yours does not make you better than anyone else. It is through God's grace that visions are granted us and indeed, a revelation such as yours comes only in the most favourable circumstances. When, for instance, a very godly bishop is leading the Church.'

Aetius bowed his head, as much to hide his thoughts as out of respect. He had, after all, only spread news of his vision in order to flatter Damasus and secure his approval.

***

Rolling up his scrolls later that evening, Aetius said to Jerome, 'I suppose it is often the fate of God's humble servants to go unnoticed and unpraised. Yet I confess that the thought of a promotion had occurred to me.'

Jerome laid down his pen. 'You refer to your discovery of the bones, I take it?'

Aetius nodded, and Jerome looked at him thoughtfully. 'Does it not seem immoral to you to be rewarded in a material sense for having been empowered by God to locate relics on this particular occasion? Does it really matter to you that people think that Damasus found the bones?' He paused. 'After all, for a man of humble beginnings — although you never did tell me much about your family — you have come far.'

Aetius clasped his hands together until the knuckles showed white. 'I am glad, sir, that you see fit to praise me — for my secretarial work at least.'

'Oh, I can't praise you highly enough, Aetius. You are invaluable to me.' So saying, Jerome picked up his pen, dipped it in black ink, and began writing again.

***

As it happened, Aetius was promoted to the post of full clerk. There were whispers that he could even become Jerome's successor as Head of the Church Archives, should Jerome himself become the Bishop of Rome. For Damasus couldn't last for ever, and Jerome was so greatly in favour.

***

Paolina said nothing about the experience which led to her miscarriage; it was assumed that it was the wine that had caused her to slip and fall into the excavations, in turn causing her to haemorrhage. Years later, she confessed to her family what had really happened that night. One other person had been there, she said, or so it had seemed. In the dim and flickering light of the oil lamp, her fevered mind had told her that it was Aetius, standing in the excavations on the very place in which the martyrs had lain, drinking red wine from a chalice of such transparent crystal that he could have been drinking blood.

Only then had she fainted and fallen.

9

Jerome was finding much to criticise in Roman life, both inside the Church and without. This particular morning he strode up and down his office, inveighing against one Helvidius, a mere layman who dared assert that the celibate state was no better than the married, and even sought to prove that after giving birth to Jesus, Mary had lived a normal married life with Joseph and borne him several more children. And all on the strength of the apostle's words, 'Joseph did not know her until she brought forth her firstborn son.'

'Maybe,' ventured Aetius, 'Helvidius's education does not permit him to appreciate, as you can, the semantic risks we run when translating from the Greek.'

Jerome stopped, surprised. 'You may have a point! We are all aware that 'know' in the Bible denotes sexual relations, but a word such as 'until' had multiple meanings and connotations, depending on context. And thus, Helvidius would have us believe that Joseph, seeing the Magi, the Star, Herod, the angels, dared touch the temple of God, the abode of the Holy Ghost, the mother of his God, and seize Mary the moment she was delivered!' He paused. 'Read out what I've said so far, Aetius.'

Aetius did so. Jerome sat down, visibly relaxed.

'Word perfect. Sometimes I think you even improve on what I say.'

Aetius said quickly: 'There is a sympathy between you and me. Like you, I was bred on Virgil and Lucretius and Cicero.'

'Indeed. Where did you get your education, Aetius?'

'Here in Rome under Victorinus, sir, at a very famous school. I had a master who paid my fees in return for certain chores. I was an orphan, you see, from the age of twelve.'

'And before that?'

'My father, who was a clerk of the City Council of Latina, had his property confiscated when I was young. A little matter of his accepting a bribe. I was forced to leave school and work for a goldsmith. Later I made my way to Rome, and got another job with a nobleman who was impressed with my abilities, sir, and for almost five years made sure I was given a classical education.'

'In Victorinus you had an excellent teacher,' observed Jerome. 'And you had the sons of the nobility for school fellows! You have a quick and well-stocked mind, Aetius. You might easily have got a position in the law or even at court, had you not left. Why then did you leave Victorinus?'

'Jealousy, sir. I was forced to leave school after an — incident. A fellow scholar claimed that I had ridiculed his performance in class. I was thrown out of my patron's house as well, as a result.'

Jerome did not miss the darkening of Aetius's face, and the quiver in his voice as he gave a bald account of the ruin of his prospects of a career.

'I worked at all sorts of things after that, sir. Even as a doctor of medicine — but physicians are not respected here as they are in Greece. Though I continued to work as a healer, I thought the Church might offer me something better. As you know, the Deacon Innocentius got me a post as exorcist.'

A slave brought in a bowl of steaming broth and set it down before Jerome.

'What's this?' demanded Jerome. 'You know I — '

'Drink it to please me!' Aetius implored. 'It was me who requested it, sir.'

'You'd have me indulge myself at the very time I'm expounding on the virtues of fasting for monks?'

'How many monks are blessed with *your* intellectual powers, sir, or your restless energy? The intellect needs feeding.

You can't go on with just a little bread dipped in oil, and wine to wash it down. How can I watch you deprive yourself when I see a bishop — sir, I name no names! — gorging himself on partridges at table last week? Such delicacies that he enjoyed — honey-sweetened pastries that made your mouth water just to look at them! He can tell you the exact spot on the coast a mussel comes from, the vineyard that produced the very wine in his glass!'

Jerome's eyes, red-rimmed, took fire. He clenched his hands as if to shield himself from his assistant's words.

'Only this morning I saw the Deacon Anemius picking his way over the puddles so daintily for fear the high polish on his shoes might suffer. Bright as a tropical bird, sir — his hair in curls and enough perfume to knock you over. Headed for the Lady Calpurnia's palace, he was.' Aetius warmed to his subject. 'Then I often see the Deacon Ascholius. He knows all the gossip. Got something on everyone. Not a lady but she's scared to cross him. He's even been seen coming from the Lady Paula's.'

'Not Paula! What could he find to hold over *her*!' Jerome's words were a statement rather than a question, and Aetius knew he had run up against hard rock.

'No doubt,' Aetius put in, 'it concerned her daughter Blesilla, who leads a very … social life.'

'She's bent on marrying,' said Jerome irritably. 'If that's what you mean.'

'She's very pretty,' sighed Aetius. 'As Tertullian says, sir, in public a girl is fondled all over by roving eyes, tickled by pointing fingers, and warms to it.'

Jerome's lips tightened. 'Your reading has been wide, boy.'

'Tertullian is all rhetorical tricks,' commented Aetius. 'Not to be compared with a scholar like you, sir! Your letters are more vivid than the spoken word and will live forever.' He paused. 'There is much in Rome to tickle your satirical bent, sir. I could tell you so much more.'

He proceeded to do exactly that. Jerome consumed the rest of his broth to tales of the excesses of bishops and deacons; so-called virgins who slept with churchmen and had abortions; and rich widows who entertained fawning clergymen to sumptuous meals …

'… and retire at last to dream of the apostles, no doubt,' said Jerome sourly.

'Pope Damasus himself, of course, is notorious for his opulent lifestyle, especially in his relations with certain aristocratic ladies,' Aetius continued. 'Don't they call him "the matrons' ear-tickler"? I've heard that in the past his intimacy with some –'

But at this point Jerome cut his assistant off, and dictation was hurriedly resumed.

***

The next day, Aetius was intercepted by the Deacon Innocentius in the grounds of the Lateran gardens.

'What brings you here, Aetius?' he asked.

'I'm delivering documents from Jerome to His Holiness.'

'Is that so? And what documents would they be?'

'Just a Biblical commentary,' Aetius answered.

'So our Dalmatian priest is now a Biblical exegete!'

'Jerome knows not only Greek but Hebrew –' began Aetius.

'Equipment enough to interpret Scripture!' Innocentius cut in. 'I hear you now work closely with him?'

'Yes. Jerome's eyesight is poor. Sometimes he can scarcely correct my drafts. He needs someone quick and well-read.'

'Well, you may go far, Aetius, in this capacity – though don't forget that I have you taken on only as an exorcist.'

Innocentius, a normally reserved and austere man, bent his swarthy Roman face to Aetius's, and said: 'And what exactly is Jerome working on now?'

'Well, it's a treatise to refute Helvidius—'

'Yes, yes. I know about Helvidius. Jerome will handle him brilliantly, I'm sure.'

'He is also translating Origen into Latin,' Aetius continued. 'The two Homilies on the Song of Songs. Perhaps also the Commentaries. But his greatest work is revising all the translations of the Bible to make a single standard Latin version. He's already begun on the Gospels.'

'A mighty task,' breathed Innocentius. 'Oh, indeed.'

***

Later that evening, Innocentius sought out the Deacon Siricius.

'So, amongst all the versions of the Bible in existence, Jerome is to determine what text is the one that most closely reflects the original!'

'At His Holiness's bidding,' said Siricius. 'The words of Jerome are always on his lips.'

'Indeed, Jerome has risen like a star,' purred Innocentius, his gaze intent. 'He feels free to air his views, interpret dogma, and to lay down the official view of the Church.'

His fingers arched in a delicate emphasis of his points, Innocentius made a rapid and cryptic speech. 'Interpreting the Bible must always be a risky business, likely to call forth the harshest criticism. Jerome expounds the Bible for His Holiness. Is Jerome therefore a theologian? His Holiness is a very old man now, his faculties sometimes failing. Jerome cites a multitude of Christian Fathers in his support. One wonders if he has read them all … Jerome translates Origen for Damasus—Origen, a great theologian no doubt, but called by some a heretic!'

'Jerome can be very persuasive,' Siricius pointed out.

'He has the gift of words—and sometimes is carried away by them. He has put his pen to the service of the Church. But is Jerome's pen more important to him than the Church? This pen spares no one. He is no respecter of wealth or person or position. Now all Rome praises Jerome for his piety, for his humility. There are rumours that he might even succeed His Holiness. There is always danger to the man so favoured. What if a breath of scandal should touch him? Scandal-mongers will feed on a mere nothing. A whisper can give birth to an outcry.'

It was Innocentius's way to leave his words dangling without giving his listener a chance to comment. So now he bowed his head in salute, and made off down the long corridor towards the chapel for Vespers, his stole fluttering up behind his left shoulder.

10

The shock of Paolina's near-death and the anxious hours of her convalescence had sharpened Paula's concern over Blesilla's future.

'Jerome has talked with you, hasn't he?' she asked, as they returned from their walk in the gardens. She had commanded her daughter's presence that morning in the room reserved for Bible study classes, for Paula now ran her own group.

Paula scrutinised the face of her eldest child. Blesilla had that radiant look that often followed on the monthly curse of women — or perhaps it was the morning exercise.

Blesilla stared back at her mother, remembering that her unruly dark hair had once been carefully dressed, that she had not always been so pale from fasting. But Paula's eyes glowed and her voice was eager.

'I don't want to be one of your chaste self-elect of God,' Blesilla said firmly, 'and give up everything.'

Paula looked shocked. 'Everything — you mean your marriage?'

'Yes! After all, you and Papa arranged the match for me.'

'Ah, my child … That was before I understood how infinitely greater is the life dedicated to Christ, and how much richer the rewards.' She smiled. 'Anyway, Furius is only an apathetic Christian if he's really one at all. If you had to marry, a man like Pammachius would have been better. I hear he grows more devout every day.'

'Yes, Paolina's got it both ways,' muttered Blesilla, swept by sudden fury at her mother's conviction.

'What do you mean, both ways?'

'I mean that Paolina's lucky to have Pammachius. And now she's even lost her baby,' Blesilla said, with heavy irony.

Her mother shook her head. 'You seek refuge from your inner confusion in sarcasm, my child... But I entreat you to weigh up your choices carefully. What do you think your life with Furius will offer you?'

Blesilla found it hard to reply. She had a confused vision of being at the centre of the social whirl of high society, but also of visits to Furius's country villas with their canopies of grape-vines, the smell of newly cut hay and the lowing of animals.

'In town I'll give parties,' she said recklessly. 'Marvellous parties, with crowds of people, with banquets of venison, pig or wild goat, and wines in silver goblets — like ours used to be.'

'In that case,' retorted Paula, 'you will be opening up your house to Heaven knows who — jumped up senators, nobodies at court and all the wives in tow. You'll have a baby, then an-other ...'

In her mind, Blesilla was already dandling a baby on her knees, feeling its little hands clutch at her. But the baby had the crumpled, fascinating little face of Bassus.

'You had Papa's babies,' Blesilla pointed out.

Paula stared at her daughter in silence for a moment before she said: 'I was overjoyed when you were born. But I married a man with great qualities.' Her eyes were full of unspoken thoughts. 'It's not unqualified happiness for a mother to see her daughter marry. Men can be brutes, you know. Most will divorce a wife if they don't produce a son — and the law is all in their favour. Then, childbirth is so dangerous — '

'Oh, I know, I know.' Again, Blesilla deflected the conver-sation back to her mother. 'You could have refused to have babies.'

'Refuse your father? When he so wanted a son?' Paula's face stiffened. 'Your father was an open and generous man. Furius is closed and hard.'

'Perhaps I know him better than you.' She spoke without conviction.

'Furius only cares about his writing,' Paula pressed on. 'He has set his sights on being a great poet. Your role will be to bring him more money and give him sons.'

'Furius is very good-looking. You said yourself that he has a nice high colour.'

'Rather too high, perhaps. He could be apoplectic, like his father. And he's quick to take offence.'

'You haven't really anything against Furius, Mamma, except his poetry. After all, what does Jerome do but write?'

Paula came to instant life. 'You dare put Furius on the same level as Jerome? Compare a dilettante to a man whose work is to save souls? Poets! Nowadays they only write for each other, courting approval and general popularity. But Jerome's work is intended for the whole world! He cares nothing for what people think and is impervious to criticism. He has no thought for money. He only burns with desire to submerge his soul in God and teach us to do the same. Compare Jerome with Furius! Why,' — Paula's eyes shone with tears — 'since his dream, Jerome hasn't once opened his Virgil or Cicero, even though he's so cultivated a man.'

Silenced, Blesilla watched her mother's passionate face. Finally she managed:

'What dream was that?'

'Years ago, when he had fallen dangerously ill in Antioch, God appeared to him and accused Jerome of being a Ciceronian rather than a Christian, because of his love of pagan literature. For years afterwards he never even touched the classics, and now as you know he concentrates all his energies on the Scriptures.' After a moment, she added: 'It transformed him, that vision — gave his life spiritual impetus. It wasn't long afterwards that he set off for the desert of Chalcis. What suffering he endured during those five years as a hermit!'

A thought struck Blesilla. 'Mamma, you aren't going to make one of those dreadful pilgrimages, are you?'

'You call it "dreadful" to visit the sacred sites? Anyway, it's nothing these days. Everyone goes.'

Paula began to talk again of Jerome's hardships in the desert. It was plain to Blesilla that he had not only inspired her with religious fervour, but had excited her womanly sympathy. Blesilla pictured her mother's departure on a long and dangerous tour of the holy places, and shuddered.

'It was so nice before you got religion, Mamma,' she pleaded. 'Those summers in the country when at your receptions all of us children watched behind the pillars, listening to the grown-ups talk and laugh while we played—and later finished up all that marvellous food ...'

'Oh, the country, the city!' Paula dismissed their shared memories with a wave of her hand. 'Such small people, with petty concerns! We have a larger vision now.'

'You know you only turned to God because you missed Papa so much and couldn't bear life without him,' Blesilla said, recovering herself. 'Anyway, Papa wanted me to marry.'

There was a short silence. 'I didn't see things clearly then,' Paula said finally. 'Marriage, especially. The psalm says: "Man was in honour but abided not; he became like the beasts that perish." Do you know what that means, Blesilla?'

Blesilla had no answer.

'It means that Adam was born with the spirit of God in him and was to live forever. This was God's will. It says in Ecclesiastes that after the Fall, Adam and Eve were married not to God but to each other. By their sex they became like the animals and died like animals, yet tried to defy death by making young ones.'

Paula turned towards her daughter. 'We, however, are free to choose. We can regain the spirit by not marrying, by turning instead to God. Jerome has explained what Paul meant when he said that the end of marriage is death; but marriage to God is eternal life.'

'Not marrying is easier for some than for others,' said Blesilla. 'And didn't Paul himself say that it is better to marry than to burn? How does Jerome get around that?'

Faced with Paula's implacable silence, Blesilla feared that now more than ever that there was no swaying her mother's mind. Paula was Jerome's now, not theirs. Paula clearly felt sorry for him — and once a woman pitied a man, anything could happen.

A maid entered to announce that the Bishop Epiphanius was asking for her. Paula stood up, pausing briefly to lay her hands on Blesilla.

'My child,' she said, 'sooner or later you'll come into the fold, I feel sure. So much work awaits us. You don't imagine that we're idle, do you?'

Lightly, she tapped Blesilla's rouged and white-leaded cheek, setting her pearl earrings swinging on their golden chains. Then Paula took a small book from her desk.

'Here, read Jerome's *Life of Paul*. It's a little masterpiece. Then perhaps you'll understand its author better.'

Thrusting the book at Blesilla, she hurried off to greet her guest.

11

'It's late, and you haven't transcribed what I dictated yesterday, Aetius.' Jerome looked hard at his assistant.

'I was with the Lady Faltonia Proba, sir.'

'Not again! You always come back exhausted. I suppose that business of exorcism takes precedence over my trifling work on Holy Scripture!'

'The ladies of the house are very religious, sir.' Aetius's tone was conciliatory. 'The aunt even wrote a poem!'

'Puerile sleight of hand,' sneered Jerome. 'Borrowing from Virgil to write Biblical history! Twisting Virgil—Christless as he was—to squeeze a Christian message from him! Oh, everyone wants to take a hand in the Scriptures, tear them to pieces and teach them before they learn them.' Jerome's dark eyes burned with exasperation. 'But their message is ineffable, mysterious, given us to ponder ...'

As Jerome talked, he quite forgot to ask about the progress of Aetius's mission at the palace of the Anicii.

***

The request by the Anicii family for an exorcist had been sanctioned by Damasus himself not long before on the occasion of one of his banquets, naturally an affair of great elegance. One of his guests had been Probus. The two formidable old men appreciated each other, each grasping and retentive of power—the one who had not shrunk from mob violence and bloody massacre to get elected to the Chair of Saint Peter; the other who had amassed one of the greatest fortunes in the Western world, supplementing his proceeds gained from marrying into the Anicii clan by private profits from several eminent public posts.

Compliments passed back and forth, particularly regarding a sermon recently preached by Damasus. The blessed martyrs, Damasus had declared, and especially Peter and Paul, had exalted the Romans as a sacred race, made priestly and royal, fit to rule the world through divine religion.

Noting the Pontiff's beneficent expression, particularly after wine had been generously dispensed, Probus decided that the moment had come to make his request. His nostrils quivered with distaste as he explained the position. As every Roman knew, family was family. What talking could do had been tried, he said, but it had been useless. There was something there that was stubborn as a mule, or else came from the Devil. Did Damasus think that religion could help?

Damasus wished that he had not let his mind wander. By subtle and allusive probing, he at last found that Probus was talking of a niece from a provincial branch of the family. She was a beautiful girl, just married, who absolutely refused to let her young husband near her. She had dreams, he said, recurrent dreams that had begun with puberty.

'Juliana's convinced that she'll give birth to snakes, like those in the Garden of Eden, who'll "whisper wicked temptation in the ears of the good at night" — these were her very words! And her voice changes when she rejects her husband — he says it is almost a growl, low, such as he's never heard before.'

Probus's shrewd old face wore a look of bafflement. 'Yet in all other respects she's a normal and obedient girl. The family's desperate!'

Damasus realised that Probus was hinting at a papal exorcism of his young relation, although he must know that she was hardly important enough for that. However, he needed to retain the support of this man who did, at least, have the discernment to appreciate his recent sermon — or the wit to appear to do so. Damasus promised to send a clever exorcist to perform privately. Grateful for this promise, Probus allowed a hint of deference to appear in his thanks.

***

At the appointed time Aetius, whose reputation in this respect was high, had been conducted to the magnificent town house of the Anicii family set on the Coelian Hill. A maid led him through its many corridors to an apartment with its own private oratory. He prepared the holy water, salt and oil which he regularly used in personal exorcisms, before kneeling in an attitude of prayer.

Finally, an aunt led the girl in. Aetius stood up to behold a Roman beauty, with features of classical purity set off by her lustrous black hair falling around her face. Juliana was only fifteen years old, they had said, but her simple, expensive robe emphasised the maturity of what was even then a voluptuous figure. A few questions revealed this girl to be childish, however, and touched — even if lightly — by the hand of God.

Aetius instructed the servants that he was to be left alone with the girl for as long as he found necessary to perform the rite of exorcism. Repeated prayers, incantations, and laying on of hands were required, Aetius told the family later, but on the details he would not be drawn. 'The utmost discretion,' he told them, 'is necessary.'

On each visit, the door of the oratory was bolted and the female members of the family would wait nervously until later in the long afternoon when Aetius would conduct the girl out and lead her back to her aunt. The older woman discerned the vibrant intensity which, despite his controlled manner, emanated from Aetius. By contrast the girl was, as her aunt had expected, pale and almost unaware, it seemed, of what was happening.

At the end of the series of visits, Aetius informed the family that the girl was now completely free of the evil spirit that had

84

inhabited her and dominated her words and actions. God's will now had an open path to her soul and her heart, and her husband would find her eager to embrace her role as his wife.

The family was relieved, and impressed with Aetius's modesty. He had, he said, simply been enabled to do good.

***

'Juliana is quite docile now,' Aetius reported, when Jerome remembered to ask. 'She will give her husband the sons he wants. Her demon has been expelled and replaced with a spirit of life.'

12

'You have a special liking for that bird, Blesilla, don't you?'

In a salon of Paula's villa, Furius watched his future wife daintily feeding nuts through the bars of the cage to her parrot.

'He's so clever,' she replied.

'"It",' said Furius. 'It's just a damn bird. Best dished up on the dining table than kept in a fancy ivory cage!'

The parrot shrieked, 'Cage, cage!' several times, reproducing Furius's intonation with surprising precision.

'Listen to that!' Blesilla cried triumphantly. 'And he's never heard the word before!'

'It's malevolent,' Furs retorted. 'It swore the other day.'

'For some reason he doesn't like you, Furius.'

Furius pushed a finger through the cage to scratch the parrot's head. The bird snapped and drew blood.

'Feeling's mutual,' muttered Furius, as a maid hurried off for acetum to wash her master's wound.

He had just attended a friend's praetorian games, and was dressed in a splendid velvet robe of dull red reflected, it seemed, in the warm colour of his handsome face. He was an imposing man of thirty with a growing literary reputation.

'That bird was a present from Bassus, wasn't it?' Furius asked suddenly. He laughed without mirth. 'Bassus is quite the ladies' man now, I hear.'

'Is he really?' Perversely, Blesilla enjoyed talking about Bassus with her husband-to-be. 'I think he laughs at them, at everyone.'

'He laughs, certainly. Oh, he can be most entertaining. He's also one of the most ambitious men you could find. You won't see him laughing at anyone he thinks important. One day he'll be Imperial Quaestor himself.'

'It's natural that he wants to get on,' she protested. 'He spent years studying the law and rhetoric.'

'Yet now he chooses to be a glorified secretary rather than to practise?' Furius's contempt was palpable.

'That's not fair!' Blesilla burst out. 'Isn't the Quaestor a sort of spokesman for the Emperor himself?'

'Spokesman? Hardly! He writes letters and drafts laws at the beck and call of others.'

'That's hardly Bassus's fault!'

Furius raised an eyebrow. 'Such vehemence!' he remarked. 'Do calm down. His way of life seems pointless to me, but he probably thinks the same of mine. The enfant terrible, the wild boy, now turned court favourite.'

'He lives *in* the world,' she said. 'You live through your poetry.'

'Ah, poetry!' Furius's face relaxed. 'Now, that's what I live for.'

She knew it was true. The vigour of his lines, his metrical ability, and his Christian themes were much admired.

A feeling of uncertainty washed over Blesilla, and she felt as though everything was a matter of perception, that no one occupation was better than any other one. It was the effect that Furius had on her sometimes.

He had just finished reading to her some verses he had dedicated to Petronius Probus. They were composed in a light vein, and celebrated Probus's villa in Campania.

He had called on all the pagan gods to grace the theme, pictured Bacchus with his entourage pausing in envy at the sight, and suggested that Venus herself might haunt the colonnaded courts and sumptuous baths. Furius drew himself up as he read, his voice gaining in resonance with each line.

Blesilla was reminded of a remark that Bassus had made down in that very villa: 'My uncle lapped up that poem. Of course, he couldn't have built the villa without the money he squeezed out of the provincials, the old scoundrel.' He had added, a wicked twist to his lips, 'Wily old scoundrel, mind you — created one of the sights of Italy.'

'Probus is a wily old scoundrel,' Blesilla said now, watching Furius.

'You'll do me no good by such remarks concerning our Praetorian Prefect for next year,' he frowned. 'My piece, by the way, has enjoyed a wide circulation!'

'It's a marvellous poem,' said Blesilla solemnly, and felt sure that she meant it.

'Not without some graceful touches, perhaps,' said Furius, mollified. 'Of course, my lady writes herself.'

Blesilla took a sudden decision. She stood up and left the room, returning a moment later holding a roll of parchment.

'You can look at this, if you like. It's an elegy.'

'Blesilla has written an elegy! Then let *my* Muse be silent!'

'There's no need to be like that, Furius,' she said crossly. 'I'd just like to know what you think of it, that's all.'

He bit his lower lip, then clapped a hand over his mouth in mock self-castigation and bent reverently over her manuscript. Blesilla thought suddenly that he looked a perfect fool. She was surprised at herself, for she was instinctively respectful of this mature, celebrated man.

Furius sat down to study the poem. Finally, he raised his eyes.

'Ah, shades of the great Propertius! Your first line recalls the spirit:

> *"Before my tomb, O Paula wife, now stay*
> *Your grieving tears."*

'Daring to challenge the master on his own ground! Only a little confusion of sentiment in your development of the theme. A few too many elisions in the first half.'

His brow wrinkled as he went on reading, this time aloud:

"'Alone, dear wife,
Rebuild the sweetness of our family life.
Be father to our little son, find husbands
For our girls, more chaste than Claudia, she
Who moved Cybele from Tiber's sea.

I'll pray that you by gracious deed and prayer
Will guide their lives with all the loving care
That we together gave. But through long nights
In dreams embrace me, and fast hold;
And for our children, guard the family gold."'

Furius finished reading. Unsure what to expect, she was nevertheless unprepared for the effect of the last lines on him. He threw back his head, and laughed heartily — the first time she had ever witnessed him in the grip of such a wholly natural outburst.

'What do you find so funny?' she demanded.

'The family gold — that's marvellous!' he said, wiping his eyes. 'And to talk of Cybele to a woman so profoundly Christian as your mother ...'

'I wrote it in memory of Papa.' Blesilla was near to tears.

'But to influence your mother, as well, perhaps? She has, after all, a reputation for giving her money away.'

Furius was scanning the whole poem professionally now, she noted. She felt her hopes rise.

'Would you circulate it amongst our two families, at least to begin with?' she asked.

'I think not.' His tone was decisive. 'Copies would be bound to leak out and it would reflect on my own reputation.' He smiled at her indulgently. 'It's not a bad little poem, though.'

She glared at him. 'Not a bad little poem?'

He saw how affronted she was, and hastily suggested they go to a jeweller's he knew where she could console herself by choosing a new pendant, or brooch, or perhaps a gemstone from the new collection that had just come in from Persia. He knew she had a weakness for precious stones.

As they left the villa, neither noticed the approach of Aetius, holding a scroll which Jerome wished Paula to read. Aetius turned away so as not to be recognised but, had they looked, they would have been surprised at the hatred that contorted his features, transforming his earnest good looks into a bitter parody of himself. Trembling with rage at the sight of the departing couple, Aetius thought back to the day when Furius had demanded, and obtained, his expulsion from the school in which his continued attendance would have opened the doors to advancement and wealth.

***

Despite Paula, despite Jerome, and despite her own misgivings, Blesilla married Furius three months later. The two joined hands in one of Rome's largest churches, one autumn day late in the year 382 AD, in a lavish double wedding with Furius's sister who was marrying one of Probus's sons. Society came in numbers not seen for years in Paula's mansion, where banqueting went on until just before dawn in her largest reception hall, decked out with what remained of the old family store of treasures.

In the middle sat enthroned the four young newlyweds, Blesilla resplendent in a specially embroidered gown of ivory silk, while speeches were made and toasts drunk by members of all the great Roman families — the Furii, Fabii, Anicii, Ceionii, Symmachi, Gracchi, Maecii and Memmi. Guests admired the silver wedding caskets and abundant gifts, the most beautiful a small chryselephantine Zeus, a perfect miniature of that sculpted by Phidias for Olympia.

After the banquet, Furius and Blesilla made the long carriage journey to Furius's country villa on the Via Appia, the music and clamour of the night still ringing in their ears. In the grounds of the villa, by torchlight, the household staff and groundsmen also feasted. Later, according to custom, Furius carried his bride up the steps and through the portal of her new home; this was the moment that sealed a marriage.

In the elegant interior of the villa, Blesilla was attended to by a circle of women. She stood in the ante-room while her maids removed her rich dress, and then two older women conducted her — a sacrificial lamb, as her mother had warned — to the bedroom, where pristine white sheets covered the bed. Ceremoniously, the women removed her heavy earrings, gold chains and other ornaments, and unpicked the rich sapphires in her hair, and stored them all away in specially prepared caskets. Finally, she stood, feeling naked in a simple undergarment, awaiting her husband.

As he threw open the door, a hoarse cry from the far corner of the room caused them both to start, and Blesilla recognised an endearment which Bassus used to use.

'Furius, it's the parrot,' she cried, terrified. 'He's in the room!'

Cursing, he barked out an order to his servants. Within minutes, the bird was caught and removed, squawking loudly.

Rigid and trembling from her long ordeal, Blesilla saw Furius, the man of poetry, of feverish bookish industry, become the male inflamed, a brute intent on his own savage pleasure. He fell on her, and unresponsive she remained through the assault until, sated at last, he cast her summarily from him, rolled over and instantly fell asleep.

Before dawn, she awoke from a restless doze to find her husband already clothed, reading in a chair. He smiled complacently and drew her to the window, quoting a line from Horace.

Later, after her maids had helped her dress, he commented: 'That old servant of yours whipped the bedclothes away very promptly this morning.'

Her heart missed a beat.

'Did you want to inspect them, Furius?' she managed to ask, 'after the manner of our ancestors?'

He laughed, cupped her face in his hands and kissed her.

'My little wife,' he murmured, and kissed her again. Then he left her to her women, explaining that he wanted an uninterrupted spell on a new poem.

13

Autumn passed into winter, a severe one, that of 382–383 AD.
On the frontiers of the Empire, the armies suffered increasing invasions from the rebellious Goths in the north to the
Persians in the south. Rome itself suffered, as snow covered
the passes of the Alps and roads blocked up. Corn from Africa, the city's main source of grain, was scarce and foreigners
were expelled from the city to relieve pressure on food.

In the office of the Lateran archives, Jerome worked in-
tensively, with Aetius's help. An additional commitment just
now was a statement that His Holiness wanted to help those
who chose to walk in the glorious path of virginity. Jerome
composed it in the form of a letter to that virgin of tender
years and most endearing innocence, Eustochium, daughter
of Paula, the exemplar of all he advocated.

Over several days, to the furious scratching of Aetius's pen
on parchment, Jerome explored, tried and juggled with glittering phrase and dramatic concept to glorify virginity, to
denounce sensual passion, and to exalt the struggle of virgins to overcome it. He lashed gluttony, drunkenness, luxury and the dangers of this world. He gave practical advice:
'As Christ's spouse, Eustochium, avoid wine as you would
poison. Wine is the first weapon used by demons against the
young … Wine and youth kindle between them the fire of
sensual pleasure … When lust tickles the senses and the soft
fire steals over us, let us cry: "The Lord is on my side; I will
not fear what the flesh can do to me."

'Remember, Lady Eustochium (I am bound to call my
Lord's bride 'Lady') … you walk laden with gold and, if you
keep out of the robbers' way … you shall see a fiery chariot
like Elijah's waiting to carry you to Heaven.'

Occasionally pausing for thought, Jerome would, in a moment of utter stillness, meet the gaze of that enticing young man Aetius. Was it such a picture of fleshly delight that sparked the erotic images borrowed from the Song of Songs that glowed intermittent and fiery through its pages?

With an effort, Jerome dictated: 'Foolish virgins may stray abroad. But you, Eustochium, should stay at home with the Bridegroom, your beloved, Christ Himself … Let the privacy of your chamber ever guard you; ever let the Bridegroom sport with you within … When sleep falls on you He will come behind the wall and thrust His hand through the hole in the door and will touch your flesh …'

Aetius raised an amused eyebrow, but Jerome pressed on: 'And you will awake and rise up and cry: "I am sick with love." Then He will reply: "A garden inclosed is my sister, my spouse; a spring shut up, a fountain sealed."'

Married women were severely dealt with.

'I do not detract from marriage when I set virginity before it. No one compares a bad thing with a good. Married women may congratulate themselves that they come next to virgins. Be fruitful and multiply, God says, and replenish the earth. But your company, Eustochium, is in Heaven.'

After a moment's thought, he added: 'I praise marriage … because it gives me virgins. I gather the rose from the thorn, the gold from the earth, the pearl from the oyster … Why, mother, grudge your daughter her virginity? … Are you angered with her because —'

'You are now the mother-in-law of God?' suggested Aetius, but Jerome paid him no heed.

They ploughed on, late into the night. The letter became longer than Jerome had ever envisaged, yet, feeling his words guided by the Holy Spirit, he felt compelled to take his thoughts to their logical conclusion. Society was in the grip of an unrestrained pursuit of profit or pleasure, or both;

dangers to virgins abounded. Under Jerome's feverish and eloquent hand many living specimens of ungodliness, lay and cleric, emerged in unmistakeable portraits.

Word got around, and the letter was seized upon, copied and devoured not only by virgins but by most of Rome, Christian or no — among them, Praetextata.

***

She stood, one morning, a good-looking woman of fifty, of considerable but graceful proportions, gazing at the blank niches in Paula's long salon where once a marble Bacchus had invitingly sprawled, where Venus had observed her own golden-tinted beauty in a small pool.

'My own brother brought the Bacchus back from Achaea for poor Toxotius,' she said to her husband Hymetius. Lowering her voice, she added: 'I saw Paula praying at a martyr's tomb the other day, her hair all over the place and dressed in rags.'

'She shouldn't appear in public like that,' he admitted.

'And little Julia Eustochium,' continued his wife, 'such a healthy, cheerful child a year or so ago and now gazing into vacancy, her thoughts miles away. The girl just copies her mother! That letter of Jerome's about Christ coming into her chamber and playing with her ... '

'Hardly the thing to say to a high-born girl, certainly.'

'It's unnatural and wicked! He tells her to put away all thoughts of worldly love and then uses these images to excite her.' Praetextata ruminated. 'I don't think that Jerome understands young girls. What really troubles them is the prospect of having babies and perhaps dying in childbirth.'

Hymetius said nothing. He thought that he understood well enough the sort of vicarious excitement a strongly repressed man might get from writing to a virgin girl in such terms.

***

Passing later through Paula's gallery, Praetextata caught Aetius admiring a marble statue of the youthful god Hermes, grasping his staff with its coiled snakes.

Aetius started. 'May I ask you not to give me away, my lady? Jerome would not like to see me wasting time.'

'You needn't worry,' she said shortly. 'I have nothing to say to your master.' On an impulse, she added: 'Tell me one thing, if you can. I would like to know just why Church virgins need to fast. I saw my niece Eustochium faint the other day!'

'The more Eustochium fasts,' Aetius explained, 'the more easily she can control her body's unconscious urges and overcome the terrors of the night ... I mean dreams, my lady.'

Reading in Praetextata's face a profound distaste, he smiled engagingly and continued:

'Don't worry about Eustochium, my lady. She still has something of the child about her and is pliant enough. She can still be tempted with sweets like mashed figs or stuffed dates to break her fast. She collects little presents for her teacher — cherries, and even apples. She might want to imitate her saintly mother, but I have heard the servant girl say that she watches other girls making up their faces ...' He paused. 'Of course, whether she stays a virgin or not depends largely on the one into whose hands she falls.'

He gestured meaningfully at the little, beringed hands which even in middle age were Praetextata's particular beauty, and gazed at her until, despite herself, she felt herself captive.

'In your hands, for instance,' Aetius was insisting, 'such pretty hands too, my lady — I don't doubt that Eustochium would enjoy a normal social life, followed by marriage and motherhood.' He chuckled. 'If not, she may find that a dream lies heavier on her than a man.'

He bowed to Praetextata and departed, and that formidable old aristocrat found a need to seat herself.

***

Jerome, meanwhile, was waiting for Paula in her private reception room. He shivered in the severe cold, for Paula's own quarters in that well-heated mansion were the only ones left — deliberately — icily cold.

'I have your latest note, Lady Paula,' he said gently, as she entered.

She looked pale and tired, for she had been outside for hours supervising food doles to the poor of the city. Nervously, she ran a hand through her hair.

'I wrote it after a very bad day. They all come to me with their problems — the family, the slaves, the estate management, finances, engagements, dowries ...'

Sinking down into a chair, she added: 'And now my Blesilla is married. I know that this life is only the flicker of an eyelid against eternity, but it's hard at times to remember it in the midst of a household.' Her voice dropped. 'The bishops leave in the spring. I still long to escape! Here, Marcella and I are only half-way to what we aspire to be — whereas the desert would offer a real challenge!'

'My lady,' Jerome urged. 'Think of your work. Your research, your critical analysis ... it is invaluable.'

'You can ponder the Bible in the desert. Saint Antony knew it off by heart. He said that he didn't need books; that a clear mind emanating from a pure heart was all that was necessary to understand the mysteries of Holy Scripture.'

Her eyes brightened as she leaned forwards, and added: 'He doesn't seem to have needed Bible commentaries!'

Jerome's face merited study at that moment, as scepticism struggled with delight at Paula's confidences.

'Even without education, Antony was so intelligent,' Paula persisted. 'Look how he bested those philosophers who tried to be so clever!'

Jerome shook his head, momentarily speechless. When he spoke, he chose his words with care: 'Our unremitting labour to unlock the spiritual meaning of the Bible is the greatest work on earth, not less here than in the desert. Besides,' — he sprang up and rounded on her impulsively — 'think of the example you set, you and your ladies. You are like an oasis of Christian truth in another desert — the desert of Roman society!'

Jerome flung out his hands.

'Ah, don't leave!' he pleaded. 'We all need you. *I* need you!'

He departed soon afterwards for his own rather better heated office in the Lateran archives. On the way, he decided to call on Marcella, who had queried his interpretation of two Hebrew words.

Outside, he pulled his cowl well over his face and assumed his 'public' walk. That humble progression amused some for, deep in his own thoughts, he would forget himself and his own resolute stride would unconsciously take over.

Just as he reached the top of the Aventine Hill, a tremendous clap of thunder, reverberating off the marble of Rome, heralded a deluge. He ran for the shelter of a nearby portico and almost collided with a cowering figure, all bedraggled finery. It was Postumianus, a priest he knew, caught in one of his well-rewarded visits to the rich and fashionable.

The thunder exploded again, and lightning split the sky. Postumianus shrank against a wall, crossing himself.

Jerome stared at him with hard eyes, and then stooped to retrieve a leather purse the other had dropped.

'Pray for the mercy of Christ, you who were made in his image!' He tossed the purse back to the priest disdainfully.

Then, turning his back on the shivering, abject man, Jerome strode out into the storm.

Postumianus, huddling in the portico until the storm passed, tried not to dwell on the contempt in Jerome's voice.

14

Blesilla experienced, that winter, all the excitements of a Rome season. And found none of it counted. By the spring of 383 AD she felt trapped, up in her villa on the Aventine Hill, by her demanding husband. He might parade her to his friends as a cultured appendage, praise her poems though he thought them trifles, but she knew now that for Furius her education lay on her like a gorgeous dress and of no more consequence.

One solace there was: despite the nightly onslaughts of her husband's body, she was not yet with child, thanks to God and all the Christian saints, frequently invoked. Her mother, who lived next door, was more concerned that Blesilla attend her classes but, despite her regular entreaties, Blesilla had stead-fastly refused.

This afternoon found her curled comfortably on a bench at the end of her garden, busily scrawling on a writing tablet. The air, crisp when Furius had left at dawn for a three-day trip to the harbour city of Ostia, now had a summery feel although it was still only May. A poem had been maturing in her mind for days past, but she was struggling with com-pressing her sentiments into the rigidity of couplets. Because the poem was really addressed to Bassus, she had allowed him to invade her mind. Sadly, only her mind, she thought.

Stuck at the fourth couplet, she threw down her stylus. As she rose, her gown swept the tablet over the low wall. Leaning over the balcony, she could see no sign of it in the rose bed below.

Quickly she made her way down to the lower terrace and along the wall. But someone had got there before her. Standing in the midst of the roses, bent over her poem, was Aetius.

'Give me that tablet at once!' she burst out.

He swung round, caught himself on briars, and pulled at his cloak until it tore free. Excusing himself, he addressed her with unconvincing humbleness: 'I have a message for your husband. But they tell me he is away.'

'You were reading my poem!'

Aetius handed her the tablet. 'Can you blame me? It's seldom that a jewel drops from the sky.'

'It's no jewel,' she said shortly.

'It *will* be a jewel,' he insisted. 'You handle that tight elegiac couplet well, my lady, with such vigour and freshness.'

He spoke with earnest persuasion, his green eyes drawing her in. Despite herself, she let him go on praising her composition, only to shiver as she heard her own lines quoted back at her:

> *'Lament my urgent flesh so oft and sweetly fused*
> *with yours, but now by separate lives is love abused.'*

Aetius stopped. 'How proud Furius must be,' he said slyly. 'All this, for a few nights' absence.'

Blesilla relaxed. 'My husband,' she said haughtily, 'is an incomparably better poet than I will ever be.'

'But of course, he is a product of the famous Roman schools.' Aetius hesitated. 'And does my lady know Ausonius's marriage poem?'

Blesilla did, for one of the girls of her circle had surreptitiously managed to get hold of, and circulate, that infamous poem in which Ausonius, by clever selection and rearrangement of innocent phrases from Virgil, had produced gross indecencies to titillate the Emperor and his court.

'I don't know it,' she said contemptuously, but Aetius ignored her.

'Carnal love. The ravening beast—or the beautiful,' he suggested. 'Like the flight of an eagle, soaring higher and higher, gloriously freed from the limitations of flat earth, approaching ever nearer the climax of his flight, that moment of ecstasy when he is flooded with the radiance of the hot sun and melts in response. And then, in a slow and relaxed glide, he returns to his place of departure.' He paused. 'Surely women, too ...'

Suddenly she was beside herself with rage, compounded by excitement. Looking into his eyes, she was in that moment at the mercy of a will stronger than her own.

'Get out of here at once!' she gasped.

'My humble apologies if I have disturbed my lady,' said Aetius in a voice more ironic than humble. He added: 'Perhaps the subject of your love poetry is further away than Ostia?'

The blood pounded in her head. Had she really heard him say that?

'No one need know of your poem, my lady.'

Her fury dwindled into impotence. 'And you a man of the Church,' she said. 'How dare you!'

Aetius shrugged. Blesilla wondered at her momentary surrender to the man.

'Put the chaste Hippolytus in Rome and a Priapus he will be,' he quipped. 'I could quote more. My memory is excellent. I could even repeat word for word your unfinished poem.'

With that, he saluted her and disappeared.

***

Worse was to follow the next day. Furius sent word that he would return earlier than expected; in fact, he would dine with her that evening. She wrote no more verse that day, and instead, dressed in good time and had her maid pile her hair up in the elaborate fashion of the day. When she entered, Furius was already waiting for her in the dining-room.

'Was it a good meeting?' she enquired, after they had exchanged an embrace.

'Oh yes, a good meeting,' he replied. His face was more florid than usual and she wondered if he had been drinking. 'A good meeting,' he repeated, 'with much good talk.'

'Very learned talk, I'm sure,' she smiled.

'As it happens, we talked about my latest poem.'

'That's splendid,' she said, with as much warmth as she could. 'I didn't realise it was ready.'

'Oh, yes. It simply needs a little emendation. Substantially it is finished.'

'I'd like to hear it,' she exclaimed.

He brushed this aside. 'And how is your own work going?' he asked, suddenly and harshly.

'My *work*, Furius? *My* little things?'

'Spare me your irony,' he said impatiently. 'Everyone knows you write. All my friends know.'

'As you have never been encouraged to read out any of it,' she began, 'I doubt that they do. And it is hardly the sort of thing … I mean, my sentiments are commonplace, really. Private thoughts, private feelings such as only few women have committed to paper.'

'Nevertheless, one or two women have done precisely that. Even very high-born, aristocratic ladies! They pour out their most intimate feelings … The lover sneers, the woman grovels, begs, implores and rages. Such women leave nothing out!'

Blesilla started. His manner was so different from how he normally addressed her, or indeed addressed any women, for whom he reserved an artificial winsomeness and, she had always felt, a rather heavy-handed gallantry.

'Perhaps such women hardly expected anyone but their husbands to read what they wrote,' she said.

He stared at her in silence for a long time. Finally, she finally burst out:

'Of course, passion is shameful in a woman, isn't it? To write of it, appalling!' Having begun, she had to go on. '*Amor*—respectable for a man, but dishonourable for a woman! Yet isn't it like the flight of an eagle, soaring higher and higher? Can't a woman too know that release from earth, the climax of flight, the moment of ecstasy?' She laughed. 'Can't women experience that passion too?'

'Blesilla!' Furius shouted. 'What are you saying!'

'A woman doesn't write down her feelings,' she flung at him. 'Only men do that. An Ausonius can even be asked by the Emperor to write a marriage song to tickle the lewd imaginings of the men of his court!'

Furius's face was thunderous, as he said through gritted teeth: 'That's enough! Do you hear me? What company have you been keeping behind my back? The *Cento nuptialis*, to which I assume you refer, and rubbish of that sort, would never be found in my library. As for lewd imaginings, I'm going to show you something, my good wife. Come!' he commanded, and swept her into the library.

She watched him take a scroll from his desk, unwind it with shaking hands, and read out the words she knew so well:

> '*Lament my urgent flesh so oft and sweetly fused*
> *With yours, but now by separate lives is love abused.*
> *In darkness, nightly, I can only make believe*
> *I hold you in my arms,*
> *Re-live our private passion's thrust and hold*
> *And from our bed the universe behold.*'

How had Furius got hold of it? Immediately, the image of Aetius floated through her mind: of course, that was it! Horrified, she heard her husband recite the story of her love, and felt the stirrings of another emotion. Only now was she beginning to see the extent of his passion and violence. Moved by real anger, Furius was impressive.

Motionless, she stood as his wrath poured over her, telling her of her betrayal of him, his house, his unborn children, his mother and her own.

'But I've only written a little poem, Furius,' she said, finally. 'And you tell me I'm guilty of all sorts of wickedness. It was just a poem—I never meant anyone to see it.'

'Didn't you, Blesilla? No one at all?' he asked menacingly. 'Come in here.'

He dragged her into his adjoining study. Volumes and scrolls lay all around in a curiously intimate chaos. Clearly, it was not a room into which he readily took people.

Suddenly there was a screech and a rustle. Furius threw back a screen to reveal the large, brilliantly hued bird, with its glorious blend of green, yellow and turquoise.

'Blesilla!' screeched the parrot. 'Blesilla! Blesilla, darling!'

'*Your* bird!' Furius said, and surprised her again by adding, 'The bird which pulls the carriage of the Indian goddess of pleasure, Rati. Isn't it so?'

'So they say,' stammered Blesilla.

'Bassus's present to you,' said Furius. Turning, he addressed the bird. 'Found you in Alexandria. You've had a long journey, from India to Egypt, then here to Rome.'

He took some seeds from the cage and held them out to the parrot. 'Here, take these.'

'I didn't know you liked him,' Blesilla whispered.

'Of course, I'm not Bassus,' Furius continued grimly. 'They say that parrots are very affectionate and mourn the loss of their first owner. Do you miss Bassus?' he asked the parrot, with heavy irony. 'Or do you love Blesilla now? Why don't you kiss Bassus—I mean Blesilla?'

He's gone mad, she thought. He's gone really mad to talk like this. 'Furius,' she said, reaching out to him. 'Don't—'

'The bird's a wonderful mimic,' he interrupted, pulling away from her. 'It'll imitate anyone you like. I think it'd even imitate you or Bassus—as you've both been closest to him. Can you say "Bassus", parrot?'

'Blesilla!' the parrot squawked instead. The bird shrilled out her name over and over and then, to her horror, repeated it in eerie fashion with Bassus's own intonation.

'Give it some more food,' Furius ordered the slave whose sole duty it was to care for the bird. 'You must keep it well fed. After all, it cost more than *you* did.'

The young African slave, frightened, offered a plate of grain to the bird, who grabbed seed after seed with its beak.

Still, Furius couldn't stop. '"Bassus" — say "Bassus",' he ordered the parrot, which was intent on finishing the grain.

'I've never heard him say his name,' Blesilla muttered.

Abruptly, Furius lost interest in the parrot. She watched, with fascinated horror, the line of spittle which had begun to dribble from the corner of his mouth.

'So now, Blesilla,' he jeered, 'let us talk of your poem, your private outpouring, your erotic masterpiece, which no doubt has occupied your leisure hours for weeks. How cunning to use your husband's absences to celebrate your sluttish adventures with another man!'

She covered her ears.

'Stop it, Furius! You've no right! How can you say such things? Have you ever seen me with another man, seen me so much as spend an hour with a man? I wrote a poem. You immediately assume —'

'I assume nothing,' he cut her short. 'Nothing.'

'But you think —'

He held up his hand. 'Will you deny that when you married me you were no longer a virgin?'

There was silence, while Blesilla thought rapidly. Was there any hope of his believing her? Should she deny everything, and pretend the poem had been written about him?

Then, shockingly, came the sound of Bassus's voice, even to the little catch which signalled a chuckle:

'Kiss Bassus, Blesilla! Kiss Bassus here, Blesilla!'

And to the parrot's shrill, incessant accompaniment, this exact and ghostly reproduction of Bassus's voice, Furius ground out the word:

'Baiae. Of course, Baiae. The trickery, the sheer duplicity of it all. The wedding-night ... Even the women knew, while I ...'

He uttered a cry, swayed, and collapsed onto the marble floor.

***

Death had struck Furius down swiftly and brutally. The fatal spasm occurred just as it dawned on Blesilla the complexity and pride that underlaid the imperturbable front which her husband had presented to the world — and to her.

Awestruck and shocked, she took up the passive role expected of her within the social bustle brought about by sudden death. Physicians and priests — even Damasus himself — came and went, offering public acknowledgment of the unexpected tragedy along with their consolation, somehow lending a greater reality to the event. Paolina arrived, accompanied by Pammachius, together with all the rest of Blesilla's extended family, and of course scores of the Furian *gens*. The palazzo vibrated with subdued voices, full and yet empty, since all of it had revolved around Furius himself, set in his family and in his Church. To Blesilla, the proceedings seemed interminable, until finally the day of the funeral arrived and the impressive procession made its slow way to the Vatican cemetery.

Blesilla had watched the servants closely in case the cause of the fatal quarrel between Furius and herself had leaked out, although as far as she knew the only witness had been the black boy slave who was fond of the parrot and of herself. Was she, she asked herself time and again, responsible for her husband's death? It seemed clear that a chronic state of emotional stress, well concealed, had triggered his final seizure. Resolutely, Blesilla buried deep within herself the knowledge that his discovery of her own behaviour was the blow that Furius's proud nature could not take. She learned to quell her thoughts, overlay her dreams with absorbing fantasies. On the whole, she was surprised at how dispassionate her own feelings about her husband soon became.

That she was for months seldom alone helped. As a widow, she immediately became a target for many. Eligible bachelors expressed an interest in meeting her; eminent churchmen suggested that bequests from the joint properties of Furius and herself would be in order.

'The Church has done quite well already from the Julii,' she said tartly to Pammachius, and even to her mother.

Jerome soon renewed his solicitations. She locked herself away but was obliged, in the end, to see him. She was inwardly amused at his effect on her. She didn't dislike these sessions; indeed, she admitted to herself that she enjoyed the sensation of his histrionic powers unleashed for her benefit alone. He was so persuasive, she thought, so very adept at making so much of nothing. His glittering words created a glorious other world in the very renunciation of the present one. And his flattery of her did not go amiss after Furius's summary treatment. Jerome praised her flawless Greek accent, the quickness of her intellect, and the tenacity of her memory. She listened to him and relished her own imposture, for she was treated as a sorrowful widow — she, who was so far from sorrowing.

'An opportunist, that's what I have become,' she told herself candidly. 'I'm as wayward and responsive as those leaves that blow around and make our garden wall seem to quiver and dance!'

She looked at Jerome and wondered if he sensed that zest for life within her that she knew attracted men; it had certainly attracted Bassus.

Oh, how she longed to see him again! She pictured him pursuing his new life up in Milan. She would visit the villa of the Bassi sometimes, simply because on the wall of a small salon there hung a picture of him made by a Greek painter when Bassus was seventeen. She agreed to go to her Aunt Praetextata's villa in Tibur later in the summer because of a chance remark that a cousin of Bassus who resided in a neighbouring villa was to be married soon and that Bassus himself was expected to travel down for the celebrations.

She had sent a poem to Bassus, entrusting it to her old tutor, whom she knew would never betray her. The poem contained no names, but two references to their love-making would, she felt sure, leave him in no doubt as to its author. As days turned into weeks and she heard nothing, she consoled herself by conjuring up Bassus's laughing grey eyes; his deep, amused voice; ran her finger along the bump in his nose which had been broken and never properly set when, in childhood, he had taken a tumble from a horse.

One afternoon, caressing in her mind a pleasurable image of herself and Bassus, she became conscious that her emerald parrot with its blood-red beak was watching her. Green and red: the colours of envy and death—or love. Fondly, she rubbed its head. It had killed her husband.

'But you set me free, parrot,' she breathed.

15

Eustochium was still on her Aunt Praetextata's mind. Just before leaving Rome with her husband to escape the worst of the summer heat, Praetextata told him that the girl would accompany them to the fashionable summer resort town of Tibur together with her sister Blesilla.

Hymetius looked dubious. 'What on earth will Paula say? Eustochium's the apple of her eye, her most chaste, dutiful daughter, whom she is preparing to dedicate as a virgin!'

'Paula herself admits that Eustochium is overdoing it and her health is suffering,' his wife replied. 'I asked if she could spend a little while with us, and Paula agreed.'

'But she'll be surrounded by noise, music, guests!'

'Yes. And amongst the guests, Hymetius, will be the man her father had in mind for her.'

***

Up in her uncle's villa in the old arcaded town of Tibur, Eustochium kept to herself in a room that gave on to a private garden, although she did, on occasion, allow Blesilla to coax her out to visit the beauties of the town—the waterfalls, the Temple of Vesta and the Sibyl, and the grotto of the Siren.

Other times, leaving her sister to her private devotions, Blesilla mixed freely with the aristocratic set. One day, while visiting with a party the ruined villa of the Emperor Hadrian, she wandered off through the olive groves to the tumbled marble and quality stone of the old baths and was arrested by the sound of men's voices.

'Nice piece of sculpture half-buried there. River god. I could do with that. They don't make stuff like that nowadays, eh?'

From the shelter of a crumbling wall, Besilla heard a man's chuckle.

'... Milan's got a bad winter. He might come south.'

'I heard he had some girl.'

'He's always got some girl, hasn't he?' Another chuckle.

'There's a rumour he picked this one up in Baiae.'

Blesilla stood rigid. There was the sound of rubble under-foot, and as the men came into view she recognised one of them as Auchenius, one of Bassus's brothers. She ducked, and turned away.

Was Bassus really coming south? In turmoil, Blesilla walked back to her own group of people. She forced herself to laugh and talk all through a picnic in the dappled shade of tall pine trees. Then she went back to the villa, where she was obliged to meet yet another set of her aunt's fashionable friends.

'Honorious will attend tomorrow's entertainment,' Praetextata told Blesilla that evening.

Blesilla stared at her.

'Your father's dearest wish was that he and Eustochium should marry,' her aunt continued. 'We've engaged the best troupe of acrobats and dancers. Eustochium says that she would much rather watch from her window. But I said to her, "Just this once, my child, I want you to be amongst us and show a little lightness of spirit!"'

Praetextata's face shone with pleasure at her own benevolence, as she turned her attention to practicalities. 'What clothes has the child with her?'

'Two grey tunics, one dowdier than the other, and an old black one,' said Blesilla.

'My girls have dresses, dresses to burn,' her aunt breathed. 'Eustochium can choose whatever tunic or dress she fancies — even silken ones — and in any colour.'

Blesilla read her aunt's intentions clearly. 'She will fancy none of them,' she said indifferently.

She smiled to herself. Ah, Eustochium was a nut that her aunt would never crack. There was a good chance that she'd go in her threadbare black tunic, and stand up to all of them.

'Who'll be there tomorrow?' she asked aloud.

'Mostly just the family and our closest friends. Oh, and perhaps the two brothers Anicii Bassi ...'

***

The next afternoon, Blesilla entered Eustochium's bedroom to find her sister regarding a long white gown, tastefully embroidered, laid out on the bed.

'It's time to get ready for the reception,' Blesilla told her. 'The maids are waiting outside.'

'The belt is very ornate,' Eustochium said doubtfully. 'And I've never worn such a gown.'

'It's loose though, and hides you. The belt just keeps it decently in place.'

Their aunt rustled in, followed by two maids.

'Your hair first, dear,' she murmured. 'Just rub her hair up with a little oil from this bottle,' she ordered a maid holding an array of unguents on a small tray.

Eustochium stood quite still, her eyes blazing in her pale face. Praetextata exuded a painful tension. The dress alone might be seemly; the application of unguents would signal Eustochium's willingness to attract.

Under Eustochium's gaze, Praetextata subsided on a chair. She was breathing heavily and sweat formed in beads on her forehead. She raised a trembling hand to her mouth.

'You would look so pretty,' she pleaded. 'Indulge us this once, to please your old aunt!'

Cornered, Eustochium bowed her head. After a moment she looked up, and caught her sister's eye. It was plain she thought the older woman's manoeuvres less offensive than pitiable. She allowed the women to comb and rub oil into her hair, and then curl it into lustrous ringlets that fell about her slender shoulders as if to protect them.

Blesilla was possessed by sudden mischief. 'She needs a spray,' she giggled. Pulling off her own headdress of waving peacock feathers, she pinned it to the top of her sister's head.

'You're enchanting!' gasped Praetextata. 'Enchanting, my darling. Come!' She led her niece to the mirror.

'A little chalk now,' she directed the maids. 'No need for eye-liner, just a hint of rouge on her cheeks and lips.'

Finally, Eustochium was led away, out to the terrace, now full with a lively crowd of guests eagerly awaiting the entertainment below. Pencil-slim the girl stood, the blue feathers swaying above her head.

There's nothing of her, thought Blesilla. She's so thin now in the chest she could be a boy. Why bother dressing her up like that? Who would ever notice her?

Music sounded, and the guests took their seats. Below, water cascaded into an artificial lake, creating a curtain of water through which the acrobats, boys and girls, shot down one by one in a chute, and in the sparkling water formed and reformed in elaborate patterns.

On the terrace, the guests were served with refreshments of cakes, olives and bread, washed down by excellent local wine and water. Shrieks of laughter floated up from the water as the men began to pelt the acrobats with flowers.

'That's going a bit far, isn't it?' demanded a young man as his friend threw an amethyst down to a smiling half-nude acrobat.

'I'll know later on,' the other returned.

'I'll show you a prettier one up here,' said the young man. 'Niece of our hostess. One of the Julii. Don't look too hard, though … they say she's dedicated to the Church. Why are you staring?'

'Well, only that … look at that profile. What class! By Jupiter, she's absolutely exquisite!'

Turning towards her sister, Blesilla became aware of a commotion as people clustered around a new arrival. She heard the man's voice rise decisively above the tumult:

'It's no rumour. News came last night. Cut down like a dog by his own troops up near Lyon!'

'What's this?' interrupted a bulky man who was being helped up the steps by a couple of dancers. 'You're not talking of gladiators are you, my boy?'

'I'm not talking of gladiators, you drunken fool,' the newcomer said contemptuously. 'I'm talking about the Emperor Gratian. There's been an invasion of Gaul, in case you don't know, and our young Emperor has been killed by his own men. We've got a new one now – a Spanish officer, Magnus Maximus.'

Bassus! thought Blesilla. Could he have been with the Emperor? Doesn't the Imperial Quaestor travel with the Emperor and his staff too?

***

'What's more,' said Praetextata next morning, holding court in her bedroom, 'he was interested. You could see that!'

Blesilla thought her aunt looked dreadful, her face mottled and her lower lip trembling. She's getting on in years, of course, she realised.

'I was right to do what I did.' Her aunt's words sounded more defiant than ever.

Surely, thought Blesilla, she was wandering in her mind?

'Once we put her in decent clothes, you could see long neck and the way she holds her little head. Such poise – so very aristocratic. That young man couldn't take his eyes off her.'

Blesilla said nothing. The young man in question had stood smiling at Eustochium as though conferring a blessing on her. Distinguished and dull, she thought. Success would make him fat later. She thought of his beringed, pudgy fingers on her slender little sister, and shuddered.

'Have you looked in on her?' her aunt asked nervously.

'She's at her devotions.'

It was an understatement. Eustochium had been prostrate, clasping a wooden cross as she prayed in a voice too soft for Blesilla to hear properly. She had probably been there most of the night, for she lifted a face drained of colour to her sister as she stood at the doorway.

Blesilla retreated, but paused behind the closed door. She sensed that the moment of submission to social niceties that her sister had shown briefly for her aunt's sake was over. And indeed, she could hear Eustochium praying, urgently and with passion, to both Christ and the Virgin:

'I have betrayed my commitment to you, my Lord, betrayed the promises I made to my teachers. Instead of standing firm, I submitted to the whims of an old woman who is doomed and lost to the ways of God.

'And I looked at the water entertainment, Holy Mother of God, and oh, I couldn't help enjoying it. It was a beautiful sight, all flashing lights and marvellous acrobatics. But also immoral, Holy Mother, with the boys and girls, almost naked, flaunting themselves. Afterwards, a man whom I knew only slightly caught me by the hand, and whispered … things into my ear. I was filled straight away with such sensations that I made me realise how right it is for girls like me to be kept apart from men in Church and everywhere.

'But the feeling lasted only a moment, Holy Mother. I think virginity is easy for me, for the very thought of being fondled by a man makes me panic. Perhaps I think sometimes that I want to be kissed, Holy Mother, but chastely …

'I was wrong to wear fine clothes and go to the party. Wrong not to cross my aunt on account of her age, wrong not to judge things for myself. My aunt applied chalk to my face, rouge to my lips and hot curling irons to my hair — she left my eyes alone, saying they were big already, and my lashes long — but she gave me fine clothes, and they were perfumed. I was led to join a fashionable group on the terraces at the hour of the afternoon when the waters, and the campagna beyond them, stretched out in the blue distance, polished and gleaming and like radiant Heaven itself. I sinned, Holy Mother, for I surrendered myself and enjoyed every minute of it.'

***

'Well, you won't get her to mix with people again,' Blesilla told her aunt.

She watched a maid rubbing cream into Praetextata's old, lined face. That mouth! Had it always sagged at one side like that? Could the heat, intense even at this early hour, account for the redness of her face and neck?

Another serving maid, pushing rings over the swollen skin of her fingers, made the old woman gasp in pain.

'What's wrong with your fingers?' demanded Blesilla. 'One is at such a funny angle.'

'Nothing!' Her aunt looked terrified. 'It's only a cramp.'

Blesilla shook her head. 'You're not well, aunt.'

'There's nothing wrong with me,' Praetextata insisted. 'I just didn't sleep well. I had a nightmare, that's all.'

Blesilla subsided, unconvinced.

16

The sultry Afer that blew at the end of September 383 AD covered Latium with fine particles of yellow dust from Africa, after which the wind took its name. Clouds mounted, temperatures rose, and pressure built. Up at her villa in Tibur, Praetextata suffered. She had been adamant that she wanted to stay on after the party, fearing a return to the stifling atmosphere in Rome. Blesilla had left some weeks previously, taking Eustochium with her.

Finally, Hymetius's temper snapped. For days he had prowled around irritably, avoiding his wife.

'Probably I've been talking too much,' Praetextata murmured to herself.

She had. Indeed, she had hardly stopped. And to compensate for her stricken hands, she spent hours at her dressing table.

'We might wait a few days longer, Hymetius,' she complained one morning, as they relaxed on the cool of their terrace. 'I can't breathe in Rome when it's like this. And now, with this rheumatism ...'

Hymetius couldn't see what staying in Tibur had to do with rheumatism. He muttered something about important public business in Rome.

Praetextata laughed. 'You're surely not rushing back just for a Senate meeting!'

'I suppose you do know that our Emperor Gratian has been assassinated,' her husband exclaimed, 'and some general has grabbed control of the Empire!'

'As though Milan cares what you Roman senators think about it!' she said scornfully.

'The court in Milan doesn't despise the Senate,' her husband shot back. 'Why do you think that your brother is to be Praetorian Prefect of Italy next year? He's full of plans to restore our temples and to get restitution of the treasures that have been stolen from them. Young Bassus is expected down in Rome any day. It's important that he's well briefed in advance on what we want.'

'The Senate this, the Senate that! I've heard you say yourself that the Senate only dances to Milan's tune.'

It was a rash remark to a man whose whole life had been centred on senatorial meetings and ceremony. Enraged at her insinuation that what impelled him and his friends was no more than a phantom, the shadow of a great name, Hymetius stood up.

'That's enough of your nonsense!' he roared. 'I'm leaving today, and the girls will come with me. You stay as long as you want to!'

By midday, the sky was darkening and a pencil of lightning glimmered now and then. No rain was falling as Hymetius and his daughters were carried down by litter to the postern gate of Tibur. He was not departing so much as fleeing, leaving his wife on the terrace, unhappy and with much on her mind. Within another hour, the storm had broken.

***

Blesilla had also learned, from one of the Anicii, that Bassus was expected to arrive in Rome any day. Her head hummed and she couldn't concentrate on anything.

Eustochium had left Tibur with some colour in her cheeks. Her eyes were brighter and she had stopped coughing. The stay had done her good, even though she had never again been seen among the guests after the water spectacle.

'There's nothing to be done with her,' Blesilla had told her aunt on their last morning. 'She's always had a mind of her own.'

'She seems as frail as a spider's web, but when her superstition is involved she's as obstinate as a mule,' Praetextata had said sulkily.

But she was also impressed, although she wouldn't admit it to Blesilla. She could see that Eustochium was altogether taken up with her Christ, a god close and almost familiar; it was as if she felt married to Christ. Any attempt to draw her into society was hopeless.

***

The journey from Tibur to Rome was not long, but bumpy and stressful. Their carriage may have been one of the finest with its canopy and silken curtains to draw against the heat, but it bounced along as roughly as any other on the increasingly busy road leading back to the city.

Blesilla and Eustochium arrived, exhausted, at their mother's villa to find Jerome ensconced with Paula and her women. Paula jumped up and embraced them warmly. To her obvious relief, Eustochium was immediately drawn into their dedicated and tranquil midst.

'My dear little sisters in Christ,' Jerome greeted them. 'May God be praised that you are safely returned from all the dangers that surrounded you.'

'We travelled with a quite sufficient escort,' Blesilla said tartly, deliberately misconstruing him. 'It was only that it took longer than usual – the road was so noisy and crowded. It's so stuffy here after Tibur.'

'One day you will welcome discomfort,' he assured her.

She said nothing. Jerome couldn't know that she was worn out far more by the daily hope, regularly thwarted, of a message from Bassus. She could not face Jerome or even her mother now. She excused herself, and left for her own villa. Crossing the garden, she was startled to see Aetius in the shrubbery, no doubt awaiting his master.

'My lady!' He clasped his hands together. 'My humble greetings to you.' Then he added: 'I am very sorry that your aunt has suffered a seizure, has she not?' He watched her closely. 'Her fingers, so misshapen …'

Blesilla scowled. 'A touch of rheumatism,' she snapped.

His eyes demolished this feeble lie.

Without a word, she brushed by him and walked on. Only inside her own bedroom once more did it occur to her to wonder how Aetius could possibly have known about the recent deformity in her aunt's hands.

***

Nerve-ridden and weary from lack of sleep, Blesilla avoided her mother and sisters for the next few days but was obliged to put in an appearance at the last of the festivities of the social season. The wealthy elite, invigorated by their summer holidays, had opened up their town mansions once more for dinner parties, lavish banquets and other, wilder, forms of entertainment. Yet Blesilla found she took scant pleasure in them now. The musicians, exotic dancers, jugglers, and even the fire-eaters and floating banquets which once thrilled her now did not touch her. Maybe I'm getting old, she thought. As a widow, she was classed with women for the most part much older.

'You look pale, Blesilla,' said Aurelia, one of Symmachus's daughters a few days later. 'It seems a long time since we were all down in Campania.'

It was one of those occasions — in this case, an engagement party on the Coelian Hill given by Symmachus, leader of the Senate, for one of his sons — that was lively for the men, less so for the women.

'Try these cakes, Blesilla,' urged Aurelia. 'They go well with a glass of Falernian. Of course, Papa doesn't like us girls to drink wine in front of the guests.'

'He won't notice. He's immersed in affairs of state.' Aurelia's sister Flaminia giggled and waved a hand towards the other side of the hall, where her father was in animated discussion with his male guests.

Blesilla turned her head, and saw the man who had scarcely been absent from her thoughts for over a year. Bassus, she thought, must have only just arrived.

'Plenty of our acquaintances are behaving no better than actresses,' she heard Aurelia say. 'Did you see Marcia, Blesilla?'

Blesilla wrenched her eyes back to Aurelia, and said, 'I couldn't agree more.'

'She throws herself at any man who takes her fancy! Did you notice, at that dinner the other day, how she was fawning all over Lucius Didius's friend ...'

Oh, moaned Blesilla inwardly as Aurelia talked on, why didn't I dress to look my best instead of snatching the first stola to hand? Aware of the two Symmachi girls, she controlled herself and made an effort to join in the conversation. It was a full hour until—after the manner of Symmachus's formal gatherings—the men and women would mingle.

Finally Bassus approached them, splendidly dressed in a full red cloak as befitted his rank, well matched to his olive skin. He had, Blesilla saw immediately, acquired a new poise and air of maturity. The boy had become a man of importance.

'You've met Blesilla, haven't you?' Aurelia addressed Bassus.

'But of course,' Bassus replied. 'We knew each other as children—our fathers were neighbours in Campania.'

Turning towards Blesilla, and said: 'I am so sorry to hear of your husband's untimely death. Please accept my most sincere commiserations for this tragic event ...'

As he launched into a formal speech of condolence, her heart sank. If only, behind the words, there was anything but that polite indifference, or a glimmer of shared memories in those fine grey eyes.

'Will you spend long in Rome?' she faltered.

'I must return to Milan almost immediately.' Even as he spoke, he was trying to catch the eye of Symmachus.

Blesilla watched his progress down the great hall, smiling charmingly at the ladies, until he merged with a group of senators in earnest discussion, and disappeared from view. Later, a flurry at the door to the vestibule told her that he had departed.

'He'll wait for me outside. Or go to my villa. It's only because he couldn't speak in front of the others,' she told herself.

Hastily, she made her farewells and sought her litter. Outside, torches lit up the courtyard thronged with carriages and litters and their attendants.

'Find out where Bassus is,' she instructed one of her servants. 'See if he has left. Go, now!'

She sat tensely in her litter until the man came back with the news that Bassus had indeed left in a hurry. He had spent two days in Rome and, after a further night in his family mansion, would be returning to Milan in the morning.

'Two days here, without a word,' she muttered to herself. 'Ah, but he must have had to confer with the Senate all the time. And just now it was for the sake of my reputation that he was all cold formality. He must be planning to come to me at my villa. Perhaps he is already there ...'

She ordered the bearers to take her home as quickly as possible.

'Has anyone called?' she demanded of her maid, Clea, who had waited up to see her mistress to bed.

'No one, my lady,' the woman said quietly.

Crumpled with exhaustion, Blesilla slept briefly, waking taut and fully conscious in the early hours. She called her maids and had them bring her most beautiful stola and shawl, and pile her hair up high. He'll come today, she told herself, even while her reason denied it. She was in a frenzy of nerves, and had the slave women scuttling here and there at her command.

Finally, arrayed in all her finery she paced the house, demanded food to be brought and then refused it, and turned away a friend who made an unexpected visit, while frail hope stuttered, wilted and finally drained away.

In mid-afternoon, a sudden thunder of carriage-wheels came from the courtyard. Blesilla sprang up from her couch and ran to the main door, then turned back and stealthily retreated to the salon. He wouldn't find her waiting for him — oh no, not this time! She sat down and adjusted a strap of her sandal. The commotion outside increased and she made out a rumble of voices.

Then the door opened and the majordomo came forward. 'My lady —'

Before he could finish, he was brushed aside by Paula, who unceremoniously walked straight over to Blesilla.

'Terrible news!' she said, holding her tight. 'A tragedy ...'

Blesilla hardly heard her mother's words, only taking in some phrases — carriage accident, dead, fall down the side of the hills.

'Bassus!' she gasped.

Paula's eyes widened in amazement. 'My child, what are you talking about? It's your Uncle Hymetius and the two girls — I've just had word. Coming down from Tibur — they had an accident, apparently they were caught in an unexpected storm. All killed ...'

Blesilla embraced her mother, murmuring words of comfort. Uncle Hymetius dead? And the daughters too? A calamity no doubt, but what had this to do with her private torture?

After Paula left, Blesilla sent a messenger for news of Bassus. It was two long hours before the man returned. He reported that he had found the mansion of the Bassi in Rome closed up, but learned that Bassus himself had stayed, not with the family, but at the palace of the Maecii. He had spent the previous night there, and left very early this morning.

Blesilla heard him out, her face impassive and, bolstered up by the strict training of a senator's daughter, said calmly: 'I see. I must pass this news on to my sister, who asked me to enquire.'

The messenger bowed and left.

So, Blesilla thought. This is the end. The end of a full year of wasted emotion. I've been brushed aside, insulted as though I were a nobody. You are completely indifferent to me. May the devil take you, Bassus, in mid-career and ruin you, inflict on you something of the agony you've caused me. I won't let it hurt me! I'll fill the emptiness you never even bothered to think about. Oh yes, I'll do that.

Unnaturally calm, Blesilla walked through her luxurious villa, drank wine, took food, walked out into her garden and back inside. She could not rest. By dusk, she had lived through many aeons, it seemed to her. She felt so hot. She flung herself down on the grass and looked up at the starry sky.

'Oh, it's very easy to forget you, Bassus,' she said aloud. 'Very easy indeed.'

It was only that the words were meaningless. She was all broken and there was no remedy, nor ever would be.

She ordered the slaves to go to bed, and only hours later did she herself finally go inside.

'Take my shawl, Lucretia. Unpin it carefully because of the jewel that holds it. I haven't got the pin? I'm not wearing the shawl? No, of course not. What are you talking about? Bed? But it's not time for bed. Besides, my uncle is dead, you know, and my probably my cousins, though I can't remember just what Mamma said. Perhaps I'll take my cloak and go out again … No? Why not?'

***

The world spun and stopped as Blesilla's fever mounted. She had never thought that Bassus would come to her in Rome, but how delightful that he had; that he was, quite often, in bed with her here, the bed she used to share with Furius …

How crazy it all is. I'm crazy with happiness, you see, Bassus. Ah, don't do that. You know it's more than any mortal

123

woman can bear without expiring of happiness. And then you disappear! Holy Mother of God, where are you? You can't do this and then leave, you fiend. You darling fiend … Don't stop now … Stuff the sheet in my mouth and no one will hear me …

Do you know what someone told me once? I can't remember who it was. That the sheer bliss of physical love was only a faint reflection of a greater union with God.

God, give me water! This raging thirst will kill me, but I can't swallow, it hurts too much. And all the water's pouring down my neck now. And the pain in my head, all over me … An ache that never stops. I'm weak, so terribly weak! Will that person holding the cup put it to my lips and wet them? Only wet them. There are sharp knives in my throat and chest, and my head is bursting.

My mother is with me now. How beautiful she is and how cool her hands are. The most beautiful woman on this earth, you know. What are those lights flickering? How many candles. But they light candles in Church, for death, don't they?

And the man Jerome. How expressive those eyes of his are, full of a sort of fire. Those eyes speak.

The blinds are open half-way and it seems it is sunset outside—a soft yellow Roman sunset, so lovely on my mother's face, except you know, Bassus, you shouldn't be here with me now. It doesn't seem the time or the place …

17

After days — or it might have been weeks — Blesilla's fever left her and the garish images in her head shivered to a stop. Her mother's lovely, anxious face leaned over her, and her cool hand clasped Blesilla's. Suddenly she couldn't get enough to drink, though she was too weak to reach for the cup of water herself. She watched her mother's face, saw Jerome. Had Bassus really gone? His presence had retreated into unimaginable distances, far beyond her strange, new little world.

Her first almost inaudible words were to her mother: 'Where's Bassus?'

'Not now — take this.' Paula's face was radiant as she bent down, but she glanced over her shoulder.

Quite clearly this time, Blesilla said: 'Is Bassus here?'

'There, don't speak yet.' Paula caressed her daughter's face. Turning, she ordered the maids to leave. There was the sound of retreating footsteps, and then peace.

Leaning over her, Paula said: 'You're going to get better, my darling.' She squeezed her hand. 'Sleep now, there's no one here but me.'

A vast thankfulness swept through Blesilla. My mother, she thought, how good she is! It was her mother's face that had saved her. Her mother was hers, not Jerome's, after all.

'Shh, now, no need to talk,' Paula murmured.

Blesilla drifted off to sleep — a deep, dreamless sleep, this time. She awoke to clear daylight. She tried to get out of bed, but struggled to even sit upright.

'It's the old weakness in her chest,' declared the family's personal physician the next day. 'You remember how she was as a child. Take this fennel for her nerves, and cucumber to calm the aftermath of fever. Give her nutmeg and cloves to stimulate her appetite and build her strength up. And rest, she needs plenty of rest.'

Blesilla was once again in the world that others inhabited. The whole family hovered around her. Weak but rational, she accepted their presence while longing for the moment when she could be alone with her mother.

'You're always with me. You haven't the time,' she said.

'I have the time,' said Paula firmly. 'Oh, I've all the time in the world.'

Warmth and gratitude crept over Blesilla and all her old resentments died away. If her mother knew about her behaviour in Baiae, she never mentioned it. Both guarded their newfound intimacy.

Jerome remained a presence in both their lives, of course. He'd soon stop pestering me if he knew the truth, Blesilla thought. Mamma hasn't told him. Why? And Blesilla would tremble again lest she lose the precious confidence that she now shared with her mother.

'Loving someone means possession of them, I suppose,' she said one morning. She was thinking of her jealousy of Jerome, whom she had feared had taken Paula over.

'Oh, no,' said her mother. 'Not possession — selflessness. Like loving Christ. It's the only way.'

No one could love Bassus selflessly, thought Blesilla. But Mamma would say that wasn't love at all — only lust.

But was it? It was more like madness. She had assumed that he was swept off his feet as she had been. For the very first time, she began to think of Bassus with a degree of calmness, and to dissect him as well as her own response.

She was filled with anger at him, and with contempt for herself. He had used her and discarded her like a common prostitute. And she asked for it, she reflected bitterly. Ah, but he knew so well how to make love to a woman. What chance did she ever have?

As she regained her strength, Blesilla embarked on a course of therapy from which Paula would not allow her to swerve. Each day, until she tired, she read — not poetry or fiction, but Jerome's diary of his time in Constantinople; his *Life of Paul, the First Hermit*, a work much in vogue; and various works by ecclesiastical writers such as Clement and Cyprian.

Finally, she was allowed to translate some Greek for Jerome. It was mind-consuming, soul-soothing work, bringing with it a degree of confidence and a fragile serenity of spirit. All of it her mother's prescription, taken by Blesilla along with her herbal remedies — with trust.

She loved and admired her mother more and more. She belongs to me, she thought, with sidelong glances at Jerome, during his frequent visits.

'We're all sinful creatures, aren't we?' she remarked to Paula one day.

Her mother smiled. 'It's the nature of human beings, yes.'

'Down in Baiae,' began Blesilla. 'Well … Mamma, you remember when I was sick, and raving on about —'

'No one is free of imaginings,' Paula interrupted.

'More than imaginings,' said Blesilla. 'Down in Baiae …'

But her mother wouldn't let her speak. Not then. Not later.

'False memories,' she said firmly. 'Giving way to fantasies is surrender to demonic spirits.'

Next morning, after breakfast, Paula said casually as her maids wiped down the last of the breadcrumbs: 'I've decided to give the Appia property over to the Church. I was wondering if, from Furius's many holdings, there were some land you want to donate, perhaps even endow a church.'

Paula's motives could not have been clearer: Blesilla was to offer some sort of expiation. She had an urge to fling herself on her mother's breast and pour everything out.

But I can't, she thought. My mother, all blameless as she is, shan't have my guilt weigh her down like lead. I'm not going to upset her any more by confirming what she half-suspects. Let the priest take that responsibility on his shoulders.

Aloud she said: 'Yes, of course, Mamma.'

***

But Paula prayed more often than ever now. Night after night, she knelt on the marble floor in her thin linen nightgown:

'Oh Christ, help me help my first-born, whom I held in my arms and suckled, my lovely Blesilla. How can I grapple with her dreadful sin of fornication, her need for contrition? She is so frail and wasted. Guide me, oh Christ, you who have the power of forgiveness.'

18

Jerome came most days to Blesilla's villa, drawn irresistibly to the prospect of capturing this beautiful young widow for Christ.

'With your advantages,' he urged her, 'you can attain a felt wisdom that transcends mere intellectual grasp of Christian concepts. Think of how fruitful a life you could lead in Christ!'

'Fruitful — a life of continence?' Blesilla objected.

'Yes, fruitful! I am not playing semantic games, Blesilla. I don't mean fruitfulness of the womb; any woman can have that if she chooses to be imprisoned in marriage. I'm talking of a higher fruitfulness.'

'What do you mean?' she asked.

His answer came with a passion that caught her by surprise. 'You have a freedom and influence granted to few. Consider your situation, my lady, I beseech you! You come from the topmost level of Roman society. You are intelligent, educated, and adept at languages. You have at your disposal your husband's superb library. I pray you, consider dedicating the use of all this to God!

'As a rich widow, you could spend hours in front of the mirror, beautifying yourself with make-up and jewels to attract the attention of young men ... perhaps a certain one in particular? Ah, you blush, but I'm simply trying to present to you a superior way of life — one to which, if I am not mistaken, you are suited. If you devote your energies to God and live celibate, you'll be free of worldly distractions and the perennial disappointments which follow excessive attachment to mere mortals.'

Blesilla composed herself and looked Jerome in the eye. 'And what would you suggest I do?'

'Above all, learn! Read, and study the Scriptures and eminent writers who discourse upon them. Read Origen. You might even read me. Discuss the deepest meaning of Scripture with scholars such as myself.' He hesitated. 'If you wish, you could translate more for me — I have a mountain of work, and my eyes are weak. You could make your books available to those who value learning or want them transcribed. Or, if you prefer a more practical approach, you could always keep open house for those who travel on behalf of the Church.'

He stood up, and she was struck, as before, by his height. 'Remember, my lady, that works of charity aren't limited to feeding bread to the poor. The hungry in spirit need your help as well. From your questions, I discern — despite a certain vulnerability to the pull of society and the distractions of marriage, and possibly widowhood — that you have a mind superior to the great majority of men's.' He paused theatrically. 'I challenge you to use it to the full!'

His words were exciting. Ah, but he couldn't know that she was outside it all, carnal sinner that she was.

'You talk of the celibate state,' she faltered. 'But I —'

'You've been married, of course. A pity. But you can choose to live chaste from now on.'

'What about second marriages?' she asked, as casually as she could. 'Are they so bad?"

'Oh, let's not condemn a second marriage, or a third, or any number,' Jerome said sarcastically. 'There are high society whores as well as those of the gutter. But I'm talking about women capable of a truly Christian life, women of your own high intelligence. You don't imagine I meant the sort you'd find down there!'

They were on the loggia, and the hubbub of the Circus Maximus drifted up, mingled with the roars of the crowd.

'Blesilla! Learn a holy arrogance. Turn to the world, and a small portion of people will know of you for a short time. Turn to Christ, and the whole world will know of you for all eternity. By adopting a holy life, you stand to gain more than you would ever sacrifice.'

He gazed at her profile and the rich auburn hair falling over her shoulders.

'You are very beautiful, Blesilla. If you could only see yourself as you are now — a hundred times more beautiful without rouge or whitelead or pearls or silks. No such adornments can make a true beauty, though they can perhaps confer the illusion of it. Because you're so attractive to men, you'll find a life of seclusion and prayer a thousand times harder than would a plain woman — this is true. But let not such a challenge deter you!

'In marriage, you've known fulfilment, and your body has been awakened to passion. But take the path I urge, and day and night you'll struggle against the enemy within. You'll have moments, undoubtedly, when you resent wasting your charm and beauty.

'But God will gauge exactly the extent of your struggle. What is hard fought for has the greatest value. To fight for spiritual delight in God brings with it an exquisite agony which is the inner joy of the true Christian. And know that your loyalty to God will bring a glorious reward!'

'But surely there is loyalty to a man, too,' said Blesilla craftily, 'such as my mother had for my father. Is that worth nothing?'

'Well, of course it is,' Jerome was startled into replying. 'But such a wonderful woman as your mother could never be anything but true. Now, she has consciously taken on a role infinitely greater.'

He brought his hand down hard on the balustrade.

'We are on this earth for but a brief moment, Blesilla! Will you misuse the moment in the torpor of common life? Become coarsened, as marriage coarsens, for a second time? Why return like a dog to its vomit? When, by embracing widowhood, you might find ecstasy?'

His voice deepened and he seemed almost to chant: 'Your eyes will see the Lord, your ear will hear His words, your mouth will kiss Him, you will know the blazing light of Christ.'

She lowered her eyes. 'I know a girl,' she began, 'who had relations with a man before she married.'

'With the man she married?'

'Someone else.'

'He was married?'

'No.'

Jerome's face darkened. 'You know what Paul says. The fornicator sins against his own body.'

'It's not clear to me.'

'You can repent of theft, say, or manslaughter—that is, sins against others. But fornication defiles a man in conscience and body. We commit it on ourselves, in our bodies. In the very act of repentance for lust we feel that itch of the flesh all over again and we sin again.'

Collecting his books for departure, Jerome added bitterly:

'I know only too well the price a fornicator pays.'

Abruptly the session was over, and Jerome departed.

***

One afternoon soon after, Praetextata paid Blesilla a visit. Though her aunt arrived in full panoply of black silk, jewels and rings, her face was pale with the tell-tale signs of sleeplessness. Restlessly, she accompanied Blesilla for a walk around Paula's gardens, talking at length of earlier and happier days.

'Did you know that Bassus is married?' she remarked, plucking dead heads off a rosebush.

Blesilla stopped. 'I didn't know,' she said finally. 'Who did he marry?'

'A rich Milanese heiress. The father has a prominent position at court.'

'Bassus has done well,' returned Blesilla evenly.

'Oh, he's bound to … to get ahead.' Praetextata stumbled over her words. Since her seizure in Tibur, her hands trembled a little and her mouth still drooped at one side. But her tongue, Blesilla thought sourly, still wagged.

Only as she was preparing to take her leave did Praetextata say: 'By the way, you needn't worry about that affair up in Tibur.'

'What affair?'

'Eustochium.'

Blesilla puzzled for a moment, and then asked: 'Do you mean putting a few feathers on her head at a party?'

Her aunt stopped, and said: 'I tried to turn her thoughts to marriage. But you had no part in it, and you mustn't feel guilty.'

'It never occurred to me.'

'It didn't occur to you?' Praetextata echoed her words in a wondering voice.

Then, rustling in her pocket, she produced a cloth bag. 'This is for you.' She thrust it at her niece.

'Aunt!' Blesilla let the glittering blue gems run through her fingers. 'But this is your sapphire necklace!'

'It was a gift from Hymetius, long ago … It's worth a lot. Oh, and I've explained to your mother about young Toxotius. He is going along very well with his studies at my brother's place, together with his cousins.'

Blesilla felt uneasy. Neither the necklace nor Toxotius seemed to belong to their meeting. The relevance became clearer when Praetextata added:

'There's something I wanted to tell you. At Tibur, the night of the spectacle.' Self-consciously, she looked around to her left and right. 'It's ridiculous, of course.'

'Go on, aunt.'

'Oh, your God has got at me.' The older woman gave a hollow laugh. 'In a dream! Because of how I tried to push Eustochium into society. An angel appeared—a Christian angel, though I don't know how I knew. Anyway, the angel accused me of laying sacrilegious hands on the head of one of God's virgins.'

'It was a dream, nothing more.'

'Except that what the angel said has come true,' Praetextata continued shakily. 'That my hands would seize up and I'd lose my family as a sign of the death that would come to me if I did not repent.'

'Oh, you are very much alive, my dear aunt.'

'Hymetius and the girls are dead—and look at my hands!' She tried to flex her aged fingers out in front of her. 'All twisted and stiff!'

Blesilla stared at them in silence.

'At the eleventh month's end I shall die. That's what the angel said.'

'What angel would talk like that?' said Blesilla. 'They say that not all dreams come from God, you know, that if demons appear, they come from Satan. This angel of yours sounds more like a demon playing mischief on you. Take no notice.'

'Of course, you're right,' her aunt replied, with a return of her old haughtiness. 'I don't know why I even mention such foolery.'

They walked back inside, and Praetextata summoned her attendant eunuch to send her litter round.

After her departure, Blesilla sank down on a couch, trembling all over.

***

In private, the next day, Marcella told Paula that her daughter looked exhausted, and suggested that a change of scene would do Blesilla good.

Paula's voice caught in her throat as she said: 'There's a weakness in her. Is it right, what Jerome and I want of her?' Her face crumpled. 'What if she's not up to our demands? What if I lose her and never see her again?'

'What's got into you, Paula? It's not like you to be maudlin! Blesilla is young and strong and will make a full recovery.'

Marcella's tone became severe. 'You're talking as though the soul is not immortal. The afterlife, Paula, is the whole pivot of our teaching!'

'What form would this afterlife take?' Paula's voice rose. 'Origen says that after death we'll take a human form of some kind that is beyond our comprehension while we are imprisoned in our earthly bodies. We will not be men and women as we are now. This life is but a moment in eternity, before we're pitched into an endless transformation …'

Paula covered her face with her hands. 'I have moments … when I struggle … If we can't comprehend it, how can we accept it?'

'Bishop Epiphanius thinks Origen is heretical in this regard,' stated Marcella calmly. 'He says that we rise in the flesh — this flesh, these bones and muscles and all — in glorified flesh.'

Paula relaxed a little. 'Please God that it may be so,' she breathed. 'What does Jerome say?'

'Jerome,' said Marcella, with a pleased expression, 'doesn't seem to know anything about a treatise Epiphanius wrote on this, or even realise that Origen has fallen out of favour with many in the Church on this very matter.'

'Jerome thinks the world of Origen, I thought.'

'Jerome,' said Marcella shrewdly, 'likes what Origen says about the virgin life. It lends weight to his own views.'

'What's wrong with having strong views?' Paula objected. 'Jerome is a staunch champion of the faith.'

Marcella pursed her lips. 'Too staunch, some say.'

'You're too hard on him! He has a difficult life—his work is unremitting, and he suffers eye-strain.'

Paula's voice softened. 'He's not very strong. Really, he needs someone to look after him.'

'Jerome,' Marcella retorted, 'is a man with the strength of ten—in his tongue, at least. A pity the man was born without an atom of tact or sense of proportion.'

'Neither have I much sense of proportion,' said Paula. She looked, Marcella thought, a shade belligerent.

'There's no holding you back, is there? You throw yourself into all you do!'

'Jerome stands up fearlessly for what he believes,' pointed out Paula.

'Indeed.' Marcella paused. 'He's under fire because of his work on the Gospels, you know.'

'But Damasus himself asked him to do it!'

'Yes, but Jerome is accused of not just translating the Gospels, but correcting them! We appreciate what he is doing, but those who don't read Greek may not.'

'Such ignorance!' Paula expostulated. 'How dare they pass judgment on one who has studied Holy Scripture more profoundly than they ever could!'

She had regained her natural colour, Marcella noted. Not for the first time, hearing Jerome criticised had roused her friend from despair to fortitude.

Marcella rose to go. As they walked through the long gallery flanked by its marble statuary, she asked: 'What's that under the dust cover?'

Paula stopped and raised the cover. 'It's Toxotius's Apollo.'

Marcella glanced quizzically at her friend.

'It was dear to Toxotius, I know,' Paula said. 'But I've made my mind up—I'm going to sell it.'

'From the quarry at Afrodisias, isn't it? A real masterpiece. This will fetch a good price.'

Embracing her friend, Marcella added, 'Don't worry about Blesilla, my dear. And I'll expect her tomorrow, of course.'

19

At Marcella's villa, Blesilla breathed a saner air. She was encouraged not only to eat and drink, but relax while she did so.

'Christ wants all the fire and warmth of your devotion, which calls for balance of mind and body,' Marcella told her. 'A body enfeebled cannot concentrate wholly on God, so make yourself physically strong. Leave aside big issues of doctrine for the moment and, if you must, turn to the smaller ones of Bible linguistics ...'

This, Blesilla soon learnt, really meant watching Marcella herself as that stalwart lady progressed through her formidable day's work — and, on occasion, assisting her. Jerome himself was frequently present, to pronounce on the relative merits of various Greek translations of the Old Testament, and their most faithful renderings in Latin. Blesilla picked up quickly that whereas Paula was all Jerome's, and his constant champion, for Marcella Jerome existed to help her and her women in their intensive textual study of the Bible. Ruthlessly she kept him at it. In return, she gave him her advice, and sometimes strong criticism.

Blesilla stumbled upon them one morning doing battle in formal style.

'My good Jerome.' Thus Marcella usually addressed him, much as she used 'my son' to lesser men. 'You're not saying that the man had no cause to threaten you with a libel action?'

Blesilla peered through the door. Jerome's face was bowed above his clasped hands, his eyes turned upwards to Marcella with good effect as he answered her.

'My Lady Marcella, I tell the truth.'

'Oh, I believe you, and I admit the truth in this case is dreadful enough.'

'Onasus is a mercentary priest!' Jerome declared. 'He is guilty of perjury.'

'I'm sure you're right.'

'I hold him up as a glaring example of the kind of malpractice that must be cut out of the Church. I didn't name him. I only referred to 'a certain person'. If the boot fits …'

'My dear Jerome, everyone knows whom you meant. And you told him he puffs out his cheeks like bladders and balances hollow phrases on his tongue —'

'So he does!'

'The man may have warts on his nose, but there was hardly need to tell him to hide it and keep his mouth shut if he wanted people to think he was handsome and a good speaker.'

'Did I say that? I don't think —'

'My good Jerome, you *wrote* it.'

***

Later that week, Marcella took Blesilla aside as she was leaving.

'You're very pale this morning, my dear,' she said. 'Let's eat.'

'I can't eat just now.'

'Come into the garden then. We've had our noses in books for hours, and a bit of fresh air will do us both good.'

They walked down a path lined with waving oleanders. It was a clear day, and in the distance the rich green canopy of pine trees bowed and shimmered, punctuated only by rooftops of surrounding homes as palatial as Marcella's own. It was, Blesilla reflected, a luxuriant backdrop to the life of self-denial and hardship practised by the ladies within their walls.

'I eat little and often,' Marcella was saying. 'It's no good fasting for days and then overdoing it.'

'My mother hardly eats anything.'

'She's younger than me, and stronger. At my age — and at yours — we need more sustenance.'

'Jerome is old enough, but Mamma says he exists on gruel.'

Marcella smothered a smile. 'It's invective that keeps Jerome going,' she said. 'There's plenty for him to use his talent on. Look how he pilloried that priest from Gaul who criticised worship of the martyrs and saints and all-night vigils, and even said that the clergy should be free to marry!'

'Jerome must have had a fit.'

'He wrote an open letter to the man. Oh, it was a model of telling argument, but very savage and abusive ...'

Marcella declaimed all down the long path to the rose garden, where the autumn sun was still warm. As they walked, Blesilla measured the moral distance between them. Marcella would certainly have a clear conscience; probably she had never done a mean or tawdry thing in her whole life, let alone a wicked one. But, the thought occurred to her, if she had sinned, she would positively relish her repentance. Whatever situation Marcella was in, she would milk it to the full.

What, thought Blesilla, would she say of *me* if she knew?

***

Marcella it was who struck terror into Blesilla a few days later. Entering her study, Blesilla came across the older woman busy scribbling. Raising a preoccupied face, she said:

'I've just been talking to a Novationist, and we had quite a long chat. I've seen him several times lately, and what he says does impress me. You know how Novatian wouldn't pardon sins committed after baptism?'

'No sins at all?' Blesilla's voice quavered.

'Not the most terrible ones like murder or adultery. He believed that when we are guilty of a deliberate turning away from the state of grace —'

'But surely,' Blesilla broke in, 'even mortal sins can be redeemed by true repentance? Is not God infinitely merciful?'

'Yes, but — and this is crucial — the Novationists hold that the Church hasn't the power to grant us absolution.'

'But … but surely to question the Church's authority would be heretical?'

'You have a fine mind.' Marcella acknowledged the point. 'Many have raised precisely this question. But the man has Biblical authority for his views, you may depend. We spent a long time discussing Paul's Epistle to the Hebrews. I imagine that you know the part?'

Blesilla searched her memory, but fright had emptied it.

'No? Well, Paul did say: "For if we sin wilfully after having the knowledge of the truth, there is now left no sacrifice for sins."

'So, the possibility of absolution is, at the very least, debatable, isn't it?' Marcella paused, her eyes bright with thought. 'As to Origen …' she murmured.

'What did Origen think?' asked Blesilla desolately.

'He insisted on the pivotal value of our free will, arguing that the Devil can ignite evil desires in us but cannot force us to act on them.' She frowned. 'I suspect that idolatry, adultery and fornication figure amongst those sins for which there is no remedy — for how could one continue to indulge in them while cooperating with God to attain salvation?'

Marcella paused once more, ruminatively, then added: 'Tertullian believed —'

'I know about Tertullian,' Blesilla snapped. 'A bad-tempered old woman-hater. Anyway, I thought we weren't talking about the nature of sin but about its absolution.'

'Well, Tertullian too held that bishops had no power to grant absolution to adulterers or fornicators, and said that second marriages were a form of adultery. Furthermore … My dear, you are *so* pale! This will not do!'

Marcella clapped her hands and a maid entered.

'Bring us some bread and cheese and wine, at once!'

'I'm fine.' Blesilla forced the words out. 'Just a bit out of sorts today.'

In fact, she felt her nerves were cracking. She gulped down some wine, and gratefully accepted the honey-sweetened bread that Marcella pressed upon her.

'Of course,' Marcella continued, 'the Novationists *are* known for being sticklers for dogma. You know that story about the Emperor Constantine losing his temper and saying to a bishop at the Council of Nicaea: "Acesius," he said, "Go and set up a ladder and climb up to Heaven on your own!"'

Her little joke fell flat.

'You don't think Novatian was right?' Blesilla demanded. 'About adulterers and fornicators, I mean.'

'I can only say that my Novationist friend argues very convincingly, strictly on the Bible.' Marcella tapped her lips. 'Of course, Paul said plenty of other things too, many in a more compassionate vein.' She pulled out a notebook.

'Paul said: "For beloved, we are persuaded better things of you, and nearer to salvation … For God is not unrighteous to forget your work and the labour of love which you have showed in His name … I will be merciful to their iniquities, and their sins I will remember no more."

'Now that sounds to me as if God is giving us a chance for remission of mortal sins through good works and repentance. But, of course, Paul's words are by no means clear.' She raised her head. 'Blesilla! Go and rest. You are not eating anything.'

'Oh!' Blesilla hastily took another bite of the bread.

'Go home and sleep now, if you can, my dear. The wine should help.'

Marcella turned back to matters that were to her of eternal fascination.

***

In her room, Blesilla lay on her bed, praying for leave to hope for God's forgiveness. Not only for her relations with Bassus, but for her littler sins too. Careless and arrogant, she had

142

flounced through life. Conceited she had been, and spiteful too – to Eustochium, for instance. Not only for years past, but even the other day when, irritated beyond measure by her younger sister's eagerness to please, Blesilla had curtly told her to take that holy-Jesus look off her face and leave her in sinful peace. How long before her uncontrollable temper would make her commit something truly awful?

Later, towards dusk, she paced up and down the garden. It would always be imprinted on her brain – that garden path, the sharp outline of a laurel tree against an amber sky. The laurel was darkening, the amber fading, when she heard footsteps behind her. Swinging around, she saw Aetius.

He bowed, and said: 'A message from the Lady Paula. The news came as I was waiting for my master, Jerome.'

His eyes bored into her. Unfolding the sheet which he handed her, she read:

'Your Aunt Praetextata died this afternoon. It would seem that she had another seizure, but quite unexpected. She had been feeling much better only yesterday.'

Blesilla was stunned. 'What date is it?' she asked, finally.

'It is the last day of November, my lady.' Aetius's eyes were coldly impassive.

A sudden instinct told her that he knew everything.

'Let me fetch the Lady Marcella. You are not well, my lady.' His voice was quite indifferent.

'Leave me!' she ordered abruptly and retreated, her whole body trembling as she ran to her room.

'If I do not repent … on the eleventh month's end I shall die.' Her aunt had died on the very day the angel had foretold. Blesilla shuddered. What else could this be but a judgment of God?

The door opened and Marcella entered. Blesilla shrank from her searching gaze.

'Your aunt was recovering from the shock of losing Hymetius and the children. But she must have been devastated! She was devoted to her children and a support to her husband in his public life and doubtless at home as well …'

So, now that she was dead, she was good, this woman who had never especially pleased Marcella! Blesilla wanted to shout:

'She schemed to get Eurochium married off. Did you know that? She dressed Eustochium up and paraded her at the party. And now she's dead, by order of God!'

Instead, she forced herself to say, 'I'd better go and stay at Mamma's.'

'That would be good. Paula always had a lot to do with her sister-in-law in the old days …'

Blesilla lay on her bed. Marcella left her, after arranging for a bowl of soup to be sent in to her. When she looked in again later, the girl seemed to be asleep, her face turned to the wall.

***

'I can't stand it, not another moment,' Blesilla moaned, at the end of that long night.

God had sent her a sign: Praetextata's sin had brought divine vengeance. And for herself, too, Judgment Day would come, and if she died in mortal sin without repentance she would be cut off forever from God's presence and the Holy Spirit, immured in God knows what sort of perpetual anguish, a ghastly culmination of everything she most feared. It was true; each sinner made their own hell—and hers was to be caught in a place from which there was no escape. Her breath came in gasps, and she was filled with an overwhelming loathing of her own body.

She muttered to herself, all Jerome's gruesome epithets ready to hand. Her body was a carcass of shame, ensnared by the Devil to sin gleefully and often. She felt as if she would choke with fear, with humiliation, but instead forced herself to take a deep breath.

At least she was still in this world! Praetextata was beyond redemption, but eminent scholars, including Jerome, were still debating the interpretation of God's will—and the nature of His inexhaustible mercy. Perhaps, just perhaps, there was still a shred of hope remaining to her.

All the old Christian precepts, long ignored when they had clashed with her own desires, came flooding back. God must be appeased, sins expiated. Money wasn't enough, prayers neither, and nor were endowments: penance would have to be paid. God demanded nothing less than the total transparency of her soul, her complete and utter abasement. She would have to grovel in the eyes of the world, to confess all. Could she do it? Instantly she pictured the staring faces in the basilica, the surrender of herself to the fascinated prurience of high and low of Roman society.

She shuddered, for she already knew the answer.

20

Blesilla confessed in the title church of Santa Prisca on the Aventine Hill very early one morning before the sun had fully risen. The dim light hid her shame, and shielded her from the gaze of the others gathered there.

Kneeling on the stone floor, she fixed her eyes on a mosaic lion, that fierce lion that had been turned loose in the amphitheatre on the young girl Prisca, noble as herself, because she refused to renounce her faith. But the lion had only licked her feet. Even torture had failed to kill her and in the end they had beheaded her, and her bones lay under the high altar.

Blesilla's knees began to hurt, her spine ached and she felt light-headed. She waited a long time in the ghostly atmosphere of the church, the silence broken only by the shuffle of feet. The penitential priest was seated behind an Ionic column in the aisle, where neither his words nor those of the penitent could be heard by the public.

Finally, her turn came.

'Terrible sins,' she heard herself whisper out her shame. 'Many sins. Perhaps too terrible for forgiviness.'

'All is possible. What sins?' She felt the eyes of the priest on her, taking in her appearance and clothes, the oldest she possessed but still costly.

'Many sins. Ungenerosity and pride, uncontrolled temper, spitefulness.' She began with the lesser.

'That is all?'

'No. Unclean thoughts.'

'Deplorable. But God can forgive.'

'There is worse,' she said wildly, her eyes filling.

'You know the bishop is as God with the power to forgive the sins of the fallen. What is your sin?'

'The sin of fornication.' The words were finally out.

The stern eyes of the priest flickered, and she knew that he once more took in every detail of her person, her delicate features, before he went on to question her further.

She told her story, haltingly but in full. The priest asked how often she had committed the sin. Mortified but determined to reveal all, she answered that it was as often as possible over six weeks of summer in a resort.

There was silence as the priest considered. At last he raised his eyes, sad but not unsympathetic. She wept further.

'You know that in such a state of sin you must be excluded from the mysteries of our Lord Jesus Christ.'

His voice was slow and sonorous. His words enveloped her, carefully chosen and respectfully delivered. He was obviously a well-educated man, not just a lowly priest, and must surely recognise her as Paula's daughter.

'I sense, by your tears, that your heart is indeed sick within you, my daughter. You will be aware that there can be no remission for your dreadful sin unless you undergo the penitential discipline.'

The dreaded words were spoken at last. In a heady mixture of terror and relief, she felt close to fainting.

'In private you will pray, you will abstain from meat, from the bath. You will do formal penance in a public ceremony next Sunday in the Lateran Basilica, before His Holiness. You will be excluded from the mysteries until Easter, when we may judge better of your condition.'

The priest paused for a moment, then said:

'You know, my daughter in Christ, that the Church will not recognise any future marriage for you.'

She bowed her head; she knew that, wanted only that. The priest concluded, and Blesilla stumbled through the heavy silence of the church and down the steps.

Outside, she sank into the waiting litter and was carried home as the first rays of sunlight appeared.

***

Back in her villa, she shut herself in her bedroom and refused all food, overcome with emotion. As yet only the priest knew of her past, but soon her shame would be public knowledge. She would become an object of cruel curiosity, could expect gossip and inquisitive looks, and her servants would be bribed to disclose what they knew.

And yet, with her confession a certain peace had descended upon her. She was sick, she knew that now, and wanted only to be made whole again and, after absolution, to live a higher life, like the angels. She had taken the first tentative steps towards cleansing herself, and was ready to pay for her sins, whatever it took.

Her mother and Eustochium had been right all along! How wise was the Church and how wise were its remedies for sin. This body of hers existed only to be mastered. She'd begin in small ways, giving up all the sweet breads and cheese and wine she loved and eating only sparingly, and work towards a deeper self-discipline. That was her goal, to conquer the urge towards the act of physical love, towards degradation.

She saw no one but her maids until the following Sunday when she crawled into the large rectangular hall of the Lateran Basilica among the other penitents, conscious only of the hardness of its marble floor. She was barefoot, her hair dishevelled, her gown gaping at the sides, filthy with ashes. In the past she had watched it all, indifferently, seen the penitents fling themselves down before widows and presbyters, clasping the gowns of anyone near. And now she herself grovelled in front of them all. Was she dreaming?

No, not dreaming. Her head might be swimming, but she was acquiring a clarity she never had before. She didn't see, but felt, the presence in the basilica of every Christian whom she knew — and there were plenty of them! Rich friends, girls she'd known all her life, as well as half-familiar faces of regular churchgoers and all the nameless faceless ones. What a scandal her presence here would create!

She cringed, making the penitential circuit across the nave and down the double aisles. Oh, never had she imagined anything so terrible. The very taste of abasement clung to her mouth, her nostrils. As they completed their circuit and sank down together, Blesilla recoiled from the feet of the man in front of her which were very near to her face — unnecessarily close. A great hulking man with hairy legs, probably from the depths of the Subura, that sink of Rome …

'How dare you!' she muttered. 'Filthy swine!'

Her anger at being caught anywhere near such a man in this dishonourable way gripped her. His soul might be as precious as hers in the eyes of God, but without the little bag of perfume hidden under her clothes she might have sprung up and fled. It was fortunate too, that after days of fasting, she had, as a precaution against fainting, eaten before leaving home, for Marcella had told her — a long time ago now, it seemed — that she would need to be strong.

She took a deep breath. It's all a formality, she told herself confusedly. God understands me. I just have to get through this, that's all.

All the penitents were groaning, and loudly weeping, and the bishop — she recognised him as old Damasus himself — with all his clergy and all the faithful slowly advanced down the central nave from the other end of the church. And they too were all weeping and wailing at the top of their voices and, as they reached the penitents, they sank to the floor … a whole church, humble and contrite.

Damasus got slowly to his feet and bent over the penitents, raising them one by one, as a solemn sign of brotherhood with those now cast outside the Church. Oh, she could believe now that they might find absolution! The whole congregation was behind them, praying for them, propelling them towards realising their highest aspirations.

At the end of the *missa catechumenorum* and the final dismissal, the penitents were released.

Walking out through the huge door of the basilica, the rise and fall of the voices still ringing in her ears, Blesilla drank in the fresh morning air. Dizzy, she tottered into the street straight into the arms of her mother and was spirited away in a closed litter.

21

'"Vanities of vanities," says the Preacher. "Vanity of vanities; all is vanity."' Jerome's voice brought out all the sombre drama of the words. 'You are acquainted with this passage, my Lady Blesilla?'

'Oh, I am.' Blesilla turned her lovely eyes on him. 'Ecclesiastes is very beautiful. And very sad. Without any hope for any lasting pleasure.'

'My lady!' Jerome shook his head reproachfully.

'Well, Solomon lived to gain wisdom, but found it only brought desolation.' She quoted: '"The sun also rises and the sun goes down and returns to the place where he rose ... The thing that has been, is that which shall be; and that which is done is that which shall be done; and there is no new thing under the sun."'

'Oh, Solomon is desperately pessimistic! Enjoy the days of our youth, he says, before we grow old and take no pleasure in anything.'

'My Lady Blesilla, you toy with me. I know your understanding is deeper than you would have me believe.' Jerome's eyes softened.

She was continually surprised at his attitude now, weeks after her admission to the ranks of the penitent. She had expected disgust from him, horror even. But she had been wrong. He did not even shrink from her physically, though she knew she stank after not having washed for so long. On the contrary, he appeared to think her worthier of his attention than previously, for she had turned all her energies on study, that opiate for her self-disgust. Sometimes he even discussed with her aspects of his translation into Latin of the Bible. At such times, Paula would join them, overjoyed at her daughter's new composure.

'"All is vanity,"' Jerome intoned. 'The implication is clear. We must despise the ephemeral things of this world and reach out for those eternal! Think of Holy Scripture like a house full of locked rooms. We must find the right key to each lock.'

'Solomon's meaning is plain enough to me,' said Blesilla. This session had lasted some time already. 'Listen to this: "One generation passes away and another generation comes …" Doesn't it breathe weariness and futility? And doesn't the Hebrew word 'hebel' mean smoke or vapour?'

'Precisely!' cried Jerome. 'That is why I translated it as *vanitas*. To show that it is our own vanity, or nothingness, that blinds us to the ways of God and creates a sense of hopelessness. Earthly life might appear to have shape and form but is in fact quite insubstantial, and trying to chase the things of this life is like trying to cling onto steam — it slips through your fingers. Far from saying that everything is futile — as you suggest — he is demonstrating the futility of attempting to find happiness in this life instead of by following the eternal ways of God!'

'Well, what about that part where he tells us to go our way, and eat our bread and drink our wine joyfully —'

'Christ's body and blood,' Jerome interrupted her. 'His body and blood, which we feed on both in the Eucharist and in our reading of Holy Scripture!'

She stared at him. She was drawn by his energy, and could feel the fascination of allegory. But she also felt a tiny spark of irritation, as reason fought with the inscrutable. She was given no chance to develop her thoughts, however, for Jerome chose that moment to introduce a name which was clearly of supreme importance to him.

'Origen.' His eyes held a powerful appeal. 'I shall send you what Origen says on the matter.'

So saying, Jerome took his leave.

***

Despite Jerome's devotion, and her mother's support, Blesilla was facing grim days. She hardly knew her former self. In the cupboards of her dressing-room were stacked her old tunics and stolas, some with ornamental borders, and cloaks and jewels — the trappings of an easy life of careless pleasure. One day, she told herself, she would dispose of the lot.

All her household grieved with her, for different reasons. Most worried about their own future in this increasingly austere household. More than anything, they feared being sold should Blesilla dispose of her wealth as recklessly as her mother was doing. Clea, Blesilla's personal maid since childhood and always adept at filching, now redoubled her efforts.

Blesilla held onto her penitential vows all through winter. Finally, on a warm spring morning, the Thursday before Easter in 384 AD, came the ceremony of public absolution, when among the other penitents, she lay on the floor of the Lateran Basilica and heard Damasus's impressive words:

'*Domine sancte, Pater omnipotens, aeterne Deus …*

'Look upon Thy servants, who have been overwhelmed by the hostile storms of the world … accept their prayers and groans, recall them from the darkness to the light … Do Thou restore them purged to Thy Church, and replace them at Thine altar …

'*Per Domine nostrum.*'

Blesilla felt Damasus's hands on her head. With a beating heart she was raised up, in a Church reverberating with the exultant sound of sung prayer. As in a trance she received the Eucharist, and bowed her head in silent supplication.

When all was over, she walked out of the Lateran Basilica, her mother by her side, to face the crowds outside.

'Ah, but just look at her!' they said. 'Look at those feet all bare and bleeding from the stones. How dainty they are, pretty as a child's, and look how under all that dirt her face is shining! Shame! Isn't it terrible to see such a high-born lady put herself down so low!'

Blesilla, drained of energy or thought, surrendered herself to the guiding hand of her mother and let herself be led home. Later, she heard Marcella insisting that, despite it being Holy Thursday, Blesilla had to eat. So eat she did, and was bathed and put to bed. Freed from the filth of weeks, her skin clean and fragrant again, she sank down on the soft bed and stretched out luxuriantly.

All afternoon she slept and through the following night, and awoke with the joyous recollection that she was free of sin, and one with God.

***

Spring passed into summer and Blesilla could scarcely believe that she was the same person. And she wasn't the same, she told herself. She shared her mother's labours, though she couldn't match her self-mortifications. Sometimes Paula even slept on the bare stone floor, wrapped only in coarse cloth. It was a wonder to see this wealthy woman — and she still was wealthy, despite her bequests — choose to live in extreme poverty. Dressed in rags, unkempt despite her heavy purse, she was renowned in all Rome for her good works. Every morning Blesilla joined her in handing out food and clothing to the indigent and the lazy in a disused warehouse that Paula had recently bought.

It was a hard life. After prayers at dawn they went straight to the almsgiving. The impact of last year's famine was still with the Romans and the city teemed with the hungry. But as always, grain there was for those able to pay, and a steady stream of money flowed from Paula to speculating merchants. The afternoons Paula spent with her women, her 'household church' as she called it, to pray or study together or visit the shrines of the martyrs.

In the evening, Blesilla would retire to her own villa and study by herself, appreciating the visits of Jerome, who arrived — usually in the company of a junior cleric — to discuss her reading of Holy Scripture and, increasingly, his translation of the Bible.

Paula's championing of her daughter, touching to many, quickly became the backbone of the girl's resolve. For weeks

Blesilla existed in a thankful glow that lightened the monotony and squalor of her daily routine.

Sometimes though, in a moment of utter exhaustion, she would hear a whisper in her ear: 'You didn't choose this life, it was imposed on you …' Evil, seductive thoughts. And she would pray, late into the night, for strength.

***

Her prayers weren't always answered, as when, after one of those disturbed nights, Marcella invited her to accompany her by carriage out to the Baptistry of Santa Constantia, where a sickly infant of Marcella's extended family was to be baptised.

Travelling along the Via Nomentana, the road leading to the Baptistry, Blesilla breathed earthiness as the sunlight danced on the paving stones and the rasp of cicadas rang in her ears. It seemed a long time since she had been in the outside world, and her heart leaped.

The carriage drew to a standstill, and she and Marcella entered the Baptistery, with its twelve arches supported by an equal number of columns. It had been built by the Emperor Constantine as a mausoleum for his daughter Constantina, whose body, like that of her sister Helena, lay in an intricately carved sarcophagus.

Under the inner dome, glowing with coloured mosaics, Blesilla watched the priest at the altar muttering over the little girl, and relived her own baptism as a girl of ten. The priest had carried out the exorcism of salt over her, too, with a warning to the Devil to go out of her and give way to the Holy Spirit. She had felt the man's hands putting grains of salt — symbol of wisdom, she knew — between her lips. He had licked his fingers and touched her nostrils and ears, uttering threats and curses on the Devil, invocations to God.

Like the child before her, she too had been lowered over the font, and had emerged washed clean of sin, and had been anointed with the chrism, or holy oil, in the name of the Father, the Son, and the Holy Spirit. How, then, could God's precepts have come to sit so lightly upon her?

The rite of baptism was completed, the appropriate exchanges made, and Blesilla followed Marcella through the Baptistry, its polished marble walls a dramatic patchwork of reflected heads and shoulders.

Outside again, they found a young monk haranguing the crowd, a giant of a man with fair hair and pale skin.

'He's called Pelagius,' Marcella said. 'A Briton, so I've heard. He's been in Rome for several years now. Half-mad probably, and utterly wrong — but very compelling. Listen!'

The young man strode among the people, his great fists punching the air as he made his points, his sandals large enough to stamp any opposition into the ground.

'You are in chains, all of you!' he thundered. 'Chains of habit, laziness and lust, avarice and hate. And yet it was you yourselves who chose to wear them! You were born pure, without sin, in God's grace — and look at you now! Of your own free will you *choose* to sin. You are damned for all eternity, unless you repent now. For the sake of Christ who gave his blood for you, follow in his footsteps and embrace a life free from sin!'

Blesilla stared, fascinated. Of course he was wrong. No man was born without the stain of original sin. But his face was ablaze with the passionate love of Christ, and his independence of mind and challenge to those around him touched a chord in her. And he was so confident and virile. In an instant, excitement flushed through her and she stood helpless. Someone had once told her that a man's private member was proportioned in size to his hands and feet.

Quickly she turned to Marcella. 'Please let us go now,' she whispered. 'At once.'

Inside the carriage she sank back on the cushions, begging silently for forgiveness for momentarily harbouring that unbidden and unclean thought. Marcella fanned her, fearing that she was sick and may faint. She did not know that Blesilla was indeed sick, but from a memory — of another young man who too had radiated confidence and vitality and was far from small. Blesilla prayed, but could not escape the shade of Bassus accompanying her all along the Via Nomentana to the entrance of her villa. Every paving stone they passed, every tree that swayed seemed to breathe his name.

***

That summer of 384 AD the heat came early and, by June, Rome was sweltering. By mid-morning the heat was shimmering off pavements and walls. People sought the shade and drank at fountains, street vendors did good business selling slices of juicy melons, the Senate was sparsely attended and senators cursed their heavy woollen togas.

One morning, Paula announced that she had purchased a substantial amount of grain, so that she and her women could continue distributing food to the needy throughout the summer.

'The poor are always with us,' she added.

Blesilla heard a murmur of assent from the group. But she herself was utterly dismayed. She had assumed that, despite everything, they would go to one of their estates by the sea or in the surrounding hills. She'd never spent an entire summer in Rome in all her life! She recoiled at the thought of unwashed people who would stink more than ever in the heat, of bandaging suppurating sores, and watching the misery of the blind feeling their way to the site of Paula's handouts. She aired her woes to Jerome that afternoon, but received scant sympathy.

'God is testing you, Blesilla. He is judging even now if you are worthy of your place in Heaven.' He threw up his arms. 'Besides, the temperature in Rome isn't as bad as all that. It was twice as hot in the desert!'

She swallowed the retort that it was different for him because while he'd been slaving away in the desert, he'd also had the opportunity of learning Hebrew, whereas she was not learning anything new here in Rome.

Relief came unexpectedly later that day.

'My dear child,' said her mother. 'You know I want to build a new hostel for penitents after they've been absolved. There's a senior government official just back from the East who wants to buy one of your own properties in Aquila. The proceeds would easily cover the cost of the hostel.' She added, smiling: 'He would meet you in Aquila and you could settle the matter there and then, if you want.'

Blesilla snatched at the opportunity, sensing that her own presence was not really necessary in Aquila, but that her mother wanted her to have this respite.

The journey, two weeks later, was like a foretaste of Heaven. Leaving the city behind, the carriage wound ever higher through the valleys and passes, and the air grew cooler and pure. Gone were the gut-wrenching smells of sweat and dirty flesh that had made her retch. And she was wearing a silken stola for a change — at her mother's insistence.

'Don't go in rags,' her mother had warned her. 'We don't want the man to think he can get the property cheap because we look so poor.'

The sale went smoothly, and even too quickly. By the end of August, Blesilla was back in Rome. As far as she could, she expunged from her mind the memories of the pleasant recent weeks. She didn't mention, at home, that the official had virtually proposed marriage to her. That hadn't affected her peace of mind — or the purchase price of her property.

22

With the cooler air of September approaching, Jerome redoubled his workload, and that of his assistant.

'My work is hard, sir,' Aetius sighed one morning. 'Though I get much pleasure from it,' he added hastily.

He bustled around as he spoke, preparing Jerome's desk with scrolls of papyrus, wax tablets, inkwells and pens, and arranging the cushions — the very picture of an assiduous assistant.

'I'm glad to hear it. But now I want you to call on the Lady Blesilla. Help her with one or two passages in Ecclesiastes that are troubling her. It will save me time. You won't have to help her much — she has a fine mind, and relishes a challenge.' Jerome grabbed a stylus, scribbled a note on a tablet and handed it to Aetius. 'Here, take this to her.'

Aetius glanced at it. 'Your commendation means a lot to me, sir. I will get no praise from the lady in question, of course. Like many women, she has no generosity to her inferiors and is concerned only to save her own soul. But if I please you, sir, that is what matters.'

'Well, you do please me, Aetius.'

Aetius hesitated, then added softly: 'If you really mean that, sir, might I ask your great indulgence in the matter of advancing my career?'

'You overestimate my influence, Aetius.'

'But master, you have the ear and the affection of His Holiness.'

'And what might your heart desire? An entrée to the choir, perhaps, or the right to hold the golden chalice at the altar?'

If Aetius heard the irony in the question, he gave no sign of it. 'Yes, that is what I should like most — to bear the chalice.'

'To assist the bishop at the holy mysteries, I suppose?'

'Yes.'

'You would have to be a deacon for that.'

'Just so, master! There are some deacons here who have earned your censure and ridicule. I think His Holiness might concede that my qualifications are better.'

Aetius watched his words register.

'Why do you want to be a deacon? It's a dead-end job. You know that a deacon isn't ordained for the priesthood but for the service of the bishop.'

'Just so, master. The deacon is very close to the bishop,' said Aetius meaningfully.

Jerome became alarmed. Aetius was going too far. He must surely realise it.

'You know that you would have to put in five years as sub-deacon before you could be deacon,' he pointed out. 'It's a long journey up the ladder.'

'The order of deacons has been conferred on laymen,' Aetius said obstinately.

'Think of the translations we work through, the letters we are obliged to compose, the Biblical exegesis — rigorous, exacting work. You'd be bored stiff as a deacon!'

'I just thought that you might give me a helping hand, sir.' Aetius hesitated. 'Senior deacons often get to be bishops.'

'Ah, so that's what you have in mind!' Jerome shook his head in disbelief. 'Never in my life have I sought favour for myself or anyone else. If I've achieved a rather special position here, it is because,' — he paused — 'there was, well, a *need* for me,' he concluded.

'And now people are saying that you might even succeed Damasus, sir. Your theological learning and your facility with languages are such great assets. Bishop Ambrose was appointed bishop straight from lay life, and he now reads and translates the works of Greek theologians to enrich his fellow churchmen in the West. A bishop has to be a scholar.'

'But a scholar doesn't necessarily make a bishop!' said Jerome sharply. 'The focus of a scholar is research and analysis, rather than guiding the faithful in the ways of the Church. Scholars can lose touch with reality sometimes.'

'Not you, master,' Aetius demurred. 'But I see you think that I am not fit to rise in the priesthood of God.'

'Make your way by hard work and such devotion to God as you are capable of,' Jerome said shortly.

Try as he might, Jerome could see no trace of piety or spiritual fire in that countenance, in those intelligent eyes, and that mouth which could curve so readily in irreverent laughter.

'You are in a temper, Aetius,' he thought. 'That's all.'

Aloud he said: 'Let us proceed with our work. That is what God has called us to do.'

***

Much later, after Aetius had departed, Jerome noticed that he had left behind a volume entitled *Coena Cypriani*. Quickly Jerome skimmed the crude verses and uttered a snort of disgust.

What rubbish, he thought savagely, and tossed it down. An obscene travesty of that marriage banquet in Cana of Galilee at which Jesus had performed a miracle by turning water into wine, that's what it was! In this pathetic attempt at satire — or was it meant to be allegory? — each guest took the form of a Biblical character, but the marriage feast was a drunken, quarrelsome nightmare in which the guests tracked down and murdered a thief, buried his body, and then, after more revelry, returned to their own homes.

Jerome's lip curled. The insolence of the author — whoever he was — in ascribing it to the blessed Cyprian, that excellent Bishop of Carthage, martyred over one hundred years ago! How dare the memory of such a man be associated with this contemptible essay for novices to snigger over! It was all part of the slime and fungus that festered round the stout abiding oak of the Holy Scriptures …

It left a bad taste in his mouth — enough to put a man off his dinner. But his slave was even now calling him to table, and Jerome settled down to his frugal repast — beans and oil, with a good bread, washed down by wine and water, and began to feel better. Then he started in as usual on the evening's work.

He worked long and hard, but once in bed that night found that sleep did not come easily. His over-active brain dwelt, involuntarily, on Aetius who had so startled him that morning with the extravagance of his visions of promotion.

***

When finally he did sleep, Jerome had a monstrous dream. He was attending a dinner party. It was one of Damasus's, a lavish affair, with God knows how many august personages, lay as well as clerical, in attendance. Splendidly apparelled, all of them, reclining on couches covered with fine silks and embroidered rugs. Petronius Probus was there, and the city prefect and Symmachus, the leader of the Senate, and every famous man in Rome.

'Let us never forget our virgins,' Damasus was saying, his face red as terracotta. 'Let us keep them ever before our eyes.'

'Even when we're dining!' yelled a deacon, holding the silver chalice of His Holiness carefully above his head. 'Let's have 'em in!'

Beaming, Damasus gave his assent.

All down the great hall, the long line of guests clapped and cheered, and the gold covers of the dining tables and all the paraphernalia of precious gold and silver vessels glittered in the light of a hundred lanterns.

'Look!' someone shouted. 'His Holiness has disappeared!'

'He's fallen off his throne,' bellowed the Deacon Ascholius. 'Hoist him up, now!'

162

But instead of Damasus's stalwart figure it was Aetius's slim frame that was manhandled into place. It was Aetius's visage that was sparkling; Aetius's voice that began preaching in deep, ringing tones; and Aetius who swayed on his throne, as if to fall, clasping a silver goblet and drinking greedily in great gulps as droplets of red wine splashed to the floor.

'The blessed blood of Christ!' he exulted. He teetered backwards, and was rescued just in time by servants.

Then everything became confused. Probus vanished and with him Symmachus and the senatorial nobles, ousted by an interminable crowd of advancing Biblical figures, easily recognisable — Peter dragging his chair, Samson his columns, while Rachel sat astride her father's household gods, and Abraham with his sacrificial lamb. Cain was there with his plough, Daniel with his tribunal. Rebecca perched on her water-jug, and Jesus was seated on the lip of a well.

The clamour was tremendous as they all fought for a place at the table. Yet finally they were all seated, and the entire magnificent dining hall reeked of boiled meats and vegetables, rich sauces and herbs sizzled in olive oil. Platters of food were served, and the wine, warmed and flavoured with exotic spices, flowed freely. The results were predictable: Adam was soon sunk in slumber, Noah drunk on the floor, and Holofernes snoring under the table, while Mary beat a drum, Isaac roared with laughter, and Judas offered his mouth in a kiss.

Now the King of Cana — who had somehow replaced Aetius — was calling for the most beautiful virgin of all to be brought before him. Someone shouted that there was no virgin as beautiful as the noble widow Paula.

'Bring her in, then!' cried all the guests.

Paula was led in then, head lowered in modesty, and all agreed that she was indeed beautiful. And suddenly, under cover of the racket, she moved closer to Jerome, and never had she seemed to him so sweet and so womanly.

'Look,' she whispered to Jerome. 'Look.' And she threw aside her mantle. Underneath she was naked, and Jerome stood gaping at her gently rounded form, her full breasts and belly with its dark triangle of hair.

He awoke sweating in agony, willing himself out of that nightmare for what seemed an eternity of moments. Then, wide awake, he struggled up, groaning. Such dreams! Ah, he was no stranger to lewd dreams — but that *she* should figure in them!

'Oh God,' he moaned. 'The only woman I ever cared for. The one woman in the world so utterly pure! I thought the bond between us a different one. Isn't it? Holy Mother of God, I've never so much as seen her at table. Can I ever permit myself to be near her again?'

He flung himself down on the ground, and prayed until the first rays of light fingered their way in through the wooden shutters.

23

Locked once more into the ascetic discipline of the women in Paula's household, Blesilla still suffered the occasional qualm. With every meal missed, every prayer sung, every psalm joined, she might move further from the old life – but was she equal to the new? She was growing thin and had spasms of coughing. She might conquer her body by wilful disregard, but its weakness was draining strength from her mind, and it was through her mind that she was increasingly living, drawing sustenance from Jerome's gratifying respect for her daily intellectual labours.

She was also discovering that not all her lady companions were free of ambition, envy, or spite. In fact, her wit and beauty, and even her courage in atoning in public for her sins seemed to arouse their jealousy, not least when Jerome smiled his approval on her.

This particular evening, Jerome was late and Blesilla wandered out into her garden. Everything was still and expectant under gathering storm clouds. As she followed the path, the sun burst forth radiantly, bathing buildings and nature alike in a golden light.

A figure hurried towards her. Blesilla saw him pick up the folds of his tunic and skip up the steps, his head turning at the sudden flight of a bird from the bronze foliage of an aspen gleaming in the shrubbery below. She caught her breath. Aetius! An unwelcome figure from her other life, and the means – she had suspected at the time – of her husband's getting his hands on her love poem intended for Bassus. Tragedy had come of that, she mused.

As she watched, Aetius tripped, recovered at once and laughed with a flash of white teeth as he stopped in front of her, breathing hard, his green eyes gleaming under their black eyebrows. He bowed. The thought came unbidden: surely there was something of Bassus in his ready laughter, dark hair and supple figure? Instantly she felt that all too-familiar shiver of excitement and quickening of the flesh that she had fought so hard to banish.

'Has the Devil sent him?' her new self asked, watching her reaction. But no, she would prove herself stronger than any emissary of the Devil. She forced calm on herself.

'Why are you here?' she demanded.

Aetius handed her a letter, and she read: 'I cannot attend you now, but if you need help with the enclosed passage from Origen, talk to Aetius as you would to me, for he and I have fully discussed it.'

Without a word, she motioned him into the library. They sat facing one another, a slave sitting respectfully at the back of the room.

'Origen explains,' Aetius began, in deep but gentle tones, 'how God, through the Holy Spirit, has veiled the form and shape of the mysteries in Holy Writ because He did not wish everyone to grasp them. The greatest truths, according to some, can only be communicated by symbols. Simple people can get confused, and can be made to believe almost anything. They will even believe that after the Resurrection we will eat and drink as we do now.'

Aetius could almost have been a loving brother the way he talked, thought Blesilla — earnest, diffident, appealing, his glowing eyes seeming only to express passionate admiration for Origen.

'He shows that interpreting Holy Scripture is only possible if we give the passages both a literal and figurative meaning,' he clarified. 'Take the treatment of love in the Song of Songs, for instance. The ignorant will confuse spiritual passion with carnal lust.'

Blesilla looked at him sharply, but Aetius continued his discourse, focusing on the nature of spiritual love.

'The Song of Songs is inspired by the Holy Spirit, and is deliberately enigmatic. If we don't discern its inner meaning, it will remain a piece of literary brilliance, but no more. But the imagery is telling us that the Christian Church is our Lord and Saviour's mystical Bride. The Synagogue was an immature child-bride, longing for her Bridegroom, Jesus Christ. "Let Him kiss me with the kisses of His mouth, for thy love is sweeter than wine," she says …'

'It's striking imagery,' said Blesilla, her interest kindled.

'Of course,' pursued Aetius, 'as Origen stresses, it must be read as an allegory—not taken literally as an erotic text. He explains clearly that just as the Church is the bride of Christ, so each one of us may hope for mystical union with Him.'

Aetius paused, and appeared moved by his own words.

'Mystical union with Christ can only be for pure virgin souls,' she said grimly.

'Fresh from penance and absolved, one is in a state of grace,' Aetius declared. 'Like one re-born.'

'The great Origen,' Blesilla pointed out, 'also had some harsh things to say about absolution. He held that there was no forgiveness on earth for the worst sins, like blasphemy against the Holy Spirit, or fornication, or unnecessary bloodshed.' She added: 'He also said that we may be absolved on earth, but that ultimately we have to face the judgement of God.'

'Yes, but he held that we pass through different phases of existence, higher or lower as we choose good or evil. And that punishment will be temporary, only lasting until its purpose is accomplished.' His voice dropped. 'Then finally everyone will be restored—even the Devil!'

'Oh no!' Blesilla burst out. 'No one could believe that! The Devil and the people who have denied God will be tortured without remission! Jerome himself says so. But those who have trusted in Christ, even if they've sinned, will be saved in the end. This is the hope that all sinners cling to,' she added involuntarily.

Aetius's eyes flashed, and she sensed a sudden shift in him. His mood seemed at one with the gathering storm outside.

'Can't you see,' he said coldly, 'that if the Devil is left out of the final restoration, then God's power is not absolute?' He did not wait for her reply but continued vehemently. 'Should I be contaminated by the Devil, why couldn't I too be saved finally?'

For some moments, Aetius faced her wordlessly, a dark figure in the now shadowy room. At last, he said: 'I suppose you know what Origen said about the man who absolves the penitents?'

'What do you mean?'

'Origen said that, to rule like Peter, a man must be of Peter's sort. But if, instead, the man who rules is bound by the chains of his sins, has he a right to rule? Surely the man granting absolution has to be a truly spiritual person himself.'

Blesilla felt a flutter at her heart.

'Perhaps people have forgotten what happened in the Basilica of Sicinius, as it was known then,' Aetius said. 'One hundred and thirty-seven of Ursinus's men killed by circus hands and ditch diggers, at the orders of the man who is now His Holiness—'

'What are you saying?' Blesilla cut in. 'That I'm not really absolved for my sins because Damasus wasn't fit to pardon me? Because he had blood on his hands from that fighting?'

Aetius raised his hands up, leaving the question hanging between them. Then he made his excuses and was gone, leaving Blesilla panic-stricken.

I must, she thought, talk to Jerome.

24

That night, Blesilla slept little after midnight prayers and that little was broken by her troubled imaginings on what Jerome might say on Damasus's qualifications — or lack of them — to grant her absolution.

By the time Jerome arrived the next afternoon, Blesilla had read what Origen had to say on Matthew, including the Lord's commission of the Keys to St Peter.

'Who has the power to remit sins?' she demanded of Jerome. 'Origen says that only men like Peter do. Is Damasus a man like Peter, or is he bound by the chains of his own sin?' Her voice quavered, but she pressed on. 'That massacre in the Basilica of Sicinius seventeen years ago — what did it do to him in the eyes of God?'

Startled, Jerome played for time with a mellifluous flow of words.

'My daughter,' he began. 'It is not given to us to understand the mystery of the remission of sin nor the means by which the Holy Spirit enters into those he entrusts with this awesome responsibility. Is it conceivable that God, who sees and knows all, would allow a man unfit for such office to be elected?'

Jerome's mind, behind his words, worked quickly.

'You have thought fit to question the authority of Damasus. Never have I felt that need. He is a great man and a great bishop in all respects. In these troubled times the Church needs a strong leader, which is no doubt why God called Damasus to office. He is a priest of the people at all levels. He is leading into the Church those aristocrats who still waver or oppose.'

He paused. 'Damasus has also shown his quality by asking me — and none other — to undertake the great work of revision of our Bible.'

Blesilla remained silent. She knew that Jerome was high in Damasus's favour and that he might even succeed him.

'You talk of a time long past when you were a mere toddler,' Jerome went on smoothly. 'What happened in the Basilica of Sicinius has been much embroidered upon over the years. When Damasus sent men into that basilica to expel those who had wrongfully occupied it, he never intended that blood should be shed. Things simply got out of hand.'

'I've heard what people say about it, quite old people, too,' said Blesilla 'It was a scandal.'

'My lady, you are very quick to question the conduct of His Holiness.' He smiled. 'And I am "old" too, don't forget — I heard all about it.'

Blesilla would not be diverted. 'Origen got everything from the Bible — you told me so. And he seems to have been very explicit about what kind of man a bishop should be.'

'He was explicit enough about sinners of all sorts,' said Jerome sharply. 'He held that only the most trifling sins could be forgiven on this earth. Perhaps our Church has come to be more understanding of human frailty now. You yourself, Blesilla, have received an absolution which Origen might have denied you.'

'That's not the same thing,' protested Blesilla. 'I'll have to think about it.'

'My lady,' said Jerome. 'His Holiness has wept with you for your sin, as you wept yourself. Can you doubt of his paternal and loving ministry? That God speaks in the person of His Holiness?

'You enjoy so many natural advantages, Blesilla. How many women are endowed with your intelligence and goodness? I beg you, put these worries behind you. No one who listens to you speak could fail to realise your heartfelt sorrow for what you did. When you cast yourself down before God, the sincerity of your repentance made all love you, all bow to you ...'

Jerome departed after still more compliments, which left her glowing, though only for a time. Outside he paused. Normally he would have gone straight to Paula but, still shaken by his dream — of no account, of course, he told himself — he shrank from seeing her and instead turned towards his office.

***

Blesilla, soon a prey once more to doubt, on an impulse made her way to Marcella's villa. As Blesilla had hoped, she did not fail her.

'Yes, yes.' Marcella tapped with her stylus on her desk. 'It is fascinating to follow the workings of your mind, my dear. You will have the truth one way or another in everything.'

Her eyes were kind as she looked at the girl.

'Now, I know all about the affair of Damasus in '66. It was a shocking business, yes. He was charged with responsibility for homicide. He was only saved by his rich friends petitioning the Emperor Valentian to quell the usurper to the papal throne, Ursinus.'

'Damasus had blood on his hands.'

'I would say so.'

'Am I absolved, then?' Blesilla was close to tears.

'My dear child!' Marcella laid her hands on Blesilla's shoulders with a loving beneficence that no bishop could have bettered. Then she went over to her neatly indexed pigeon-holes and sought out a volume.

'Bishop Ambrose on penance,' she explained, and quoted: '"Only God forgives sins. The instrument is human in baptism or absolution. The bishop is God's instrument."

'So you see, my dear, that whatever his past, a bishop is able to transmit God's forgiveness of sins.'

Marcella turned to face her. 'You can accept what Bishop Ambrose says, Blesilla. He is a wise man and was a lawyer before becoming bishop. He is related to me and I am an old friend of his sister, a dedicated virgin. He writes lovely letters to her, and she shows them to me. If you had asked me before, I could have set your mind at rest, my dear.'

Blesilla stuttered out her thanks and went home to examine what Marcella had told her.

There, she sat down on a couch, picked at a few grapes and drank a glass of wine, for strength. She suspected that no one had really answered her questions. If it was God and only God who remitted sins, why should there be bishops and other priests who heard confessions, set penances and, when they had been carried out, pronounced the sin extinct? Yet bishops and priests must surely have that power because otherwise the whole earthly process such as she had gone through would be superfluous. Indeed, if people needed no intercession to commune with God, the whole institution of the Church would be superfluous, and this simply could not be. So the priests must have the delegated power to forgive sin and, to her mind, that implied that they must be in a state of grace themselves when pronouncing forgiveness. But had Damasus been in that condition when he had absolved her? No one, other than Damasus himself, really knew.

Had any of them, Jerome, or Marcella or Ambrose really answered her?

***

Towards the end of the afternoon, her youngest sister Rufina called—a rare occurrence. Blesilla was aware that whenever she could, Rufina escaped the austere lives of her mother and sisters. Now almost thirteen, Rufina was pretty, vivacious and engaged to be married.

'Everyone's still talking about you even now,' said Rufina, regarding her sister rather as though Blesilla were a sideshow in the marketplace.

'I believe you,' said Blesilla drily.

'I would never do public penance,' Rufina said.

For the hundredth time, she wished that she had the nerve to ask just what her sister's sin had been. Amongst the wilder speculations which had brought a blush to Rufina's cheek had been Blesilla's secret murder of her husband (how else could such a healthy man as Furius, and not as old as some husbands, die so suddenly?); or perhaps Blesilla had misbehaved with a high-ranking churchman, noted among society women for his wandering hands, who had left Rome abruptly just before Blesilla's remarkable conversion to the ascetic life. Rufina had plied her mother with questions but had been given short shrift.

'The confessional is between God and man,' Paula had said, 'and your curiosity, repugnant as it is, is a sin in itself.' Rufina had never again dared to ask, but she could not help wondering. After all, there were not so many sins.

'I couldn't have done it,' said Rufina again. 'Penance like that, I mean.'

'You never would have to,' Blesilla returned bitterly. Shame bit at her for her public grovelling in the basilica. 'It took a lot of doing.' Her voice shook with anger at all of them, herself included.

'Well, I have to go now.' Rufina stood up and smoothed down her pretty blue tunic, the jewels nestled there catching the light. 'I'm on my way to a reception with Paolina at the villa of the Valerii.'

She left a faint trace of musk and cinnamon behind; she had always loved her perfume. Blesilla caught up a hand-mirror and scowled at her unkempt image and strained face. From the Valerii, Rufina and Paolina would hear all the latest gossip; they would eat sweetmeats and fruit tarts, drink honeyed wine; and mingle freely with young and old.

Blesilla sank down on a couch, a prey to the disturbing tremors of the old world of lightness and laughter and indulgence.

She felt weary. Truth eluded her and she was too restless to study. On an impulse she went to her bedroom and ordered Clea to fill her private bath with warm water. While she waited, she flung off her clothes and stood naked to the caress of the soft wind drifting in through her window.

***

It was in the early hours of next morning that she awoke in ecstasy, sated. Long cries of fulfilment had been wrung from her as she writhed joyfully under the gorgeous body of Bassus — or was it Aetius? Finally waking, she was still giddy with delight and deliberately she re-lived it all, lying on her hard bed.

So many truths, her senses told her in the clarity of mind that followed her dream, but against this she could do nothing. No wonder that lust — for she recognised her weakness for what it was — constituted a mortal sin.

She lay spreadeagled, and finally dozed off again. Long past the hour when she was accustomed to join Paula and her women at early prayers, she turned a flushed face to a maid who put her head around the door, gazed expressionlessly at her for a moment, and then disappeared.

'I heard that her maid said that Blesilla looked exactly as though she had been making love,' the widow Antonia whispered later to Asella.

Blesilla meanwhile had dressed hurriedly and walked out into the dawn light, across the garden, to a side door that led directly to her mother's premises. Crossing the courtyard to Paula's oratory, she felt herself caught between two worlds.

'Hail, gladdening Light, of his pure glory poured …' chanted the women inside the oratory.

Moving like an automaton, Blesilla pushed open the door of the oratory, and knelt beside the little group of women.

'Who is the immortal Father, heavenly, blessed …' intoned the others.

Blesilla raised her eyes and met those of a woman who had turned to look at her. There was no warmth in those stony eyes, and later, as the group dispersed, Blesilla encountered Asella, who ignored her and moved on in her black cowl, like a hostile sail in a safe harbour.

She went through the rest of the day with an outward composure that had little to do with her turmoil within. She shivered, remembering her fevered response in the dream. Hadn't it pointed to her real nature? She was no slave of Christ, but of man. Slut! Asella's loveless eyes had accused her. And so she was. Masquerading as a lady of high mind and character, she would never belong with these pious ones. Her head seemed to spin like a two-coloured top whipped into speed as one image blurred into the next.

She ate nothing that noon but, once back in her villa, Blesilla prayed until late in the afternoon. She repeated prayers that she had learned as a child, simple and innocent words that she felt might wing their way directly to God. Again she asked forgiveness for herself, asked for God's blessing on her mother for all the love she had shown. And all the time, a real part of her innermost being lay outside these prayers as the darkness lies beyond the flickering light of an oil lamp.

***

By the afternoon, Blesilla had a sudden, compulsive need to go out and immerse herself in the living city. She had to get away from herself. She called for her litter bearers; late afternoon had always been her favourite time in the city, especially on such a day as this when the sun touched the old buildings to golden life and the noise in the streets was still muted.

A string of noble carriages passed her slow-moving litter down the Viale Aventino. They were probably on their way to the Temple of Venus and Rome, the largest and most ostentatious temple in the city, designed by the Emperor Hadrian himself. Although the festival commemorating the goddess Roma Aeterna — one of the two goddesses to which the temple was dedicated — was long since over, the goddess was still in imperial favour and much in vogue.

Blesilla watched the carriages pass, catching fragments of idle talk and laughter. They brought back memories, for she recognised nearly all the occupants and could well piece together the sort of conversation they were enjoying. She smiled. Ah, it was comforting to be outside again, to see these familiar faces that reassured her that life outside a cloistered stronghold was not all bad, that pleasure could be innocent, and that married love could be beautiful and good. Though of course, she thought wearily, all this was too late for her now, sinner that she was, betrayer of her womanhood and of her class in society. A noble girl with the instincts of a wanton, that's all she was, perhaps all she had ever been.

Listlessly she watched two splendid horses trot past her litter, going in the same direction. Gradually the occupants of the carriage came into her field of vision and then slid away. Her heart beat violently. The man was Bassus and with him was a young and attractive woman, her head close to his. Bassus and his wife.

Blesilla put her hand to her throat and felt the blood pounding in her veins, her breath shuddering through her. In a haze, she ordered her bearers to turn and take her back home as fast as they could. Oh, she still wanted him. She should be the one sitting beside him in the carriage, lying against him in the night — not some rich Milanese heiress. Her repentance was worth nothing. Nothing!

When her litter finally stopped, she ran into her home and straight to her private quarters. Her dear familiar bedroom shadowed by oncoming dusk hid her, but did nothing to calm her. She sank down on the floor to pray, though she did not know for what. Later, she sent word that she wanted food and wine, but when they were brought she took only the wine, greedily, until the fumes swirled in her head, obliterating thought.

She dismissed her women and went to bed, but sleep was long in coming. Hours later, or so it seemed, she awoke whimpering from a tortuous dream of Bassus and his wife, and lay staring into the darkness of the sleeping house. The air was heavy; she felt unbearably hot. She fumbled for the water-jug, and in the darkness knocked over the cup. Tilting the jug, she put her lips to it and drank, again and again.

Then she undid the shutters and opened the doors. It was cooler outside, and a light ground mist softened the outline of Rome. There was nobody to see her now; even her nightwatchman had disappeared. She envied him his untroubled slumber.

She stole along the terrace, trying to think coherently. Hadn't she truly repented and proved it by embracing her public shame? She had felt then that she was entering the infinite world of the love of God. But now, she was not so sure. One glimpse of Bassus had been enough to reawaken the old craving for him that would damn her for all eternity. She knew now that until the demands of her body were met she would never find peace.

Standing at the top of the steps, she moaned. Forgetting for a moment where she was, she started forwards, lost her footing and crashed to the bottom of the long flight of steps.

*****

It was the nightwatchman who found her, as dawn was breaking. At the sight of his mistress lying there unconscious, her limbs awkwardly splayed and her breathing shallow, he turned pale with fright. If he'd been doing his duty instead of sleeping peacefully in his own small room, he would've found her much earlier. There was no doubt: he was to blame.

She would die and he would be thrown into prison and tortured. And under torture he would confess to anything they liked. Briefly he debated throttling Blesilla. He was strong enough to carry her body the short distance to the River Tiber. It could look like suicide. But the light was getting brighter and the risk of being seen was great—and then his own death was a certainty.

He ran to wake Blesilla's maid.

25

'It's got into the lungs,' said the physicians when Blesilla's fever raged on and she grew weaker. 'We can do no more. Look at her!'

Blesilla looked back at the faces surrounding her bed, drifting in and out of consciousness. Her eyes were over-bright, her throat parched, and her lips cracked.

'Mamma,' she murmured.

'Shh,' murmured Paula, stroking her hair. 'No need to speak.'

***

She had stayed with Blesilla from the moment she had been summoned in to find her daughter in a roomful of wailing, chattering servants and had her carried, swathed in linen, to the comfort of her own home. There, she had girded herself for the same vigil as before, the physicians' chill pronouncements at her heart—her fever mounting, her lungs congested, and her body too wasted to withstand that night of exposure.

Taking up her place by her daughter's bed, Paula herself had regularly wiped her forehead with damp cloths, moistened her lips, and clasped her hand in her own, trying to instil courage and hope in her by touch alone.

Listening to her irregular, hoarse breathing, Paula lived again those days only last year of Blesilla's torment of spirit, of her sickness, her terrible confession babbled out in delirium, and her own furtive efforts to hide the story from everyone. She had been sick enough then, but not like this—skin translucent, face emaciated, and eyes blue rimmed.

Jerome was often there, a male presence of more avail than the physicians who could only tell what they could see, and had no remedy now. God's will would prevail, Paula would repeat to herself, as she knelt yet again in prayer.

***

On the thirtieth day, towards dusk, when Blesilla had closed her eyes and seemed to breathe more easily, Aetius appeared at the door with a message from Jerome.

'He will be here within the hour, my lady,' he said, his eyes downcast. 'He implores you to take some air, for you are very tired.'

It was true. Paula had not slept for the last two nights; she was aching all over and her head throbbed. She waved Aetius away, but a little later, leaving Eustochium to take her place for a few minutes, she crept outside. Ah, but she was afraid now.

Passing through the gallery that led to the garden, she heard a voice. It came, she knew at once, from the statue of the Apollo.

'I am the gaiety and laughter and music of life, the poetry and light, woman, which you've renounced for yourself and your children. And I am the spirit of Rome and for centuries past protector of the Jullii family and your dead husband as well.

'Disaster is coming upon you, woman, for you have forsaken the ways of your ancestors. You are guilty of impiety in worshipping the mortal body of a man who died nailed to a cross. You taught your husband's children to renounce me, you allowed his eldest child to fall on her knees and grovel before the priests of this man — a performance as unworthy as it is wicked ...'

The voice reverberated through the empty gallery, gathering pace until it seemed that a great roaring wind swept through — unless the noise was in her head. Paula tried to speak, but her words were stuck in her throat; she tried to move, but her feet seemed chained to the floor. How to struggle against this great force of a god who seemed to burst from his restraining marble?

The voice thundered on, the voice of the idol that had caused Toxotius to murder those Christians at Ephesus years before. It had alienated her husband then; it was destroying her child now.

A chance sound intruded from outside—the small shriek of a child, quickly muted. The spell was broken; reality reasserted itself. Paula snatched at the opportunity to exercise her will. She ran across the gallery, heart pounding.

She summoned all her strength. Placing her hands in the grooves of the marble head of Apollo, she pushed it out onto the terrace and, with a cry, sent it crashing to the flagstones below.

***

Back in the bedroom, Jerome was kneeling by the bed. The only sound was Blesilla's breathing, once again harsh and irregular. Her eyes opened, seeking Paula. Seeing her enter, she opened her mouth to speak. Through her swollen lips, Paula just caught the words:

'Pray to the Lord Jesus to pardon me that I could not do what I wished to …'

'My child.' Paula laid her cheek on her daughter's and Blesilla whispered one last confidence which only her mother heard. Then her ghastly, laboured breathing stuttered and finally petered out.

Paula felt a hand on her shoulder, pushing her gently aside so Jerome could sprinkle the girl with holy water in the form of a cross. For Jerome was pronouncing the Viaticum, holding the cup to Blesilla's lips, and easing the wafer between her lips.

'It's too late,' Paula moaned. 'She's already gone!'

Laying her head down on the bed, she wept loudly, clasping the limp body of her daughter, refusing to let her go.

She was still crouching there when Jerome's voice uttered the final invocation: 'May the Lord Jesus Christ protect you and lead you to eternal life.' Those gathered around the bed hardly heard him above Paula's wailing.

Finally Paula gave way to her other children, and allowed Eustochium, Paolina, Rufina and Toxotius to lead her away.

'You must not weep.' Jerome stood over her. 'Rather let us rejoice that she has at last done with her wretched body that very nearly was her downfall. Blesilla has purged away her sins by penance, and now by God's grace has left this corrupt and sinful world behind to live again in Christ!'

Paula struggled to her feet, her eyes blazing.

'Leave me alone!' she cried. 'Go and leave us all alone! Leave us to our grief. I want none of your sermons!'

PART THREE

EXPULSION
FROM ROME

26

'Don't we all grieve?' asked Marcella of Paula, with unaccustomed gentleness. 'I've kept away until now because I saw you needed to be alone, but we all fear for you. You seem so bitter and angry, impervious to everyone and everything.'

Paula did not reply, and Marcella shook her head. 'It's no good, you know. You're denying Christ.'

***

Blesilla's funeral had been a splendid affair, with all the nobles of Rome attending the bier which was covered in a cloth of gold. A tremendous crowd had followed its progress through the streets, and as many as possible had squeezed themselves into the Basilica of Saint Peter. There were far more people, Paula had observed through her tears, than at her husband Furius's funeral.

She had fainted in the middle of the ceremony and had to be carried out. At this, the mutterings of the crowd swelled to a hostile crescendo in pity for Paula, for the family, who had been trapped — as they saw it — into fanatical excesses. Blesilla had died from fasting, they murmured, from mortifications following her penance; the mother would doubtless follow soon. At the sight of Jerome, the rumblings became violent as a burly soldier shouted that they should throw Jerome and all the monks with him into the River Tiber. The cry was taken up quickly, and became louder and louder.

Pammachius, aware of the hatred of the ascetic movement among the great mass of Romans, had arranged with the city prefect to have troops in readiness. They had swung into action without delay and, by the time Paula came to, order had been restored.

***

It was three days after the funeral, and Marcella had found Paula crouching by her bed, in an attitude of prayer, her eyes fixed on a charming portrait of Blesilla on the wall above her.

'She never did like that dress,' Paula said. 'She only wore it for the picture because I asked her to.'

'Paula, listen,' said Marcella.

'I remember down in Campania, when her cousins brought over a little chariot with a pony. A child's chariot. No one could keep Blesilla from trying to drive it and she was better than any of the boys!'

Paula's tears were flowing again.

'Paula!' said Marcella again, more severely.

'How he would have suffered! Of all his children, she was the only one who counted in his eyes, apart from the boy.'

'Pagans grieve, Paula, but we Christians know better.'

'I've failed them both,' sobbed Paula. 'Toxotius and Blesilla!' She wrung her hands.

'Come outside.' Marcella pulled Paula to her feet.

Listlessly, Paula obeyed, and they went out through the long gallery into the garden.

'I see you that you've got rid of that Apollo,' remarked Marcella, as they passed a conspicuous space in the line of statuary.

Paula paled. 'It spoke. The head spoke. I smashed it and she died.'

Appalled, Marcella put her arms around Paula. 'There there, my dear,' she said.

'I'm not raving! Apollo spoke, as protector of Toxotius and his family, telling me how wicked I was to turn against him.'

'It was a fantasy.' Marcella spoke gently. 'The fantasy of an upset mind.'

'I was sane enough to destroy him. And then Blesilla died!'

'She was ailing ... you did everything you could. There was no hope for the girl.'

'Toxotius could have handled her,' persisted Paula. 'He might have been able to save her ...'

'You mean pluck her from our sort of life? Because that's what he would have tried to do. And you know that Blesilla was a very determined girl who decided things for herself.'

'Oh, she did, she did!' Paula began crying again.

'Come now, Paula. Blesilla has given herself to God. Through our mourning, let us remember how little death counted with her — and ought to with us.'

'Can't you understand, I feel responsible for her death! Of course, you've never had a child.'

This waspishness was so unlike Paula that Marcella simply disregarded it. She said only:

'You haven't let Jerome near you since the funeral.'

'Oh, but Jerome sent me one of his very best letters! Replete with Bible exempla, Job included.' Paula's bitterness acquired a dangerous edge. 'I should act like the holy Melania, who shed not a tear when she lost her two sons and her husband too! He has the nerve to tell me how she was better able to serve God once she'd been freed from a heavy burden.'

'My dear, he doesn't mean —'

'I know exactly what he means!' Paula's laugh was near hysterical. 'The death of my child is my gain! And he has the nerve to picture Blesilla in Heaven thoroughly ashamed of me and interceding to God to forgive me. Do let me show you.'

Paula took Marcella's arm and led her back inside and through to her study. Opening her desk, she rifled through a sheaf of papers and extracted one.

'There! Read this!'

'Oh, you know what he's like,' said Marcella impatiently. 'For him, a display of grief by one of us over another simply betrays weakness or lack of a deeper vision. As a Christian, you should find cause to rejoice that her soul is now in a better place, at home with God rather than in this fraught world of ours — *this* is what he means. Jerome thinks the world of you. He only meant to comfort you!'

'I wonder,' said Paula ominously.

'Yes, it's his way. You know what he wrote to me about Lea's death — bringing up poor old Praetextatus who had died only a few days earlier and picturing him naked in the foulest darkness while the Lea exults amongst the choir of angels! And everybody liked Praetextatus, too ...' She tut-tutted. 'Something comes over Jerome once he takes a pen in his hand! Look at the letter he sent to Eustochium to thank her for her gifts on the festival of Saint Peter. He just had to expound their mystical significance. And she'd only sent him a few cherries.'

'She sent him more than a few cherries!'

'Well, of course, she sent doves, bracelets and a letter too, and in each one he saw hidden meanings, lessons to draw ...'

Marcella added carefully: 'Jerome is very dependent on our friendship, you know.'

Paula shrugged. But she had, Marcella observed, regained her self-possession.

'After you fainted at the funeral, the situation almost got out of hand. I was scared for Jerome. Public hostility is growing day by day — people blame him for spreading insane superstition, which is what they call the life we lead. Lacking our faith, they distrust our practices, and in particular they hate Jerome.'

'Perhaps they don't know any better.'

'True. But it's the way Jerome criticises everybody. People don't take kindly to being told, for instance, that marriage is only a second best — when for so many it's the only thing they've got.'

'Jerome will always have Damasus behind him.'

'My dear Paula, Damasus is ill. He isn't expected to see the year out.'

'Jerome might succeed him.'

'With his propensity to stir people up the wrong way, I very much doubt it! I hear things, you know. Both his tongue and his pen have run Jerome into serious trouble at the Lateran. He's a lonely man ...'

***

When Marcella got home, she immediately sent a message to Jerome asking him to visit her as soon as he could. A reply came quickly: she could expect him at noon the following day.

He arrived punctually, his lean face hard to read in the shadows of the portico.

'You have been neglecting us,' Marcella reproved him after they had greeted each other. 'You are busy, of course — but we miss you.' She sensed his unease. 'And you have avoided Paula.'

'Paula won't receive me,' he said abruptly. 'I've written to her.'

When she made no answer, he thrust a bundle of papers at her. 'Here are the answers to your questions on Psalm 127 and those Hebrew words which puzzle you. Written at night, I may say,' he added. 'I have scant time, my lady. As you know, I am collating Aquila's Greek version of the Old Testament with the Hebrew.'

'I shan't keep you then,' she exclaimed, but continued to ponder aloud as, slowly and deliberately, she turned the pages of his manuscript.

A maid announced that the Lady Paula had arrived.

'Really? I didn't expect her,' said Marcella ingeniously. Then, dropping her voice, she added: 'In fact, I am worried about her, she's lost weight and her grief is destroying her.'

'My lady,' Jerome bowed deeply.

Marcella left the room. Jerome and Paula stood before one another, separated by a vast sea of incomprehension.

Shocked at the change in her, he began formally: 'My lady, let me ...'

Then he lost control and burst out: 'What nonsense this is!'

She trembled. 'I should have thanked you for your letter.'

'The letter needed no reply.'

'What? Not reply to such a long letter, when I've been so privileged as to have had everything so graciously explained to me?'

Jerome glared. 'I felt her death as much as you,' he barked.

Paula looked directly at him. 'No, you didn't. You haven't the faintest idea what I feel. And you tell me to stop mourning her!'

'I may have been hasty, perhaps, in my approach,' he conceded. 'Of course, it is natural to weep when such a saintly young person, whose glowing faith was matched by an earnest and brilliant intelligence, departs her body so unexpectedly. Indeed, I considered myself her spiritual father and could not hold my own tears back as I wrote that letter!'

For a moment Paula didn't answer, and it occurred to him that she may have starved herself into a state of aberration.

'But now, it is time to stop your mourning,' he continued urgently. 'You weep for her, crowned in Heaven as she is, just as though she grovelled in hell. Weep for any of the wicked you like, but not for your saintly daughter!'

'Not mourn my lovely girl?' When Paula finally spoke, her voice was low. 'I'll never be able to see or hear her again. I wanted her with us, of course. I wanted to save her from marriage. She broke her heart because of a man.'

'She overcame her passion and did penance and received absolution,' Jerome said deliberately.

Paula's eyes rested on Jerome's for an instant. You don't know of Blesilla's final words, she thought. No one but I knew that she had in some way relapsed, and the knowledge is weighing heavily on my heart. Had she once more sinned after penance? Was she with the choir of angels, as Jerome and the others thought, or was she in hell? I will never know.

'How little you understand,' she murmured.

Jerome's face was a mask. 'It's impossible to talk to you!' he expostulated, and then added: 'But I may not be here much longer to plague you, my lady.'

She remembered Marcella's words about Jerome, and felt a surge of sympathy. After all, it was not his fault that he could not understand a mother's love for her daughter.

'How can you talk to me like that?' she asked gently. 'You know our feelings for you, how grateful we are, how we have loved you, how we look up to you.'

His face came to life. 'If you only knew how much encouragement you give me by expressing such things,' he said.

'But tell me, what did you mean by saying that you mightn't be here much longer?' she asked.

'Oh, sometimes I think I've finished with Rome — or rather, Rome is finished with me.'

'You can't leave Rome!' she cried. 'Your work! What would happen to your work?'

'Ah, my work will go on wherever I am. It might even prosper in a quieter retreat, away from this Babylon.'

'But what will happen to us without you?'

'You will all continue to serve Christ in the way you have done up to now,' he answered simply.

Soon afterwards he departed, leaving her contemplating the long years ahead, which suddenly seemed emptier than ever before.

27

Early one morning, Anicia Fausta, sister-in-law of Petronius Probus, received an old friend, the Deacon Siricius, in her villa on the Coelian Hill. She twirled her bracelets impatiently; she had much to say to him.

'Rome seethes with gossip, of course, and great families are a favourite target. But a certain cleric of yours has sneered at what is surely above criticism – my aunt's poem.'

Siricius looked at her sharply. 'I assume it is her Virgilian cento to which you refer?'

He did not approve of such poems either, particularly this one, composed by a lady so confident of her right as a Roman aristocrat to write Biblical history, using Aeneas as the prototype for Christ.

'A mole ...' Anicia Fausta was saying. 'He called my aunt a mole, destined to burrow blindly beneath the foundations of our Holy Church. '

'Impossible!' Siricius declared. 'It is true that the man in question has a hasty tongue, but –'

'And he seems to have the capacity to drive some women to frightening extremes of religious devotion,' snapped Anicia Fausta. 'Who is he and where's he come from?'

Siricius summarised Jerome's recent history.

'Ah, so he's been in the desert! And brought monkish habits to our ladies over here. A few of them might just as well be in the valley of the Nile as in our glorious city what with their rags, wallowing in dirt, and sleeping on the ground! And in noble villas, under the eyes of slaves, of neighbours, of all Rome!'

'Such ladies,' said Siricius gravely, 'feel that their lives are closer to that laid down in the Gospel. Now, there are other matters I wish to discuss ...'

Much later, as he prepared to take his leave of her, Anicia Fausta brought him back to what was really on her mind.

'You'd better be careful, Siricius, visiting us like this,' she said. 'You might get put in a letter by this man, like that scathing one he wrote to Julia Eustochium ridiculing certain members of the clergy and in particular men who want to be deacons only to see women more easily!' She laughed uneasily. 'I half expect my own daughter to receive a letter warning her against my own decent way of life, serving God but not forgetting family responsibilities; and telling her that she must remain barren, pledge her virginity to the Church, and enjoy the blessings that come from remembering its ever-present need for funds.'

***

Siricius still had Anicia Fausta's complaint on his mind the next day at his weekly meeting with Damasus on administrative matters, when accounts and estimates of expenditure were submitted for His Holiness's approval. Siricius bowed himself into the holy presence, followed by his retinue bearing the heavy bound books and account sheets. When these were placed carefully on the oak table before His Holiness, Siricius waved his assistants out except for a young and nervous sub-deacon. Damasus's face was, he noticed, wan after an exacting morning spent on a visit to the shrine of a new martyr. Rapidly, he made a silent prayer to Christ and the Blessed Virgin to watch over the elderly man and grant him strength.

First on the agenda was the management of an estate near Laurentum which had recently been donated to the Church.

'All the documents prepared by the notaries have been signed and witnessed,' Siricius explained. 'The estate is in Appia, little more than a day's journey from Rome, and belonged to the Lady Paula. Sabinus here knows it. Her cousin is the village notary.' Siricius indicated the sub-deacon.

'If Your Holiness would like to read out the particulars ...'

Damasus assenting, the sub-deacon stepped forward tentatively and began speaking, his words pouring out in a high-pitched voice:

'The estate comprises some fifteen hundred workers and is in a well-favoured part of Appia between the forest and the sea. The farm workers —'

Damasus raised his hand, his ring glinting in the light. 'Slow down please, young man. Rest assured, I am not going to bite you.'

'I beg you to excuse me, Your Holiness.' The sub-deacon took a deep breath. 'As I was saying, the farm workers, both slaves and smallholders, have been treated most generously by the Lady Paula, but it has been discovered that the bailiff has been selling a considerable part of the produce on the local markets for his own benefit. The bailiff has now been removed and punished.'

'The produce of this estate will be a timely addition to church funds for the provisioning of our urban poor,' commented His Holiness comfortably.

The sub-deacon was suddenly seized with the courage to speak in his own right. He badly wanted to blurt out: They work, these peasants do — but here in Rome the poor don't!

All he said, with a glance at Siricius, was: 'The workers on the estate, Your Holiness, still remain miserably poor.' The words sounded oddly in his falsetto. 'They ask that they be allowed to retain one third of their own produce for themselves that the Lady Paula always wanted them to have.'

'Yes, yes,' agreed Damasus. 'I wouldn't wish it otherwise.'

'I've arranged for an annual delivery to Rome,' said Siricius. 'This year it will comprise three hundred cattle and one thousand pigs, as well as substantial quantities of wheat, wine and honey. Then, in season, four sacks of a special mushroom grown on the estate will be brought to us weekly.'

He saw His Holiness's eyes gleam as he contemplated this delectable contribution to his banquets, and remembered that had he a special weakness for mushrooms.

'That seems in order,' Damasus nodded.

Siricius motioned the sub-deacon out.

When Siricius and Damasus had approved the accounts, Damasus murmured, as though to himself:

'We must never forget our duty to the poor.'

Siricius wondered if the elderly man had simply forgotten his presence. He cleared his throat discreetly, and waited.

Damasus came out of his reverie and said quite normally:

'I intend to make this the subject of a speech to our episcopal conference.' His hand toyed with a sheet of paper on the table. The speech had been carefully written in an especially large script adapted to his failing eyesight.

'"You will see others build churches,"' Damasus read out, '"adorn them with marbles and precious ornaments, cover church doors with silver and altars with gold. Your duty is of a different kind. Yours is to clothe Christ in the poor, to visit Him in the sick, to feed Him in the hungry, to shelter Him in the homeless ..."'

Siricius bowed his head, thinking of the splendour of Damasus's own quarters, his banquets, his churches too. His Holiness saw nothing incongruous in a division of duties; his own was obviously to court the great families of Rome with the sort of luxurious entertainment to which they were accustomed. Siricius knew the words that Damasus had read out were Jerome's but, with the deviousness which his role forced upon him, said:

'Your Holiness's words are particularly fine, in the manner that your audience has come to expect of you.'

Damasus clasped his hands together. 'You know, when I am preaching, I feel the Holy Spirit speaking through me.'

Siricius took a sudden decision, and said:

'I should like to bring to Your Holiness's attention a matter which causes me alarm. Complaints have been made about one of your staff and his harsh criticism of both clergymen and certain prominent Romans. I myself have been begged by a lady of our noblest family to curb the man's virulence.'

'I know precisely to whom you refer.' Damasus's attention was riveted on Siricius. 'But do remember the man's goodness of heart and devotion to Christ. Our Jerome is a moralist, the most eloquent of moralists. You can't deny that we need one. Jerome's pen exalts virginity, the most direct path from this earth to Heaven. Besides, he is in the middle of his most important work, the translation and revision of Gospel truth, for the enlightenment of all the faithful and the greater glory of the See of Peter!'

Damasus got slowly and painfully to his feet, indicating that their session was concluded. Siricius felt extremely irritated; it wasn't the first time that Damasus had recovered without warning from a lapse in attention and confounded his listener. Siricius hadn't even had the chance to mention Anicia Fausta's particular complaints.

As Siricius was leaving, Damasus said: 'I suppose those mushrooms are safe?'

Siricius's face betrayed a hint of disdain. 'Your Holiness may be absolutely assured that they are. I would eat them myself without hesitation.' Then, on an uncharacteristic impulse, he added, 'Or perhaps Jerome could be the taster.'

***

'I had a dream,' announced the Deacon Anemius that evening, leaning back and tenting his pudgy fingers across his stomach. 'On a wall were the shadows of two men—one was His Holiness reaching towards the other as if to offer a gift, a transfer.'

Siricius set down his wine, careful to betray no sign of interest.

196

'The man facing His Holiness could easily be seen in profile,' continued Anemius. 'That high forehead and beak of a nose were unmistakeable. And then, I found myself in the Lateran Basilica, and all inside were shouting, "Jerome, Jerome!" in acclamation.'

Siricius said nothing, which prompted Anemius to add: 'In the dream it was plain that His Holiness was forestalling any attempt by his old rival Ursinus to grab the Lateran when the election of his successor comes up, for Ursinus is in North Italy and only waiting for His Holiness's death to pounce.'

Siricius swallowed. He knew that the Deacon Anemius was flattering him by telling him his dream. They all fawned on him, the other six deacons, since Damasus's health had begun to fail. Siricius was the deacon closest to Damasus. Years before Jerome's arrival in Rome, Damasus had mentioned the succession to Siricius in a way which encouraged Siricius to hope—and his hopes were known to all.

Siricius waved a disparaging hand. 'People would never stand for Jerome as Bishop of Rome,' he said.

'A mob paid by his supporters could easily crush any opposition,' Anemius protested. 'Then what choice would people have? Anyway, Jerome would preach them into submission.'

The thought that Jerome might become the next Bishop of Rome made Anemius's well-fed belly churn. After all, Jerome had publicly referred to him as that Golden Apple and the Gas-filled Bladder. Clumsily, Anemius pressed his warning further.

'Jerome's words are always on Damasus's lips.' He added in a low voice: 'Damasus is old and wandering but his public support for Jerome as his successor might well be decisive.'

Anemius's round, protruding eyes irritated Siricius, but this was not why he said, severely:

'Jerome is a scholar. He's wrapped up in his important work. I don't think he cares much for either a pastoral or priestly role.' Facing Anemius, he said with emphasis: 'Your worry is without substance.'

And yet, Siricius himself was also worried. Even disinterestedly so. He was a deeply religious man and, being an obvious contender for the seat of the Bishop of Rome himself, he had weighed not only his own capacities but those of others as well. Jerome, holding this lonely office, with absolute discretion to choose his ministers, would be a dangerous man. Full of learning as he was, he was also enormously self-centred, impetuous and unrestrained in invective.

Siricius smiled to himself, remembering how he had once laughed at a young cleric doing a parody of Jerome preaching. Jerome had been haranguing God.

28

On a day in early December in 384 AD—a day which ever afterwards would remain etched in Jerome's memory—Jerome sat beside Damasus in the gilded papal carriage which carried them back from the Cemetery of Saint Agnes on the Via Nomentana. Here, Damasus had wanted to inspect the new marble slab on which his panegyric in honour of the young martyr had been inscribed in a beautiful neo-classical script by the celebrated calligrapher, Dionysius Filocalus.

Lately Damasus had been insisting on Jerome accompanying him on his local devotions. Just two days earlier, Damasus had celebrated the feast day of Saint Eutychianus, bishop and martyr, in the crypt of the Cemetery of Callistus on the Via Appia. It had been a day of lowering skies which had opened in a sudden and heavy downpour that drenched high Lateran dignitaries, clerics and laymen alike. Since then, despite not feeling well, Damasus had persisted with his engagements. Jerome felt that the old man was turning to him as one would to a member of his own family. Jerome's impatience at lagging behind his own exacting timetable was tempered by affection for the old prelate.

'I think my little sister Irene saw that vision of Saint Agnes,' Damasus confided to Jerome later. 'After she died by the sword—such a terrible death for a child!—the parents of Agnes saw her passing in a crowd of virgins, all clothed in gold. My sister spoke so often of that vision I believe that she too must have been blessed by God to see it, even so long after the event. Perhaps that's why she used to spend all those hours praying at her tomb …'

Damasus paused, and then stated calmly: 'I won't be here to see Saint Agnes's feast day in January.'

At the quaver in his voice, Jerome could believe him, although with Damasus one never knew. Age came on him in waves of forgetfulness, but then he would surprise listeners by snapping back with his old vigour. This afternoon he seemed frail and shrunken, and Jerome did not like his flushed countenance, but nonetheless he was sure that this present indisposition would pass. He himself depended on Damasus and his patronage for his great work of scholarship; surely God would protect that work to ensure that it yielded the correct translation of His own truths and shield Jerome from the petty jealousy of so many Roman clerics.

As their carriage bumped back towards the Lateran, they were held up by a huge crowd surging noisily towards them.

'Gladiators,' said Damasus. 'They're coming from watching the gladiators. It's one of the days of the quaestorial games. Rufius Albinus's son is giving them today, I believe. It'll set his father back a good few pounds of gold.' He sighed. 'The crowd's got blood in its nostrils and it won't even notice their bishop, Jerome.'

'Wait.' Jerome swung himself down from the carriage and faced the attendants. 'Drive your horses into them if they won't get out of the way,' he ordered angrily. 'His Holiness is exhausted and at this rate we'll never get through!'

Then he turned to the crowd. 'It's the Holy Father!' he shouted. 'Make way, make way!'

'You are my strength now, Jerome.' Damasus regained his hold of Jerome's arm, and the carriage swept on.

***

That afternoon, in the depths of the Lateran, the Deacon Anemius had hurried up the stairs to the room used by his fellow deacon Siricius for settling the accounts.

'I have something very important to show you,' Anemius said breathlessly. 'Is His Holiness not back yet?'

'He's not likely to return for some time. He's at the Cemetery of Saint Agnes today, remember. With Jerome.'

'We've got him!'

'What on earth are you talking about?'

'Jerome. We've got him at last!' Anemius was too excited to curb his enthusiasm. 'He can rant as much as he wants about saints and martyrs and virgins, and wax lyrical to Damasus about Agnes. But just let Damasus see what Jerome has written here. If he ever did think of Jerome as his successor he certainly won't now!'

'What have you got there?' Siricius frowned. 'Show me!'

Anemius brandished several sheets of parchment. 'It's a letter addressed to one Ephraim,' he said. 'The fellow died about a year ago. He was a Jew, one of Jerome's friends for a time. He procured Hebrew books for Jerome and copies of texts that Jerome couldn't easily get his hands on.' His eyes gleamed. 'Just listen.'

He read the letter aloud. Motionless, Siricius heard him out, a flush creeping up his face. As Anemius concluded, the two men looked at each other.

'Of course, Jerome is ever happy to ridicule and abuse the lives that some of the clerics lead!' Anemius said. His jowls trembled with rage as he recalled Jerome's scathing words about himself.

'Anemius,' Jerome had once commented, 'will mince his way to Heaven, a very model of purity. Can't you see him there? The pristine freshness of his robe, the scented rolls of flesh above the collar, the shining leather of the pretty shoes he wears on visits to the richest ladies. See the downcast eyes, the bashful face and the catch in his voice as he allows himself — oh so reluctantly — to be coaxed into accepting a gift.'

'That is bad enough,' Anemius spluttered, still shaking. 'But to call the succession list of Roman Bishops a *fraud*?'

Siricius waited.

'The cunning devil! The serpent in the grass! And this is the hypocrite who waits daily on Paula and Marcella, who licks their feet and takes their money. Say something, Siricius, will you? You sit there with clasped hands while this viper hisses out his poison … to a Jew!'

'Jerome could not have put it more eloquently himself,' Siricius replied, after a moment's reflection. He took the other man's arm. 'Leave the letter with me,' he ordered, 'and go now, Anemius. Please take it no further. Have you told anybody else about the letter?'

'Not more than one or two others.'

'Then let that suffice, or you will find yourself in disgrace. Now leave me in peace to consider the matter further.'

As Anemius rose to leave, Siricius called after him:

'How did you come by that letter, by the way?'

'It was found amongst Jerome's papers.'

'Who found it?'

'Jerome's assistant, Aetius, who transcribed it. Jerome had apparently told him to deliver it, but the Jew died suddenly before Aetius had a chance to do so. Aetius told me that, after months of hesitation, he decided that we should see it.'

After Anemius had departed, Siricius sat puzzling over the matter for a long time. He was shaken. Jerome had an almost slavish regard for hierarchical authority. Was it possible that he had been so dismissive of Liberius's succession list of Roman bishops, which so neatly underlined the claims to primacy of the Roman Church? Jerome had been under an obligation to the Jew who had helped him in his work on the Hebrew books of the Bible. Naturally, he never suspected that his letter would go further. But what a risk to take!

Then Siricius chuckled to himself. The provincial Jerome, close as he had become to Damasus, obviously had no idea that it had been Damasus himself, a deacon at the time, who had drawn up that list for Liberius.

It was Siricius's clear duty to show Jerome's letter to Damasus, a task distasteful to him. But first he must question Aetius.

***

The morning of the eleventh of December found Jerome alone in the room in the Lateran Palace that he used now and then to be nearer to Damasus. Aetius hadn't appeared yet in the archives office, and Jerome was in urgent need of a scribe. Rather hazily, for he had been up until the small hours crouched over a translation into Latin of Didymus's *On the Holy Spirit* for which His Holiness had specifically asked, Jerome became aware of a commotion outside his door.

Going down to the administrative offices shortly afterwards in search of a replacement for Aetius, he sensed an air of excitement and urgency amongst those he passed in the corridors. Then again, he thought, the Lateran was usually simmering over one rumour or another.

Outside the administrative offices he met the Deacon Ascholius. The man's eyes flickered over Jerome without expression and then moved somewhere beyond. Jerome was taken aback. Ascholius had always behaved in a correct, if not particularly friendly, manner towards him. The deliberate cut hurt.

Entering the offices, Jerome sought out the man in charge of the clerical staff.

'I haven't seen Aetius since yesterday morning,' Jerome told him with a touch of asperity. 'Please find me another scribe immediately.'

'Yes, well, of course we'll supply one as soon as we can,' the man replied. 'Everything is in confusion just now.'

'Why?'

'*Why?*' A man standing behind Jerome repeated.

Jerome swung around to face the Deacon Anemius. His round eyes shone, and his teeth—large yellow ones, Jerome noticed—were bared in a malicious smile.

'You are so immersed in your important work that you don't know why!' whispered Anemius. 'But perhaps you needn't finish that work now.' Anemius's smile broadened.

'What the devil are you talking about?'

'You see, His Holiness ...' Anemius's words trailed off.

'He's taken ill?' Jerome demanded of the archives man.

The man stared, frightened.

'Surely you ... kn- know,' he stuttered. 'His Holiness was found dead in his bed this morning!'

29

There followed dark days for Jerome. Alone in the archives office of the Lateran Palace, he worked. But even his work had lost some of its savour. The new scribe that had been promised never came, and Aetius had disappeared. 'Assigned elsewhere,' was all Jerome was told. Was he to understand 'somewhere more promising'?

The Lateran, meanwhile, was a court without a head, and seethed with the feverish angling for position and patronage produced by the imminent election of Damasus's successor.

'It has taken no time at all for them to show their claws, their fangs,' Jerome complained bitterly to Marcella. 'Once they looked up to me, or pretended to. I was at the very centre of things, my work respected and eagerly awaited. Now nobody talks to me!'

'But you did find all those calls tiresome,' Marcella began. 'Think of all those times when—'

'Well, I knew them for what they were,' he interrupted testily. 'I despised most of them, but I always treated them with courtesy.'

Jerome was profoundly unhappy or even more egotistical than usual, Marcella thought. She marvelled how it never occurred to him that he had himself provoked the clerics' hostility.

'You know I had become Damasus's dear friend—his right hand, even,' Jerome was saying. 'He was always calling for my company and asking my advice. Without him you simply cannot imagine how I'm being treated! They always envied and hated me because I was so close to His Holiness, the man they thought might try to succeed him.'

He scowled. 'They are so worldly that they can't appreciate

that my highest ambition is to serve God in my work. If anyone ever insinuated that I might be the successor to Damasus, I told that Satan to get behind me!'

Marcella knew that he was speaking the truth.

'I have heard that Siricius ...' She let the sentence hang, unsure how to put it.

'He is a quiet one,' Jerome fretted. 'You never know what he's thinking. Of course he'll be elected. The other day Bishop Ambrose arrived in Rome. He and Siricius were closeted together for hours. I did not even speak to him!'

Ambrose, who had come to Rome for Damasus's funeral, had stayed on for several days and had indeed spent many hours with Siricius. The powerful Bishop of Milan, himself a Roman, got on well with Siricius. Their discussions on the sort of Church both envisaged stretched far into the night, and ranged from issues such as excommunication and the treatment of repentant heretics to, perhaps most importantly, the urgent need for the issuing of imperial-style edicts on matters of church practice and discipline.

They had also discussed the men they wanted in senior positions.

'Now that the Danube frontier has collapsed,' said Ambrose, his eyes intense in his melancholy face, 'and the Goths and the Huns are threatening civilisation itself, we urgently need to defend ourselves. Civil war is inevitable ...'

He went on to talk of a Church whose divine authority would be a bastion against the invading barbarians as well as the ever-present threat of Arianism from within. He spoke eloquently and with assurance, moulding his words to suit his listener, drawing him into his vision of things. As always, he used no notes. No wonder, thought Siricius, that he drew the crowds at his sermons.

'... and the living symbol of that authority will be seen in the integrity of our priests — our celibate priests.' Ambrose smiled and held up his index finger. 'Now, my dear Siricius, we must talk of the erudite man Jerome. I've corresponded with him occasionally. I know all about his admirable work on the Scriptures, of his years as a solitary in the desert, of his championship of virginity. Indeed, we are at one with him, you and I, in our notions of virginity, that very pinnacle of Christian virtue.'

Ambrose leaned forwards. 'But you tell me also that there is a darker side to him—dangerous views, a certain letter that our Jerome has written to a Jew. You are in a dilemma, Siricius, and would like some advice, perhaps.'

Siricius handed Jerome's letter to Ambrose and waited. Ambrose's face grew grave.

'Indeed, to question—especially in writing!—the succession list of Roman Bishops is inflammatory at best. What in God's name could the man have been thinking! We must tread deftly. The knowledge and circulation of such a letter would bring only divisiveness to a delicate situation, yet regretfully it has been already seen by some. Leave it with me ...'

Ambrose put the letter away carefully. 'Now, you had another equally pressing concern, I believe.'

Siricius nodded. 'It's Ursinus again — Damasus's old rival. He's hovering in northern Italy, waiting to pounce. We must foil any attempt by him to put his name forward for election—'

'But of course,' Ambrose cut in. 'Ursinus will at all costs be held in check. The bloody scandal of his battle with Damasus at the last election must not be repeated!' A hint of a smile played around his lips. 'In fact, the Emperor assures me that units of the Imperial Army in training near Milan will be deployed to prevent Ursinus's supporters from gathering in Rome for the election.' His smile broadened. 'Furthermore, arrangements are already in place to pack the Lateran Basilica with your own supporters when the time comes.'

Ambrose stood up to take his leave. 'Your election to the seat of the Bishop of Rome, Siricius, has never been in doubt.'

***

Rome was in turmoil. It was the seventeenth of December, the beginning of the ever-more popular Saturnalia celebrations. Saturn himself, the Roman god in whose honour the celebrations were held, could hardly have improved upon the exuberant displays of beneficence, public and private. Sacrifices were offered at his temple in the Roman Forum, followed by a lavish public banquet; private homes and villas were given over to partying which lasted days, slaves relishing the temporary reversal in roles which saw their masters serving them; and in the streets and squares there was unrestrained revelry, carousing and gambling.

Meanwhile, masses were being said for the recently entombed Damasus, who had been laid to rest with all the pomp and ceremony that traditionally attended the Bishops of Rome at such a time. His body, clothed in crimson and clasping a crucifix, had lain in state surrounded by flickering light of countless candles. For days, people gathered around him in prayer.

After the Mass for the Dead, his body had been transferred to a small church on the Via Ardeatina where, according to his wishes, he was buried next to his mother and sister. The funeral procession, thronging the streets, had provided a sombrely incongruous backdrop to the preparations for Saturnalia.

After Damasus's funeral, Jerome had taken refuge in the records office near the Theatre of Pompey, and was kept informed of activities in the Lateran Palace mainly through Paula and Marcella. Marcella was, as always, well informed, all the more so now because of her friendship with Bishop Ambrose's sister Marcellina, at whose villa Ambrose was staying in Rome.

Jerome was therefore able, like Ambrose before him, to forecast accurately the outcome of the papal election that followed Damasus's death. The Lateran Basilica was overflowing with the genuine and paid supporters of Siricius who was duly elected and acclaimed by the entire congregation.

30

Jerome waited weeks to be bidden to attend on Siricius. When at last he was, on the dark and nebulous morning of the tenth of February 385 AD, he found himself — to his chagrin — relegated to the role of mere onlooker at a session devoted to papal correspondence.

'"Siricius to the Bishop of Tarragona. Siricius duly announces his ordination,"' Siricius dictated to his scribe. '"*Eius cura et quod ei a Petro subsidium*. Your report directed to our Brother Damasus of sacred memory has come to me, now consecrated in his place, as our Lord has ordered."'

Siricius gazed with black and unfathomable eyes at Jerome. 'Have you an objection?'

'But I've already dealt with that letter from the Bishop to Damasus, asking him to address those issues!' protested Jerome. 'I outlined Damasus's response before his death.'

'From now on I wish the style of such letters to be changed,' said Siricius shortly. He crossed his arms, slowly and deliberately. 'And this letter, you see, will be particularly significant.'

With effort, Jerome held his tongue. Damasus had never treated him in this high-handed fashion! Jerome had drafted all his letters and, if discussion were needed, the two had usually sat down together to take a glass, in Damasus's private sanctum, when the old Pontiff would throw off his heavy robe, sit back and take his ease.

But Siricius had left Jerome sitting rather awkwardly on the other side of a vast expanse of shining oak table. He was dictating at length on Church discipline — less of a letter, thought Jerome, than the sort of directive the Emperor might write.

'We bear the burdens of the heavily laden,' he intoned, 'or rather the blessed Apostle Peter present in us bears them ...'

His eyes wandered to Jerome and rested on him for a long moment, to Jerome's discomfort and puzzlement, before he proceeded with his peremptory rulings on the readmission of heretics into the Church, and on to what Jerome realised was his real interest: the urgent need for clerical continence.

'Priests and deacons are constrained by the indissoluble law of continence. From the day of our ordination, we surrender our hearts and bodies to sobriety and modesty ... *Qui autem in carne sunt, Deo placer non possunt*: 'Those interested only in unspiritual things can never be pleasing to God.' Your interests, however, are not in the unspiritual, but in the spiritual, if so be that the Spirit of God dwell in you. And where, unless in holy bodies, thus we read, can the spirit of God dwell?'

As he spoke, Siricius's eyes sought Jerome's. Jerome felt uneasy. Siricius's words on continence were the sort that Jerome himself might well have uttered. Yet he sensed that they were directed at him, as though Jerome's own flesh had erred, or was erring. Siricius seemed, in short, on the verge of reproving the very champion of virginity himself. Jerome frowned. What was he getting at?

Only when the long series of decretals was finished did Siricius address Jerome directly.

'Periodic continence might have been acceptable in the Old Testament for the purpose of begetting children,' he said, 'but the New Testament makes it clear that priestly observance — including continence — is a daily task, and that to observe it absolutely ensures a greater degree of perfection.' Siricius looked at him pointedly. 'If licence amongst the clergy is to be curbed, it will be by directives such as this one — not by letters by lesser members of our order which are read by all and sundry and do grave harm to our Church.'

It was a cruel slap. Jerome left His Holiness's presence, smarting and full of words which — fortunately perhaps — he had no chance of uttering. Jerome was unaware that Siricius, recently exposed to the driving force of Ambrose, all the stronger because solicited, had reached a momentous decision about him.

***

Of course, there was his work. And his ladies were a solace.

'I'm being eased out, all the same,' Jerome exclaimed to Paula one morning. 'The very ones who used to come to me for advice now close up like molluscs on a beach when I pass. I can't even be sure of finding a scribe now that Aetius seems to have disappeared into thin air.'

Jerome was sitting in Paula's salon, getting up often to stride impatiently up and down. Maids were cleaning up around him; others sewed at the far end of the room.

'To possess the Lord, in return to be possessed by the Lord,' he said bitterly. 'I was an idiot to try for this in Rome!'

His urgent need of sympathy caught at Paula, and she felt his resentment as if it were her own.

'Then why not leave?' asked Paula. 'Leave the Lateran before they make you!'

Jerome stared at her. 'I was given a commission,' he said slowly. 'I intend to complete it.' He pondered. 'I suppose I might go to the country. I have friends not too far from Rome. I will need access to a good library, however.'

'I wasn't thinking of the country here,' said Paula. 'I meant the Holy Land.' She added: 'You've told me often that in Caesarea there's a magnificent library.'

Jerome's eyes gleamed. 'Oh, there is!'

'It's not so far from Caesarea to Jerusalem.'

'Jerusalem,' he mused. 'It's a city like any other, no better than Rome.'

'Bethlehem?' suggested Paula. 'The centre of our world.'

'The Holy Land haunts me sometimes, of course. And it would be Heaven to leave this hurly-burly, the noise ...'

212

His eyes rested on her face with sudden apprehension.

'The only thing is,' Jerome said abruptly, 'I'd lose you.'

There was a silence.

'Perhaps you wouldn't,' Paula said, returning his gaze. 'The Holy Land haunts me too, you know.'

The maid Clea, who had preternaturally sharp ears, got up and swiftly made her way from the room. This news had value.

***

For some days, neither Paula nor Marcella saw anything of Jerome.

'I warned him!' Marcella expostulated. 'I warned him about his letters attacking the clergy, that they'd come back at him. All he said was, "Let them reform, let them hear God's truths and I'll praise them as vigorously as I now condemn them."'

'There's no halfway in Jerome's world,' said Paula quietly.

Then, on the morning of the fifth day, Jerome did come to Paula's mansion, shocking her by his pallor and wild eyes.

'Like a starving beast, he is,' reported a servant to Clea, 'like he'd eat you!'

'What's happened?' cried Paula.

'When I tell you, you won't believe it!' Jerome burst out. 'I can hardly believe it myself—yet I have it in writing—*I am to stand trial!*'

His fury and despair filled the room. He had been summoned: he was to attend in the papal apartments the very next morning to answer charges of behaviour deemed unseemly to his position and damaging to the Church.

'As though I'm not devout, not the chastest of men,' he roared, throwing his arms wide. 'I'd have thought that they would at least be grateful for all the writing I've done for them! But no, they prefer ill-founded gossip over true scholarship, and will do anything to bring me down!'

'Don't upset yourself,' Paula begged, frightened. 'If the charges are fabricated, I'm confident that you can have them dismissed.'

'You underestimate their treachery! They'll stop at nothing, that Senate of Pharisees,' he ground out. 'Nothing!'

He departed soon afterwards, hardly in better shape than when he arrived. That morning, not even Paula could raise his spirits.

31

Jerome had slept little when, grim-faced and tense, he presented himself next morning to face an assembly of some twenty senior churchmen. From where he was sitting, a patch of blue sky was just visible through the high-set windows of the Lateran meeting-room. Aloof yet dominant, His Holiness Siricius sat apart on a raised platform, surrounded by the clergy.

Jerome took some small comfort at the presence of the resolute and open countenance of one Basilius seated at a table below the papal throne with documents spread out before him. He was obviously the spokesman of the clergy. Jerome knew Basilius to be a man of moral stature and thought he could trust him to be fair. He listened intently to Basilius's reasoning tones, his dispassionate words:

'You have been summoned before us to answer four charges, Jerome. You will be given full opportunity to respond to each. The charges are as follows.

'First, you have publicly espoused views on marriage which give offence. Second, you have unforgivably slandered members of your own clerical body. In the third place, your personal conduct has been grossly at variance with the standards expected of you and indeed espoused by you. Lastly, you have shown grave disloyalty to the Church which could seriously damage it.'

Jerome quivered with anger. Could they really be talking about him? Controlling himself, he rose and stated proudly that these accusations were false from beginning to end and that he welcomed the opportunity to refute such a tissue of lies.

Sitting down, he braced himself for Basilius's indictment on the first charge. He didn't have to wait long.

'While extolling the role of virginity for Church virgins and clerics,' Basilius began, 'you have denigrated the standing of married couples who make up the great majority of Christians. You forget that marriage of ordinary devout Christians intending to bring children into the world is pleasing to God.'

Basilius's expression was troubled as he continued. 'Just a few passages from your writings will suffice to illustrate this point. For instance, you say: "I do not detract from marriage when I set virginity before it. No one compares a bad thing with a good."

'You will not deny that you wrote these words just last year, in a letter to Eustochium.

'Nor is this a one-off. To the contrary, you have voiced such opinions on many an occasion. For instance — and, again, I quote you: "I praise marriage ... because it gives me virgins. I gather the rose from the thorn, the gold from the earth, the pearl from the oyster ..."

'You have even referred to marriage as simply a remedy against sin,' Basilius concluded.

'On that last point I was, in fact, quoting Ambrose,' Jerome began, but his voice was drowned out by the mounting protests from the audience.

'So our parents are no better than the beasts of the fields, eh?' someone growled.

Jerome was already on his feet.

'Who amongst you would deny that Adam and Eve embarked on marriage only after their sin, that while marriage was intended to replenish the earth — I quote Genesis! — virginity replenishes Paradise?

'Is Paul to be scorned when he warns us that married people can't give themselves wholly to God, when he calls them divided in heart, taken up with worldly affairs and pleasing to their wives, whereas the celibate man is the true follower of Christ, pale through fasting and squalidly clad, a stranger to this world? Like Paul, we do not condemn marriage—we only leave it far behind!'

Scriptural quotations flooded effortlessly from Jerome's lips. He recited authorities ranging from Origen to the late Pontiff Damasus. Ambrose, as well.

'And why should I not keep Heaven ever before men's eyes?' Jerome's voice rang out. 'Everyone amongst us should strive to throw off the shackles of this earthly life and seek spiritual union with our Lord.

'Ah, as long as I have breath in my body I will urge women—and men—to follow the virgin life, outside of marriage or within it.'

He looked fixedly at a cleric who, as everyone knew, kept a woman, though discreetly.

There was silence. No one dared to enter into the debate with Jerome on this. Basilius looked up at Siricius, who nodded. Basilius turned back to Jerome.

'After listening to you, Jerome, and noting the strength of your beliefs regarding virginity, we can accept that you have not intentionally distorted the Church's teachings. Rather, we observe an excess of zeal and this, together with a lack of sensitivity to the feelings of ordinary people, blinds you to the pain your words can inflict on devout, married Christians. Do you wish to say more?'

Slowly Jerome shook his head. From Basilius's tone, he understood that he was being warned rather than condemned on this count. So be it.

'His Holiness asks me to pass on to the next charge. A number of our letters, most of them widely copied and read—and not only by Christians—pillory the lives of lay and cleric, often on the basis of'—Basilius paused for emphasis—'unsustained gossip.'

There was a chill in the air as Basilius read out extracts scolding luxury and greed and sloth among clergymen.

'You have written, Jerome: "There are some of my own order who seek the office of presbyter or deacon so they may
see women more freely. Such men think of nothing but their
dress; they use perfumes freely, see that there are no creases
in their leather shoes. Their curling hair shows traces of the
tongs; their fingers glisten with rings ... When you see them,
all primped up, you would take them for bridegrooms rather
than clerics."'

Basilius swallowed. There wasn't a whisper in the room.
Some half dozen clerics trembled under their robes, fearful
that the monkish scourge arraigned before them might, even
in this gathering, name names.

The vignettes continued. Wealthy widows of unseemly
behaviour and clergymen who took money for visiting them
were not spared Jerome's tongue. There was a horrified laugh
or two at Jerome's caustic wit: '"The hand outstretched in
blessing often closes on a golden coin."'

Extract followed extract. By now, the hostility in the air was
palpable.

When Basilius was done, the meeting waited for Jerome's
inevitable tirade that he had told nothing but the truth, dis-
graceful as it was. Instead, he surprised them by simply remaining silent, allowing the tension in the room to build up.
Finally, Basilius addressed him.

'You do well to say nothing, Jerome. I think you can hardly
deny that you are guilty of slandering Roman clerics and no-
tables.'

Jerome was thinking furiously. How could he win over this
hostile company? Everything he had written was true, and the
actuality was even more damning. The more honest clerics
amongst them must be acutely uncomfortable.

'Is it their actions you condemn, or my words that portray
them?' was all he said, at last.

For a time no one spoke, and the silence was broken only

by some shifting of feet. Then Siricius lowered his eyes and inclined his head, and Basilius spoke:

'Again we note your words, Jerome. You are not withdrawing your accusations, and make no mention of refraining from such attacks.'

'Truth drives my pen, suffer for it though I may!' thundered Jerome. 'And that pen is at the service of our Lord!'

There was a murmuring from the clergy, their eyes fixed on the man before them, as if daring him to continue.

In the charged atmostphere, Basilius continued.

'We will proceed to the next charge.' Basilius beckoned to a tall, lean priest whose name Jerome could not recall, though he had seen him in conversation with certain deacons whose dislike of him was well known. The priest walked forwards. His face was haughty, and he addressed the court in acid tones.

'I speak of the Lady Paula. For years she has led a strictly secluded life and — as we are all aware — is noted for her charity and piety. But now it is rumoured that she will accompany Jerome to the Holy Land! Would this noble lady ever have thought of such a thing if she had not been seduced by a ruthless conjurer who deals in words? Of course, the Lady Paula is — as we are also all aware — extremely wealthy. It's only her money that makes Jerome's expensive adventure possible.'

'And that is not all.' The priest paused, turning slightly to take in Jerome. 'Far from it! It is no secret that Jerome and the Lady Paula are close friends. They meet frequently by day, admittedly always in the presence of others. But Jerome has been seen leaving the Lady Paula's mansion just before dawn.'

The priest turned and flung his accusation directly at Jerome: 'He preaches chastity and practises fornication!'

Jerome was quite unprepared. His face darkened with anger. 'Lies, lies, all lies!' he roared. 'I'm used to calumny and hatred. I expect nothing less from men like you! But that the Lady Paula of all people should be singled out as your target reveals the stinking depths of your squalid envy! Had she chosen the empty life of fashion—frequented smart spas, dressed in scented fingery and gorged herself on expensive delicacies, then you'd fawn on her in the most disgusting way. But because she has given up everything and spends her time fasting, in prayer and study and good works, you insult and slander her. Christ, who sees all things, will condemn you to everlasting damnation!'

Angry mutterings followed this outburst.

'And who,' continued Jerome, 'is the liar who claims he's seen me leaving the mansion of the Lady Paula at dawn?'

The priest stated that it had been a slave of Paula's, her nightwatchman Livius, who had informed them.

Jerome laughed harshly. 'You'll believe a slave, but not me? Do you realise that the fellow was responsible for the death of the Lady Blesilla? When she collapsed in her garden that night, he was asleep. Had he been doing his job, and brought her into the house, she'd be alive this day—'

'And had you been doing your work of translation and research rather than persuading young girls to adopt a life of extreme asceticism, the Lady Blesilla might also be alive today!' the priest shot back.

'So now you insinuate that, because I encouraged her to renounce the values of the world and embrace those of Christ, I am responsible for the death of the Lady Blesilla too! The Lady Paula had the fellow flogged for his negligence. Can't you see? This is his revenge!'

'Enough!' His Holiness intervened. 'The evidence of the slave is to be investigated immediately.'

There was a silence. They all knew what that meant: torture.

***

There followed a break of some hours during which the clergy deliberated. Left alone, Jerome fulminated to himself.

'A farrago of lies, an outrageous concoction,' he mumbled, his teeth clamping together as though he had his enemies between them rather than a crust of bread. 'There's a good chance the slave will not survive.' He shivered. 'Though then there'll be none to disprove his lies! But God will protect Paula. I will not despair.'

***

When the meeting resumed, Basilius called for the slave Livius to be brought before them.

'Unfortunately, Livius' — the messenger spoke euphemistically — 'is not in a condition to give evidence. He has, however, retracted.'

A surge of relief left Jerome weak and trembling. Then, seeing the hostile faces before him, and feeling his isolation, he asked quietly:

'You will now leave the Lady Paula in peace?'

Basilius's honest face twitched with distaste. 'His Holiness is satisfied that the charge of inappropriate personal conduct is without foundation,' he said. 'But the gravest matter we have to investigate is yet to come — your disloyalty to the Church. This charge must receive our closest attention, but as time is short and our brothers all have business elsewhere, we will resume tomorrow morning.'

***

Jerome chose seclusion that night, much of which he spent in prayer, invaded by gusts of anger and loathing at his fellow clerics. He was totally unprepared for the thunderbolt that they were about to deliver.

32

The next morning, the clergy settled down in expectant silence as Jerome, grim-faced and taciturn, moved to his lonely place before them. Basilius rose and addressed them.

'I will now read out a letter written by Jerome a year before to a certain Ephraim, a Jew who had been a friend of his for many years—one of those, in fact, who had helped Jerome gain mastery of the Hebrew language. Because the Jew died just after it was written, the letter was never delivered, but remained among Jerome's papers. Aetius, to whom Jerome had dictated the letter, brought it to the attention of His Holiness. The relevance of the letter will soon become clear.'

'What letter?' Jerome demanded. 'It is much more than a year since I last wrote to Ephraim.'

'It is hardly strange if this letter has slipped your memory, then,' Basilius rejoined mildly. 'You have written so much.'

Jerome shook his head. 'I am well aware of what I have written—the Lord has blessed me with a flawless memory. Whatever this so-called letter is, it is not from my hand. And if Aetius produced it, why isn't he here? I haven't seen him for weeks!'

'His Holiness has been in possession of the letter for some time,' Basilius told him. 'He takes a grave view of its contents. He has instructed that the letter be read to this inquiry—and to you—in full.'

Basilius motioned to a young cleric who had been taking notes of the proceedings. The cleric stood up, cleared his throat, and read:

'"Jerome to his dear friend Ephraim.

"So you have found yet another stick to beat me with in our long-standing wrangle about religion. A wrangle only between friends, thank the Lord.

"And the latest is a very big stick indeed. You deny that Peter was the first Bishop of Rome. The Catalogue of Bishops drawn up by Damasus's predecessor Pope Liberius, which has Peter as the first Bishop, a fraud! Not a word of this conclusion outside, I beg of you, in this city of all cities, for you'll call forth howls of fury from every Christian in the place. They'll murder you, my dear Ephraim, for taking Peter from them in this way. Damasus himself will take the lead, and not even I could dissuade him.

"You've got some arguments, Ephraim.

"You point to a tradition among the Jewish people that it was Roman Jews converted abroad who first brought back the message here; that far from founding it, Peter and Paul found the Church already flourishing on their arrival here.

"Then all sorts of discrepancies exist in previous lists of Roman bishops for those early years. And you remind me that the learned Eusebius made not Peter but Linus first bishop.

"But now in Liberius's catalogue we have all inconsistencies ironed out as bishop follows bishop in an unbroken line beginning with Peter. To fill a gap, a single bishop is even made into two (it happens twice!). Liberius has put Clement as the bishop following Linus, even though Clement never called himself a bishop at all, let alone successor of the apostle Peter.

"Of course you are right, my dear Ephraim. The list is a fraud, at least for its early entries. In the apostolic age, churches were ruled by groups of elders or presbyters, not by a single bishop.

"But as a churchman you will not find me admitting in public that our profession of an unbroken line of bishops from Peter to Damasus is a deception. Such an admission from a man of my standing would do incalculable damage to our Church. On the contrary, in public I shall uphold the validity of Liberius's Catalogue, in company with all other churchmen, none of whom criticise it even if truth urged them. But few of our clergy give their minds to this sort of thing. Indeed, many live far too well to make over-much use of the mind at all. Nothing is so destructive to the mind as a full belly, fermenting like a wine vat, giving forth its gases on all sides. Ah, Ephraim, men can hardly embrace wisdom if their thoughts are on a well-laden table, if fine meats and wine incite their lust. And I see those very clerics sunk in such filthy pleasure sniffing after preferment like dogs after a bitch on heat, lost to the eternal verities.

"Do not, however, think me a coward in publicly upholding the validity of the Liberian Cataglue. On the contrary, I would gladly face any danger on behalf of my Church. If I were a cowardly creature I should not be seeking your help in going beyond the Greek version of our Old Testament to the Hebrew, the original language of mankind, so as to present an accurate translation in Latin. What an outcry I must face from filthy swine who grunt as they trample on pearls if I so much as cast doubt on the Greek versions in use now!

"That the Jewish people do possess a deeper wisdom even our Origen himself has admitted. But do not imagine, my friend, that you have inveigled me into following in your footsteps, after this easy victory of yours over the seat of Peter. You have not shaken my faith and I am not quite a Jew yet!'"

The young cleric finished reading the letter and sat down.

After a moment of stunned silence, pandemonium broke loose. The clerics could hardly believe what they had heard. The enraged chorus that it unleashed might have come from the rabble at the arena rather than from a staid group of Roman clergy.

'The Synagogue on Saturday, the Church on Sunday! That's Jerome for you!' yelled one.

'Out! Out! Jerome must go!' bellowed another, as others took up his cry.

Jerome rose, demanding to see the letter. As soon as it was handed to him, he sat down and became engrossed in it, even now his legendary power of concentration shutting out his immediate surroundings.

Meanwhile, his opponents in court scented victory. During the last three years they had been obliged to put up with much from this arrogant man whose intellectual capabilities undeniably surpassed their own. Envious of his growing intimacy with Damasus, many had also squirmed under the bite of his wit. But what Jerome had said of certain clergymen was largely true, and Siricius knew it. Thus far, they had felt that Jerome might yet escape them. But now, surely, this letter must seal his fate! To deny that the Pope's authority derived from Peter — could anything be more subversive? And the shamelessness to share his wicked doubts with a Jew! Jerome must be finished.

The hubbub subsided as Jerome rose to his feet again. 'I absolutely deny having written this,' he said, his voice low but firm. 'Yes, I knew Ephraim — he more than anyone else helped me learn the Hebrew language. And yes, we engaged in many a lively discussion on the finer points of difference between his religion and my own — but I repeat, this letter is a forgery!' He turned towards Basilius. 'I demand that Aetius be brought face to face with me.'

Ignoring the request, Basilius's eyes bored into Jerome. 'So you wholly deny the contents of the letter and admit that the Catalogue of Bishops drawn up by Liberius is true and valid?'

Jerome hesitated. He knew, as they all knew, that this was the crux of the whole inquiry. He chose his words carefully.

'This is not a matter to be answered by a simple yes or no,' he said. 'In one sense, what is said in the letter is true, certainly so. But complete truth can sometimes be elusive. One truth can distort a more basic underlying truth — a spiritual truth. We must accept that there can be more than one understanding of the one truth. I must answer in my own words, standing before you.'

All eyes were trained on Jerome as he continued to make his points clearly and deliberately.

'Peter did not found and become the first leader of the Christian Church in Rome. As is said in the letter with which I am falsely charged, when he arrived here there was already a vigorous Church governed by a group of elders or presbyters. Who can deny Peter's own words in his first epistle general: "The presbyters amongst you I exhort, who am your fellow presbyter"? If he had chosen to be first Bishop of Rome or had been held so by the elders, why did he not nominate his successor when once he knew his martyrdom was inevitable? Had he done so, that man's name would have been emblazoned from that time on in Church memory and there would have been no uncertainty about who had taken over from Peter.

'The reason is that it was not necessary. Only later — and we do not know how much later — did increasing numbers make it necessary for the presbyters to choose one to preside over the others and so to become Bishop of Rome. This was done to remedy schism and to prevent any self-elected individual from rending the Church by drawing it to himself. The duty of one duly elected and that of his successors was the same as that exercised today by His Holiness Siricius. But this first Bishop of Rome was not and could not have been Peter.'

Jerome paused to give time for the clerics to absorb his words. The silence was absolute now, and he continued.

'But in another sense the letter which you have — to your shame — foisted on me gives a profoundly wrong impression.

'Christ said to Peter, "Thou art Peter, and upon this rock I will build my Church." Because the words are Christ's, and he has all power, they must be fulfilled. But what did he mean by "rock"? You are aware, of course, of the play on words here: the name Peter, or *petros* in Greek, signifies a stone, and the word for rock is *petra*. Throughout Holy Scripture, the concept of a rock is used to signify the living stone of God Himself on which we must — metaphorically — build the foundations of our faith and on which we must place our trust for salvation.

'Peter delegated to the early elders of the Church this power and authority given him by Christ, and as a group they exercised them. Whoever were the first individual holders of the office that subsequently came to be known as the Bishop of Rome matters little. For instance, I have no difficulty in thinking of Clement (considered by many the first successor to Peter) as the type of shadowy but splendid figure who has earned the right to be included in any catalogue of Bishops of Rome even though it is most unlikely that he was ever consecrated in that office. Clement is often referred to because he is the first successor of St Peter about whom much is known; in fact, he was the fourth Bishop of Rome.

'The catalogue therefore, as this makes evident, is only the imperfect record of the actual God-given continuity of the presence of the Holy Spirit which makes us an elect race, a royal priesthood, a holy nation, a people for God's own possession. It is *that* which matters, and it is *that* which is the fundamental, underlying truth, obscured in that forged letter by its concentration on outward form at the expense of the inward spirit of the past.

'Can you not see? It is the delegation of power and authority from Christ through the apostle transmitted in an unbroken line of apostolic succession, at first through groups of presbyters, which is the essence of the words of Christ—not that every early individual in that line should happen to have been addressed as Bishop!'

Again Jerome paused, and then adopted a sharper tone.

'I suspect that many of you would secretly agree that the early part of the catalogue drawn up by Liberius is largely fiction. But, as even your forged letter points out, to admit the fact publicly would damage the Church. It would only serve to confuse the ignorant, who are incapable of distinguishing simple factual accuracy from deeper levels of spiritual truth. Pagans, heretics, and all who are jealous of the Church would shout that we claim unfounded authority for the Bishops of Rome—while our faithful would be upset at the suggestion that Siricius does not stand in due succession from the apostle Peter. Therefore, outside this room, and for the good of our beloved Church, I freely support the validity of the catalogue as the visible evidence of authority of our Bishops of Rome. Freely will I proclaim that in this city of Rome, the Prince of Apostles, the glorious Peter, founded the Church and by his faith strengthened it.'

'Of course,' Jerome added casually, 'those not endowed with subtle minds need not concern themselves with my reasoning as to the underlying truth of the catalogue, but may rest content with a simple belief in its historical accuracy.'

He sat down, arms folded, suggesting the teacher before a class not well endowed to pass their examinations.

Basisilius rose and, with obvious irony, said:

'Nevertheless, Jerome, our simple minds must try to grasp how a subtle mind can at the same time believe and disbelieve something.' He paused. 'You have stated that Ephraim was your friend. Did you know him well, as the letter clearly indicates?'

'Yes, I knew him well,' Jerome admitted.

Basilius then turned to address the whole gathering:

'Do you consider,' he asked them, 'that this letter is truly in the style of Jerome's writings, which are known to us all?'

There was immediate and vociferous assent:

'Of course it's his!'

'Who else could have written it?'

'It's got the mark of Jerome all over it!'

For a moment Jerome himself shrank at the wave of vindictiveness that swept through the room and seemed to threaten his physical safety.

Basilius angrily called for order, then turned to Jerome.

'Jerome, you have asserted that the Catalogue of Bishops is a fraud, but that it is also true. You have asserted that whilst you disbelieve its contents, you can at the same time defend its validity in public.'

He paused and then, raising his voice, flung these words at Jerome:

'You offer to our Church this gift of disloyalty! This hypocrisy in a Christian writer! And to whom do you offer it? To a Jew. To a Jew, no less! At the same time as you ruthlessly excoricate your fellow churchmen.'

'I never wrote that letter!' Jerome shouted. 'Where's Aetius? He has not even appeared here! Have him brought before me!'

'Aetius is not in Rome. His Holiness satisfied himself by exhaustive inquiry that Aetius had spoken the truth before allowing him to depart. You wrote that letter, Jerome.'

Basilius turned to the roomful of clerics.

'Do I hear any dissent?'

There was none; the silence was complete. The eyes that were fixed on Jerome were hard and unforgiving, and the expressions exultant.

Jerome realised that he had lost.

'The decision of His Holiness as to your future will be sent to you in your rooms, Jerome,' Basilius told him, his tone softening a little.

***

The next day, Jerome received written notification of Siricius's decision. He was to leave Rome by the end of the summer, never to return.

Part Four

Afterwards

33

A week after the inquiry, Paula and Marcella and the other ladies had been informed only that Jerome had left Rome for the country. Their anxiety deepened, and with it a sense of confusion.

Then one morning Paula had a visit from a pale and harassed young monk who introduced himself as Vincentius.

'Jerome sent me to tell you that he's with me and my little community out beyond San Sebastiano, down south.' He paused, unsure how to proceed. 'He wanted you to know that they asked him to — well, he is to be banished from Rome. My lady, are you alright?'

Trembling, Paula sat down. 'How is he?' she begged. 'What have they done to him? Please tell us, is he alright?'

But Vincentius could not tell her clearly how Jerome was. 'Just that ... well, he's not the man we all know,' was how he put it.

Paula looked searchingly at him, but all she saw was a terror in the young man's face that matched her own.

'You must take me to him,' she said. 'At once.'

It was a tense and miserable journey that they made in her little-used carriage over the flat, airless land that lay between Rome and the hills to the south. When they finally reached Vincentius's quarters, Paula found an older, defeated man sitting in a dim room, hunched over a pile of books — all, he said, that was left him of his former world. Jerome, in short, had retreated into himself.

But his weakness called forth all the firmness of a woman who had brought up five children. Hiding her dismay, Paula sent the monks and slaves scuttling away while she herself turned to the task of reawakening in the dejected figure before her the old Jerome—the one who was rarely silent, equally passionate in love or hate, praise or denunciation.

'You bother to visit a leper?' he asked bitterly. 'A worthless outcast?'

'Come, Jerome, I am asking for an explanation of what's happened—not self-pity and recrimination.'

Listlessly he answered her questions, but she refused to give up. Bit by bit he found himself recounting the proceedings of the inquiry in detail, keeping from her only the accusations of his alleged visits to her by night.

'You've got friends,' she declared. 'Many! Marcella and the rest of us—and others at the Lateran, too.'

Uncharacteristically, he shrank from meeting anyone. 'Never will I see them again - never!' he stammered, breaking into a fit of coughing.

'Well, you can't stay here!' She glanced through the window at the humble farm buildings around the house. The land lies too low; it's damp. You'd be better up at my villa in the Alban Hills.' She raised a hand. 'It's no use objecting. I've made my mind up—I'll send a carriage in the morning.'

Outside, she tackled Vincentius.

'He's a sick man. It's your duty to accompany him—there's plenty of room for both of you in my villa.'

'Of course, if you insist ...' Vincentius nodded, marvelling at how this slim woman with the intense eyes swept aside his every reservation, and departed once more, taking with her most of Jerome's library. It was pressure of the most effective sort, though it brought Jerome close to panic.

Shaken at Jerome's transformation, Paula prayed long that night for strength to deal with it, and bring back to full life this man so richly endowed in spirit and mind, yet so prickly in character.

***

After some days in the cool heights of Paula's villa in the Alban Hills, Jerome, despite himself, began to revive. Marcella arrived, and for a time they all debated the particulars of the recent inquiry, and its implications.

'Uncanny,' fretted Jerome, hunched in an arbour of the villa overlooking the deep blue of the water in the centre of the crater, known as the Lake of Diana. 'As though a second self had invaded my brain, taken possession of my pen and written that letter to Ephraim. Everyone believes that I wrote it. I'm half-way to believing it myself!' He would shudder, and beads of sweat break out again on his forehead.

'From what you've told us,' said Marcella, who had dragged out of him a full account of the letter's contents, 'you said too much. You should simply have denied writing it.'

'It was so devilishly clever,' he returned. 'I couldn't help discussing the arguments within it! Ephraim and I did debate, all the time. But there really was no danger of his converting me!'

'That's not the point, though,' Marcella broke in. 'It is that, as you yourself said, you couldn't resist taking up the challenges posed by the letter — as its writer intended. The more you discussed it, the more you gave the impression that you'd written it!'

'Was I to save myself at the expense of the truth?' Jerome demanded. 'Before that Senate of Pharisees?'

'You couldn't bear, before that Senate of Pharisees, not to show off your learning, more like it,' Marcella said tartly. 'Was it really the place for a lecture on the several shades of truth? One truth would have been enough. A flat denial that you wrote the letter, and a repudiation of the views expressed in it!'

Marcella spun around to face Jerome. 'And why did you have to fulminate against the clergy? These were, after all, the men who were judging you! Do you think they liked being told that they looked more like bridegrooms than churchmen?'

'Someone has to tell them the truth, whether they like it or not!' Jerome retorted, with a suggestion of his old fire. 'One or two might even listen.'

'Holy Mother of God, where is your common sense?' cried Marcella. 'The problem with you, Jerome, is that for all your intelligence and learning and piety, you've never understood people!'

'Well, I understand Jerome and have intuition enough for both of us,' interrupted Paula, walking across from the other side of the terrace where she had been following their conversation. 'And it's not the time to provoke him, Marcella—not now, just when he's starting to get a bit of colour in his cheeks again!' Dropping her voice, she added, 'It's that letter, you know—he keeps coming back to it …'

'It was Aetius, of course,' Jerome was muttering, unaware of the two women while unwittingly proving both their points. 'He wants to destroy me. He's the only one close enough to me—and has a quick mind as well as education. But why? Perhaps he was bribed, or his own envy and restentment might have been fuel enough. I remember now, I refused to recommend him for a post—of deacon, if you please!—on which he'd set his heart, and for which, as I told him, he would have been quite unsuitable.' He frowned. 'Yes, perhaps that was it.'

As they gratefully reached for the refreshments of olives and dates placed before them by a maid, Paula was careful not to mention a small piece of news that Marcella had recently obtained about Aetius: he had been appointed head deacon to an ailing, elderly bishop up in Ravenna, far away from Rome.

***

The late summer heat peaked. A great storm brought cooler air, the thunder reverberating around the walls of the crater, lending a dull, metallic glaze to the waters of the Lake of Diana beneath them.

As Paula had predicted, benefiting from a combination of the invigorating, fresh air of the hills and the attentions of his close-knit group of women, Jerome grew stronger. His cough disappeared, his appetite increased, and his spirit returned. The day that Paula heard him revile one of the slaves with all his old vigour, she thought it time to reveal a plan that she had been hatching ever since his trial.

Their conversation swayed back and forth over various matters during the afternoon. But it was when Jerome began talking of his work, and the interruptions he had suffered, that she said:

'You must concentrate on the future, on your translation of the Old Testament, the work which only you can do. You did start on the Book of Job—'

'Ah, Job! Now there's a challenge!' cried Jerome, his eyes lighting up. 'It was Ephraim, my linguistically brilliant friend Ephraim, who helped me peel back the layers of metaphors to pin down the meaning of that obscure Hebrew text—which, by the way, uses Arabic and a dash of Syrian. I will labour to make Job whole and free from stain, even if people here prefer ancient faults to new truths. They'll cling blindly to the Latin whatever state it's in. As far as they're concerned, if it makes their response easier, the blessed Job can go on lying amidst filth and swarming with the worms of error!'

'Well, soon you'll have left Rome far behind,' said Paula quickly. 'And so shall I.'

'You can't still be thinking of going to the Holy Land in company with a pariah dog! You couldn't possibly leave your family — and all this!' Unclenching his fist, Jerome gestured at the panorama of the lake, shimmering like a mirror under the emerging sun and encased by the lush green of the surrounding hills.

'As though that meant anything to me!' she said scornfully.

Jerome looked at her intently. 'Paula, you must be sure it's what you want,' he said, at last. 'I can't foretell how my life will be from now on ...'

She waited, and he took a deep breath. 'It's not only that. There's hardly a person in Rome doesn't sneer and rage at me for our friendship! Do you think I want to bring all this down again on your head?'

'I know what they accused you of—with me, I mean,' she said gently. 'Of course it's all leaked out.' She smiled. 'What does it matter? It's not true. "By honour and dishonour,"' she quoted, '"By evil report and good report ...". Paul suffered before us. Take heart, dear Jerome. We're going to see Palestine together!'

She handed him a paper, and her eyes were shining.

'What's this?'

'Oh, places I've always longed to see! Jerusalem of course, but all the rest too. I've read everything that Eusebius wrote about Palestine, you know. All the places in the Bible—holy Sinai, the mount of God, the valley where the calf was made, and where God spoke to Moses from the burning bush—'

'Mount Sinai!' Jerome exclaimed. 'Do you realise the hardships and dangers that we would encounter? And you're a woman!'

'I'm aware of that,' said Paula. 'And yes, of course there would be hardship, and dangers too. But anyone who can travel there, does—you know quite well. We could go by way of Athens ... We could see Ephesus! Oh, if you knew how I once craved to see Ephesus!' Abruptly, she stopped. 'Anyway,' she continued more quietly, 'Sinai is only twelve staging posts from Pelusium.'

He laughed out loud, for the first time since the inquiry. 'You've done your research, haven't you!'

But Paula was not laughing. 'It would be easiest to go straight to Alexandria from here, and then to Nitria—the cradle of the monastic life, and only forty miles from Alexandria. What better way to restore your energy for your work after the despicable accusations and falsehoods that have assailed you here?'

She paused, and added guilelessly, 'Of course, the Seer Didymus is in Alexandria, isn't he?' She knew of his unbounded admiration for the blind Biblical scholar.

He smiled, appreciating her little stratagem.

'We might see Memphis,' she said. 'There are pyramids in plenty in the twelve-mile stretch from Memphis to Babylonia. The guides have a tale that Joseph made them to store corn —'

'And you'd like to see them all, I suppose?'

'Well, it would be a shame to miss them as they are practically on our route ...'

So the talked of her plans through the long, sultry afternoon.

***

Marcella, visiting her friend again several days afterwards, raised her face to Paula expectantly as she descended from her carriage.

'Better,' said Paula immediately. 'He's much better. Listen!'

Indeed, from within the villa, Jerome's disdainful tones were clearly audible.

'I prefer to go forward quite openly as the translator of another man's books than to deck myself out, as certain people do, like an ugly croaking crow in another bird's plumage ...'

'He's dictating a preface to his translation of Didymus's treatise on the Holy Spirit,' explained Paula.

'Quite himself again, by the sound of it,' Marcella commented drily. 'Anyway, who are the "certain people"?'

'Oh, there's a book out on the Holy Spirit. He says that it's largely plagiarised from the Greeks — Didymus, Basil the Great and Athanasius included.'

'You surely don't mean Bishop Ambrose's book?'

Paula hesitated, remembering Marcella's close family link with Ambrose.

'Anyway,' Marcella shrugged, 'it seems to be doing Jerome a power of good — and Ambrose has broad shoulders.' She added: 'I've got a letter here for Jerome. It's from Rufinus, in Jerusalem.'

'I hope there's nothing in it to upset him.' Paula frowned. 'Rufinus doesn't approve of Jerome's translating the Hebrew of the Old Testament. They've already written to each other about it.'

'Who *will* approve of bypassing the Latin and Greek versions that people are so used to?'

'The Church should!' Paula spoke with vehemence. 'Damasus understood the futility of trying to revise a Latin translation of another translation.'

'You're really serious about this plan of travelling to the Holy Land, aren't you?'

'Yes, I am.'

'And Jerome agrees with it?'

'I think so.'

A ripple of panic entered Marcella's voice. 'Paula, do you realise the risks you'll run? In Rome, the talk … it will get worse. You must know that it's highly controversial for a woman in your position to leave her family! And outside the city, you'll meet another, rougher world, one from which you've always been shielded … If you survive it, you'll be one of the highest-ranking pilgrims ever to undertake such a perilous journey! As your friend, my dear, I can't help but worry. Do you really want to put yourself at such risk, when God is here in our midst? Are you quite sure you know what you're doing?'

'Oh!' cried Paula, 'I know just what I'm doing! I'm going to hear quite enough from the family on the subject. Don't *you* start!'

34

There was no time to lose, Paula realised, if they were to board the ship before winter set in. Leaving Jerome to pursue his work in her villa in the Alban Hills, Paula returned to Rome and to her complicated preparations.

Her immediate task was the distribution of her wealth amongst the members of her family, her children especially. What she didn't reveal was that she had also set aside ample sums of money to draw upon later at her own discretion should Jerome require, as she predicted — accurately as it would turn out — additional funds to enlist the help of those people necessary to realise his plans.

She braced herself for the family protests, which were not long in coming. A visit from Toxotius's father, so aged by now that the rarely left home, marked the outrage felt by the Julii. Her father-in-law was accompanied by his only remaining son Gnaeus, now virtually head of the clan. He had, Paula knew, been summoned from Sicily, where he normally resided.

'Young Toxotius — your only son! What will happen to him?' the old man demanded.

'Of course, it will be hard to leave my boy,' Paula admitted. 'But little Toxotius is on the verge of manhood, when a mother must surrender a son, anyway. Pammachius will ensure that he'll be safe over these years.'

'A wise choice, certainly.' Gnaeus compressed his lips. 'Indeed, with Pammachius to guide him, we may be reasonably sure that that the boy will adopt a sackcloth over the toga.'

His father put his hands to his head. 'Paula, for the sake of your family, reconsider! There are bandits and thugs everywhere out there!' He shuddered. 'Disease too,' he added, as an afterthought.

Paula noticed him eyeing her two chests. Rather unfortunately, her father-in-law and his son had surprised her supervising the packing of valuables and gold coins.

'We shall be well protected,' Paula reassured him. 'We'll have soldiers to take care of us on the road. In Jerusalem, the governor is an old friend of the family and I'm sure he'll invite us to stay with him.'

'If you take him up on the offer,' said Gnaeus sarcastically. 'Isn't the whole point of a pilgrimage to spurn all offers of physical comfort, and suffer when you can?'

'My point,' she repeated, 'is that the offer of protection is there should we need it.'

'"We"? Are you really travelling with that monk who has been banished from Rome?' Her brother-in-law regarded her with distaste. The downturn of his mouth, and indeed his whole countenance, reminded her of her dead husband.

'Think of the scandal,' quavered his father. 'It's his reputation as well, after all. Think of him if you won't think of your family. Isn't this monk disgraced enough?'

'We will not be alone,' she replied quietly. 'Eustochium comes with me. And servants and maids, and other monks.'

'By Jove, I'm thankful my brother isn't here this day!' exclaimed Gnaeus. 'Come, father, our business is done.'

'You'll never come back, will you?' asked his father, getting to his feet.

Paula hesitated.

'Truly, I don't know yet,' she said slowly.

'I don't understand what you'll get out of it all!' burst out the old man.

Paula didn't answer. For she could only have said:

'Freedom.'

She watched them leave without looking back. In their eyes, she knew, she was betraying the memory of her husband as well as her extended family. How could they know that she had

long ago tacitly opted out of their narrow world, bound by loyalty to family and clan? If worldly considerations counted for
her now, it was rather the suggestion that, by association with
Jerome, she might damage him further.

But she could eat nothing that evening. Instead she sank
down and prayed to Anne, mother of the Virgin, for whom she
had felt, since girlhood, a special reverence.

***

Paula tossed and turned on her bed hour after hour that night.
Only nocturnal fears, she told herself, but the words of her husband's family had struck deep. She was right to go, she knew
that. God had set her on that path. But what would become of
her when their travels were over? And what would become of
Eustochium?

But from her daughter she was getting all the support she
needed, almost as though their roles were reversed. Gentle and
self-effacing though she was, Eustochium was showing herself
to be quietly resolute, and unwavering in the face of criticism.

'What would happen to Jerome without us?' Eustochium
had said, quite simply. 'And what would happen to us without
him?' Her grey eyes glowed. 'I want to see it all too. And we'll
be safe in a way no one here understands. *You* know, Mamma.'

Paula smiled at her. 'Yes, I know,' she said.

She was remembering something Damasus had once said to
her about Eustochium.

'The child has the innocence and goodness we have all lost.
Nothing can hurt her, wherever she is.'

***

It was the merest chance — or fate, she felt later — that at Marcella's house the next day Paula encountered two monks, friends
of Jerome's, who had brought presents for him. One had just
come from the Holy Land. With mounting excitement, she
heard places described that she would soon see for herself.

They talked of the Church of the Resurrection, built by Constantine over sixty years ago, in the very heart of Jerusalem.

'There was a room carved into the rock where the Tomb was, or so I've heard,' said Paula. 'Is it still like that?'

'Ah, it's not a cave any longer!' the first monk exclaimed, pressing his hands together in excitement. 'The earth has all been carefully carved away around it and it's left standing like a little building—and Golgotha, site of our Saviour's crucifixion and resurrection, is in an adjoining atrium.' He shook his head in wonder. 'A vast church, such as is hard to describe, spans them both. Finally, the holiest and most sacred site in all Christendom, built in the full glory it deserves! Thanks to our Emperor Constantine, God rest his soul, and his pious mother Helen, who consecrated these places in honour of our Saviour, purifying them from the taint of pagan cults—'

'That's not all, either,' interrupted the other monk. 'The grotto where the Holy Family took refuge, and where Our Lord was born, just out of Bethlehem, is now covered by the Church of the Nativity. To think that it was once a site of heathen worship!' He crossed himself hurriedly. 'It's octagonal in design, and in the nave is a fine mosaic floor ...'

'In blue and gold, isn't it? And you go up steps from the nave of the basilica and look down into the grotto,' said Paula confidently. The words came by themselves—almost, she thought, as if spoken by someone else.

'Yes,' said the monk, in surprise.

'And there's a big building east of the basilica? A convent filled with women, isn't it?'

The monk shook his head.

'There's no building there. Only empty fields.'

'Exactly!' Paula beamed at him suddenly. Then she fled as quickly as she could, unable to contain her elation.

She had no doubt now what God intended for her.

'First, I'm going to travel all over the Holy Land and see all the sacred sites,' said Paula to Jerome, two days later, back up in her villa in the Alban Hills. 'Because once I'm established there it'll be harder to leave.'

'You're planning a long stay there?'

'If the holy Melania did it, why shouldn't I? Build in the Holy Land, I mean.'

Jerome looked startled. 'You mean that you want to settle in Jerusalem?'

'No, in a village,' she stated. 'Preferably out in the country, close to where Christ was born — that's where I want to spend the rest of my life. I'll build a convent — no, two convents,' she added grandly. 'With the proceeds from all this.'

She waved her hand, dismissing 'all this' — the villa set high above the lake, the fine mosaics which Toxotius had bestowed on it, the marble statues in the garden, the slaves. Her gesture also embraced, Jerome realised, other properties, the extensive farmland in several Italian provinces, much of what Toxotius's clan and hers had so assiduously drawn to themselves over generations.

'Don't look at me like that,' Paula spoke confidently. 'We'll have funds enough.'

'Your children,' he cried. 'Your son, your family —'

'They have accepted it,' she said.

'What a sacrifice!'

'Sacrifice?' Paula wished that he could understand how fervently her whole being was waiting for departure.

Jerome shook his head. 'You, who have so much — to give it all up ... I never thought — I can't believe ...'

'I never thought I'd see *you* at a loss for words!' Paula could not hide her amusement. 'Besides,' she said, 'I've always wanted to travel to the Holy Land.'

'You'll need to use all your money, you realise that? My funds are depleted, my situation precarious.'

'Then my wealth will be put to good service at last,' she declared.

By the end of the afternoon they reached agreement. They would be together, but leave separately. He insisted on that. He would voyage at the end of the month by ship to Cyprus; she and Eustochium and the others would follow some weeks later and meet him there.

***

At last the day came for Jerome's departure. He set out at dawn from Paula's villa for the harbour town of Portus. He was leaving Rome — that 'Babylon' — for the last time in his life, with only Vincentius and a handful of monks and his young brother Paulinianus — who had reached Rome just in time — and their slaves. He made his goodbyes in Rome, for the monks, seeing the highly charged state he was in, judged it to be in his interests that that none of the ladies should come to Portus to see him off.

As he climbed into the carriage, Paula impulsively reached out her hands towards him, an instinctive gesture of love and trust.

'I'll not be long joining you in Cyprus,' she breathed. 'Wait for me. May God calm the waves and guide you safely there.'

Jerome stood motionless at first, and then grasped her hands and held them for a long moment. Then gently he released them. It was the first and only time that they ever touched each other.

35

Paula and Eustochium knew that they had little time left in Rome if they were to avoid a dreaded winter sailing. Paula's frantic preparations left her less time for anguish at the leave-takings to come. Nevertheless, the set faces of her two youngest children haunted her. Once the shock of grasping that their mother would be leaving, Rufina and Toxotius regarded her activities gravely, Rufina's arm often thrown protectively around her little brother's shoulder.

Paula sold off as many of her estates as she could in the time. Pammachius helped her in quantifying her assets, in transforming her land into gold, and in facing buyers who tried to drive too hard a bargain with a woman in such a hurry to sell. Quickly Paula grew accustomed to the daily arrival of wealthy Romans clutching their bags or chests of gold coins to complete their purchases or secure them by making large deposits. She hired more guards as her stocks of gold mounted. Pammachius undertook to organise regular instalments of money from the uncompleted sales to be forwarded to her for her future building projects in Bethlehem.

To their regret, most of her slaves and staff had to be sold along with the estates, though Paula granted a few their freedom, among them Clea, her scheming, avaricious ways finally rewarded.

Marcella helped keep at bay the dozens of visitors who each day crowded the doors of Paula's villa, some to pay their respects and wish her well, but many — thought Marcella sourly — who hoped to benefit in one way or another from Paula's hurried departure.

***

Quite deliberately, Marcella said nothing about a visit she had had from Furia, sister of Blesilla's husband and wife to a son of Probus. Furia had whispered to Marcella a chilling story about Juliana, that troubled young woman of the Probus clan, who on her marriage nearly three years before had begun to suffer the strange delusion that she nurtured serpents in her womb, making her repulse her husband. The young cleric Aetius had so successfully exorcised Juliana and banished her serpent-demons that, within the year, she had given birth to a premature but fine and healthy son. Visitors remarked on his lovely green eyes, flecked with yellow, never seen before in the families of either parent.

Within weeks, Clea, now taken on by Juliana as nurse after her manumission by Paula, had with a word wrought havoc. Casually — or so it seemed — the woman remarked one evening to Juliana's husband that his son's eyes were the very same as the eyes of the exorcist Aetius. Clea said no more, but that night Juliana, again heavily pregnant, miscarried.

As her life ebbed away, Juliana, clinging desperately to the last vestiges of coherence, chose to reveal to her husband certain details of the exorcism which until then she had refused to acknowledge even to herself. During the rites of exorcism the fixed, intense gaze of Aetius had affected her in a way she'd never been affected before, transporting her far away from all the rules and responsibilities and customs which made up her world. She wasn't quite sure what had taken place, but while all her delusions had indeed been banished, she'd also found herself responding helplessly yet without hesitation to his wishes.

After her funeral, her husband had sought out Probus and the two men travelled north. Christian they may be, but to the proud old aristocrat Probus, family honour was an older code still.

A few nights later, Aetius was found brutally murdered in the grounds of the palace of the Bishop of Ravenna, one of the young man's known haunts. His head had been bashed in and he appeared to have been knifed, and had been left to die among the oleanders, encircled by rivulets of his own blood. The screams of the slave who had stumbled across him awoke all within a radius of a mile.

Marcella had paled as she listened to Furia's recital of the tragic events. She had vowed that neither Jerome nor Paula should ever know of them. Aetius was dead and she did not want even the shadow of that flawed young man to play any further role in the lives of Jerome or any of them.

***

Paula's last act before she left Rome was to visit the tombs of Blesilla and Toxotius out on the Via Appia. She stayed long, in silence, grasping at memories, denying a desertion. Those stone tombs, she told herself, did not hold souls; only God did. She prayed, looked at them one last time, and left. Her courage wavered then, and again when she gazed for the last time at the familiar old villa on the Aventine Hill which had been the setting for almost all her adult life, first as wife and then as mother.

Taking a deep breath, resolutely she turned her attention back to her preparations for her departure and the journey ahead. She gathered together the loyal Eustochium, a few chosen women and her slaves, her portable wealth and her provisions. Finally, all was ready.

Her children, her kin, and the ladies of her class, sheparded by Marcella, travelled with her as far as Portus. As long as she lived, she would never forget those hours before she boarded the ship — a far smaller vessel than that which had taken Jerome away — that would transport her south. The fond embraces, the pleas, the promises — and, above all, little Toxotius's outstretched arms as he cried, 'Mamma, don't leave!' and the tears which the onlookers could not hold back, and nor could she.

But the moment came at last when she stood on deck, tasted the chilling reality of the voyage ahead, heard the raucous voices of the porters and deckhands, smelled the salt air and watched the shifting light on the sea.

The rowers took their places and the vessel moved out into the open sea. Paula watched as the strip of water between her and those left on shore inexorably widened. Holy Mother of God, she thought, can I really do this? She pressed Eustochium close at that grimmest of moments, watching the figures on shore become smaller and smaller, until her little son shrank to a mere dot, and all that was left of the land was a blurred line before it too disappeared.

***

Once the letters began arriving — months later — the ladies left behind in Rome travelled too, vicariously. Paula's letters came from Cyprus, from Antioch, from Jerusalem, then later from Bethlehem, Jericho and Nazareth. She seemed to be forever on the move, looking down on the site of the desolation of Sodom and Gomorrah, visiting the shores of Lake Tiberias where Jesus miraculously fed the thousands, spending time with the monks in the desert of Nitria, the very cradle of monasticism in the Nile Valley where, as Jerome wrote, she had wanted to stay, forgetting sometimes that she was a woman amongst men.

Some letters arrived quickly, others took many months, but all contained her reflections blended with Jerome's vivid descriptions, ringing with the delight of the travellers.

Then one day Marcella opened a letter from Jerome, and read: 'This village has real charm. Nestled in a hill, with the silence of the countryside around, still but for the cries of the peasants and the chanting of the psalms in the Empress Helena's Church of the Nativity ...'

And there, in Bethlehem, in the burning summer of 386 AD, they settled and stayed for the rest of their lives.

HISTORICAL POSTSCRIPT

With her wealth, Paula built two monasteries in Bethlehem, one situated next to the Church of the Nativity for women, which she would run, and one close by for men of which Jerome would be in charge. She also built a hospice for pilgrims – in a nod to those who shared the plight of Mary and Joseph when they arrived in Bethlehem and found no accommodation.

Paula supervised her women strictly. She housed them separately according to rank, lest the senatorial ladies be tempted to treat those of lowly status as their servants. They worshipped together and daily work was shared by all. Paula and Eustochium, 'shabbily and sombrely clad' as Jerome put it, took their turn in 'trimming lamps, lighting fires and sweeping floors'. Infinitely compassionate if any of her brood fell sick, Paula also displayed toughness when necessary, dealing swiftly with any stealing, arguing or show of pride. Unhappy the woman ever suspected by Paula of sexual leanings; redoubled fasting was Paula's prescription. As the reputation of both monasteries grew, so did their numbers, and towards the end of her life Paula's monastery boasted some fifty nuns.

Meanwhile, Jerome's fervour continued undiminished and, though loath to accept any formal title, he became in effect the local Christian leader, preaching in Jerusalem as well as Bethlehem, retaining his links with Rome without being shackled to its administration and falling prey to its politicking. As spiritual guide to Paula and her nuns as well as the wider community, he finally found the freedom to live the ascetic ideal to which he had long aspired, as well as devoting himself – with Paula's financial and intellectual assistance – to his literary endeavours.

The hours were too few for the vast outpouring from his masterly pen of translations of Greek theologians, satires, treatises, his great series of commentaries and, above all, his creation of a definitive translation of the Bible in Latin—the Vulgate—about which he remained passionate and which he eventually completed which, as his first patron Damasus had shrewdly anticipated, helped consolidate Christianity as the established religion in Western Europe. And to the end he urged, in a spate of letters of advice to virgins, that they should ever be on the watch for the foe shut up within them, that dark beast of the forest—sex.

True to form, Jerome's ardent faith and moral fearlessness unfailingly generated controversy that was the stuff of his life. As a gambler cannot resist the dice, so he could never stand aside from disputed interpretations of Scripture and faith. He savagely inveighed against those whose views he deemed heretical, notable amongst them Pelagius, the British monk who spread his dangerous doctrine of free will, and Origen, from whom he had learned so much in his earlier years but later condemned for his unorthodox views on the freedom of the soul.

For this reason, Jerome also pursued his one-time friend Rufinus, who remained loyal to Origen, with bitterest invective until the day Rufinus died. Ambrose, Bishop of Milan and leading light among Christians in Western Europe, was another of Jerome's targets—perhaps as much for his role in approving the clergy's expulsion of Jerome from Rome as for Ambrose's plagiarism of certain ancient Greek writers.

Through their many years in the Holy Land, Paula and Eustochium, in addition to their own duties, cared for Jerome, ensuring that he was free to work to the limit of his prodigious capacity. Moreover, Paula's sharp intelligence and aptitude for languages made her invaluable in assisting with Jerome's exegetical work.

Yet theirs were lives of hard work, teaching, prayer and mortification; lives sometimes turbulent, and increasingly dangerous. The Roman Empire, which had been buckling for some time, finally collapsed, and in 410 AD Rome was sacked by the Visigoths, led by Alaric, who brutalised and starved its citizens, forcing them to yield up their assets and gold to save their lives.

Shock waves reverberated throughout Western Europe, and beyond. 'In one city,' Jerome wrote, 'the whole world perished.' Marcella, brutally beaten up in her own residence, suffered it with courage, more concerned for a young pupil than for herself. Impressed by the composure of the eighty-five-year old lady, the soldiers granted her sanctuary in a nearby church, where she died shortly afterwards.

Refugees from the West poured into the Holy Land, many seeking shelter with Jerome in his monastery. 'Who would have believed,' marvelled Jerome, 'that the daughters of that mighty city would one day be wandering as servants and slaves on the shores of Egypt and Africa?'

Respite was moderately short-lived. The monasteries in Bethlehem, including Jerome's library, were set on fire and destroyed by bandit supporters of Pelagius. Monks and nuns were assaulted, a deacon killed, and Jerome and Eustochium forced to flee to a fortified tower.

Paula had died in January 404 AD at the age of fifty-six. Her death was a crushing blow to Jerome. For twenty years they had shared each other's lives; he was the person she most admired; she was his 'consolation'—words wrung out of him in the dazzling eulogy he wrote on her death. She had met his need to be close to a woman, and Paula herself found fulfilment in loving and serving Jerome, but doing so on her own terms.

Eustochium, who took Paula's place as head of the monastery, died fifteen years after her mother. Again it was a blow to Jerome. She had been his spiritual daughter, a virgin whose life embodied all the qualities he so passionately preached.

Jerome survived Eustochium by only a year. Disillusioned and exhausted, he died in September 420 AD, his prestige in the Church high, reflected in the immense body of writings he left behind, and in particular his translation of the Vulgate. He was buried in the place of his choice, a grotto beneath the Church of the Nativity, in Bethlehem, close to where Paula and Eustochium were buried. His remains were later transferred to Basilica of Santa Maria Maggiore in Rome, where they still lie today in the Crypt of the Nativity.

GLOSSARY OF NAMES

Ambrose, Saint (Aurelius Ambrosius), born *c.* 330 AD, in what is now Germany; died 397 AD, Mediolanum, Italy. One of the four original Doctors of the Church, Ambrose was Bishop of Milan from 374–397 AD. He was famous for his compassion to the poor and his defence of orthodox Christianity. A consummate orator, he was noted for adapting liturgy to the situation at hand. (When Saint Augustine arrived in Milan and commented that the Church did not fast on Saturday as in Rome, Ambrose responded that if he were in Rome he would fast on Saturday, but if in Milan he would not — which led to the saying, 'when in Rome, do as the Romans do'.)

His writings, put together in the form of notes by his many listeners, consisted of commentaries, theological and dogmatic works, and homilies. Within his theological works is the highly regarded *On the Faith* (written around 379 AD), a five-volume defence of the divinity of Christ against the claims of Arianism, and *On the Holy Spirit* (written around 381 AD), in effect a sequel in which he draws heavily on ancient Greek writers (incurring the wrath of Jerome) to define the Holy Spirit as being the spirit of God and equal with the Father and Son.

Patron saint of bee-keepers — the 'Honey-Tongued Doctor' in reference to his rhetorical skill (although legend also has it that a drop of honey was found on Ambrose's face as a baby), his feast day is 7 December.

Antonia Melania (or Melania the Elder), born *c.* 342 AD, Spain; died *c.* 409 AD, probably Jerusalem. Moving to Rome when young, she lost her husband, Valerius Maximus, and two children early. Leaving her remaining son, Valerius Publicola, in the care of a tutor, she sold her possessions and travelled to Egypt, where she spent time among the desert fathers before founding a monastery on the Mount of Olives in Jerusalem, the remains of which survive.

A well-known and scholarly figure in the ascetic movement of the day — although her firm defence of the controversial Origen tainted her later reputation — she was close to Paula and Jerome as well as other eminent thinkers. Her granddaughter, Melania the Younger, also adopted an ascetic life and accompanied her on her travels.

Antony, Saint, born *c.* 251 AD, Upper Egypt; died 356 AD, Mount Kolzim, Egypt. Also known as Antony the Great and Antony of the Desert, he is renowned for being one of the first ascetics, inspiring a whole movement of asceticism and firmly establishing the role of prayer in Christian life.

Much of what is known about Saint Antony comes from Athanasius's *Life of Antony* (written around 360 AD), famous in Christian literature, which describes his twenty-year period in solitude and prayer in the Libyan Desert. The temptation of St Antony is also a staple fare in Christian art, where the saint is variously depicted as fending off devils, phantoms, and other supernatural phenomena.

Patron saint of basket-weavers, swineherds and those with infectious diseases, his feast day is 17 January.

Apollinaris (the Younger), born *c.* 310 AD, Laodicea; died *c.* 390 AD, Laodicea. Bishop of Laodicea, in Syria, Apollinaris is noted for denying that Christ had a human, rational mind. In his impassioned defence of Christianity against Arianism — a movement which repudiated Christ's divinity — Apollinaris swung to the other extreme, stressing the deity of Christ. He argued that Christ had a human body and soul, but not a human mind — which in his view would have been inherently sinful.

Although esteemed by scholars such as Jerome for his classical learning and staunch defence of the Nicene faith, Apollinaris's views were pronounced anathema by Damasus I in Rome, and condemned as heretical by the Second Ecumenical Council in 381 AD.

Arius, born *c.* 250 AD, Libya; died 336 AD, Constantinople. Christian priest in Alexandria, whose teachings on the nature of the Trinity sparked one of the great theological conflicts of the fourth century. In brief, he argued that as Christ was created by God, there must have been a time when God existed but Christ did not, concluding that Christ was not fully divine but rather was subordinate to God.

Matters came to a head in the Second Ecumenical Council in 381

AD, where the 150 bishops issued a statement defining the equal divinity of each aspect of the Trinity — Father, Son and Holy Spirit — the orthodox stance held today. Arius was accused of heresy and excommunicated, although his legacy, in various forms, lingered on.

Athanasius, Saint, born *c*. 296 AD, Alexandria; died 373 AD, Alexandria. One of the four Doctors of the Church, and Bishop of Alexandria for many years. He was a distinguished theologian and defender of orthodox faith against Arianism, which denied Christ's divinity. He was exiled five times — including a six-year stint in the Egyptian desert — for his beliefs. After spending time in retreat with Saint Antony, he wrote his famous *Life of Antony* which inspired many to try to live the ascetic life.

The feast day of Saint Athanasius is 2 May.

Ausonius (Decimus Magnus), born *c*. 310 AD, Bordeaux; died 395 AD, Bordeaux. Roman poet and teacher of rhetoric. Although derivative, his poems illuminate many practices of the time, such as winemaking. As a tutor he was very popular; many of his students became famous, such as Emperor Gratian who made him Praetorian Prefect of Gaul and, in 379 AD, Consul.

His poems include *Mosella*, describing his journey down the Moselle River; *Ephemeris*, an account of daily life; and the infamous *Nuptial cento*, where he borrowed phrases from Virgil and rearranges them to apply them to a traditional wedding night. He wrote one poem to a slave girl, Bisulla, with whom he was rewarded the year he became Consul.

Blesilla, Saint, born *c*. 363 AD, Rome; died 384 AD, Rome. Eldest daughter of Paula and Toxotius, Blesilla was married when young to Furius but widowed within a year, after which she renounced her life of pleasure and, following in her mother's footsteps, adopted the ascetic life. Within months, she developed a fever and, despite the efforts of her family and friends to save her, died in agony.

The premature death of this young and beautiful woman prompted a public outcry against Jerome, whose rigorous practices of self-mortification, such as fasting, Blesilla was known to have embraced. In Jerome's much-quoted letter to Paula he deplores Blesilla's death while reproaching her mother for the extent of her grief.

The feast day of Saint Blesilla is 28 September.

Constantine (Flavius Valerius), born *c.* 272 AD, Naissus, in what is now Serbia; died 337 AD, Nicomedia. The first Roman Emperor to convert to Christianity, Constantine reigned from 306–337 AD and is considered the founder of the Eastern Roman Empire. Its capital, Byzantium – present-day Istanbul – was therefore renamed 'Constantinople'. Claiming to have been inspired by a vision of a shining cross with the words 'in this sign you will be victorious', Constantine defeated his rival Maxentius at the Battle of the Milvian Bridge in 312 AD and captured Rome.

As Emperor, he proclaimed the Edict of Milan in 313 AD, granting people religious freedom, which effectively ended the persecution of Christians and helped establish Christianity in the Roman Empire.

Damasus I, Saint, born *c.* 305 AD, Egitania, in what is now Portugal; died 384 AD, Rome. Bishop of Rome from 366 AD until his death, Damasus overcame early controversy in his papacy, when he was accused of murder and adultery, to commission – with the assistance of his secretary, Jerome – the translation of the Bible into the Latin Vulgate, or vernacular. This, together with his vigorous defence of the Church against heresy and schism, is considered his most significant accomplishment.

A capable administrator, he presided over the Council of Rome in 382 AD and issued a decree that listed definitively the 73 canonical books in the Old and New Testaments (46 and 27 respectively), settling years of wrangling over which books should make up the Bible. (This list, which included what he considered the divinely inspired deuterocanonical books, remains the basis of Catholic and Eastern Orthodox Bibles.)

It was during Damasus's pontificate that the supremacy of Rome as seat of the Holy See was established over competing claims from Eastern churches. Christianity became fashionable under Damasus, who was not averse to targeting women so that they in turn would convert their husbands – a strategy which, thanks in part to his personal charisma, achieved some success along with accusations of adultery. Damasus also encouraged the veneration of Christian martyrs, restoring their catacombs and crypts, and preserving their relics.

Patron saint of archaeologists on account of his dedication to works of restoration, his feast day is 11 December.

Didymus (or Didymus the Blind), born *c.* 313 AD, Alexandria; died *c.* 398 AD, Alexandria. Distinguished orthodox theologian who, although blind from childhood, possessed a rare memory and intelligence. Versed in dialectics as well as geometry, his knowledge of the Scriptures was unparalleled in his day, and he was highly esteemed for his textual analyses, insights and allegorical interpretations.

A follower of Origen, he was head of the celebrated Catechetical School of Alexandria where he opposed Arianism. He was a prolific writer, his works including *On the Holy Spirit* (translated into Latin by Jerome), *On the Trinity*, and many Biblical commentaries of which only fragments survive. Jerome considered him his 'master', and referred to him as 'Didymus the Seer'.

Eusebius, born *c.* 265 AD, Caesarea, Palestine; died *c.* 339 AD. Bishop of Caesarea and noted historian, referred to as the father of Church history. One of the most respected of the early Christian scholars, he was part of the school of Pamphilus, founder of Caesarea's famous library and follower of Origen. Most of what we know of Eusebius comes from his considerable literary output, of which a large portion survives. His major works include *Ecclesiastical History* (a ten-volume history of the Church), *On the Life of Pamphilus*, *Chronicle*, and *On the Martyrs*.

Eusebius was also responsible for compiling a historical list of Roman bishops. Despite some controversial claims (listing Linus rather than Peter as first Bishop of Rome); repetition (counting the third pope twice under the names Anacletus and Cletus); and omissions (notably John XX), the list was highly influential, helping to form the Liberian Catalogue, which in turn became the basis of the definitive *Liber Pontificalis*.

Eustochium, Saint, born *c.* 370 AD, Rome; died 419 AD, Bethlehem. Third and much-loved daughter of Paula and Toxotius, Eustochium displayed signs of piety early on. Resisting efforts to be married off to economic advantage, she made a vow of perpetual virginity (about 383 AD, which prompted Jerome's celebrated letter *On the Care of Virginity*, in which he praised her as a 'paragon of virgins'.

In 385 AD she accompanied her mother to Bethlehem where, under the direction of Jerome, they established three monasteries of which Eustochium became abbess after her mother's death (no easy task as their finances were much depleted). A fluent speaker of Latin and Greek, Eustochium also read Hebrew, and assisted Jerome in his translation of the Bible as well as reading and writing for him when his eyesight failed. Jerome's many letters to her are testimony both to her intelligence and to her strength of character.

The feast day of Saint Eustochium is 28 September.

Gregory, Saint (or Gregory of Nazianzus), born *c.* 325 AD, Cappadocia, Turkey; died *c.* 389 AD, Cappadocia. Bishop of Constantinople and friend of Saint Basil, Gregory was one of the greatest theologians of his day, and a champion of orthodox Christianity against the threat of Arianism. He is particularly renowned for his contribution to the doctrine of the Trinity. A skilled orator, his sermons were hugely popular, and his literary epistles are among the finest literary achievements of the day.

The feast day of Saint Gregory is 2 January.

Helvidius (full name and dates unknown). Primarily known as the author who disputed the perpetual virginity of Mary, prompting (in around 383 AD) Jerome's treatise *The Perpetual Virginity of Blessed Mary* in which Jerome bolstered his defence of virginity, placing it above marriage. Helvidius cited references in the Gospels to brothers and sisters of Jesus to claim that, following Jesus's miraculous conception, Mary and Joseph had more children; Jerome levelled by arguing that any later children were cousins, or offspring of Joseph by a former marriage.

Hymetius (Julius Festus), dates uncertain. Brother of Toxotius, husband to Praetextata, and uncle to Eustochium. Proconsul of the Roman province of Africa, Hymetius was exiled by the Emperor Valentinian after having used wheat destined for Rome to relieve the famine in Africa of 368 AD (despite having replaced the wheat and returned a profit to the Emperor).

Like Toxotius, Hymetius was a pagan. Jerome recounts how Hymetius, as guardian of Paula's children, together with his wife Praetextata, tried to block Paula from dedicating her daughter Eustochium as a virgin. He died soon afterwards, which Jerome considered divine punishment.

Jerome (Eusebius Sophronius Hieronymus), born *c.* 347 AD Stridon, Dalmatia, in what is now Croatia; died 420 AD, Bethlehem. One of the four original Doctors of the Church, Jerome was a priest and theologian as well as scholar and historian. A dream of being chastised by God for lacking Christian values was credited with giving him new direction and prompting a five-year stint among the hermits in the desert of Chalcis, Syria. While doing penance, he added Hebrew to his knowledge of Latin and Greek—linguistic skills seized upon later by Damasus when commissioning him in Rome in 382 AD to translate the Bible from Greek into Latin.

This creation of a single, authoritative Latin Bible—known as the Vulgate—remains Jerome's main claim to fame, together with his prodigious literary output. As secretary to Damasus, he was assisted by a circle of highly educated, aristocratic women, including Marcella and Paula, who shared his monasticism. A strong-willed and outspoken man, his refusal to court popularity coupled with his acerbic criticism of the Roman lifestyle won him the respect of some while alienating others. Hostility to Jerome was exacerbated when Paula's daughter Blesilla died after embracing his ascetic practices. Following the death of Damasus, he was put on trial by the Roman clergy for his alleged relationship with Paula and, despite a spirited self-defence, was forced to leave Rome in 385 AD, followed by Paula and Eustochium.

Jerome spent his remaining years travelling, ultimately settling in Bethlehem where, with Paula's financial backing, he devoted himself to his writing, sealing his reputation for scholarly brilliance in his commentaries to the Scriptures, his dialogue against the Pelagians, and his treatises against Origenism. Buried in Bethlehem, his remains were later transferred to the Basilica of Santa Maria Maggiore, in Rome.

Patron saint of librarians and translators on account of his extraordinary literary achievements, his feast day is 30 September.

Livy (Titus Livius), born *c.* 59 BC, Patavium, northern Italy; died *c.* 17 AD, Patavium. Roman historian noted for his monumental one hundred and forty-two-book series (of which thirty-five survive) on the history of Rome. Well educated, Livy was wealthy enough to indulge his love of writing. Rich in detail and rhetorical flourish, his books remain—despite their patriotism and inaccuracies—a classic source of information on Ancient Rome.

Marcella, Saint, born *c.* 325 AD, Rome; died *c.* 410 AD, Rome. Born into a wealthy family, Marcella married an aristocrat, but he died seven months later. Refusing an offer of marriage from the Consul Cerealis, the young widow decided to model herself on the ascetics of the East about whom she had heard as a child from the Patriarch of Constantinople during his vists to her home.

Devoting herself to a life of prayer and poverty, Marcella abstained from wine and meat, exchanged her fine clothing for simple garments, gave up elaborate hairstyles and make-up and ensured that she never spoke with a man alone. Inspiring other aristocratic women – including Paula, Asella and Lea – to live a life of piety, she transformed her magnificent home in the Aventine Hill into a Christian community for the poor and a centre for spiritual study and prayer.

Possessed of a formidable intellect, Marcella guided her ladies in the study of the Scriptures. She mastered Greek and Hebrew, and her academic rigour won the respect of Jerome, whom she assisted with his translation of the Bible into Latin. Referring to her as 'the glory of Roman ladies', he often sought her opinions and corresponded at length with her. Refusing to be intimidated by his irascible nature, she was one of the few who could calm him when he threatened to lose his temper.

Marcella was still alive when Rome was sacked by the Visigoths in 410 AD and tortured for refusing to give up what remained of her wealth, and died soon afterwards.

The feast day of Saint Marcella is 31 January.

Novatian, born *c.* 200 AD, Rome; died 258 AD, Rome. Roman priest, theologian and antipope who opposed the re-admittance into the Church of those who had committed mortal sins, and especially those who had, during persecution, renounced their faith (known as *lapsi*). His uncompromising stance inspired the Novationist movement which spread rapidly in reaction to the perceived laxity of the Roman Church.

Although the sect was labelled heretical by Rome for its denial of the Church's power to grant absolution, and its leader excommunicated, it continued to flourish for several centuries, thanks in part to Novatian's orthodoxy in all other respects, and in part to his eloquence and learning. The first Western Christian theologian to write in Latin, his most influential work was *On the Trinity*, in which he defends the doctrine of the trinity against contemporary heresies.

Origen (Adamantius), born *c.* 185 AD, Alexandria; died Tyre, Lebanon, *c.* 254 AD. The most distinguished theologian of the early Church, Origen wove some of the traditions of Greek philosophy into a systematic and comprehensive interpretation of Christianity – a shrewd approach which won him an immense following. His homilies on Jeremiah, Ezekiel and Isaiah were translated into Latin by Jerome.

Some hypotheses attributed to Origen were, however, considered controversial – namely, his references to the pre-existence and transmigration of souls; his suggestion that ultimately everyone, Satan included, may be reconciled with God (*apokatastasis*, or universal reconciliation); and his view that the Son of God was subordinate to God the Father.

Tortured during the persecution of Christians under the Emperor Decius, he died prematurely, leaving behind a rich body of work. Foremost was his treatise on Christian neoplatonism, *On First Principles*, in which he sets out his main theories, including – and here he departed from the fatalism that characterised so many teachings of his day – the freedom of the soul and the importance of free will.

Pammachius, Saint, born *c.* 347 AD, Rome; died *c.* 409 AD, Rome. Roman senator and friend of Jerome, he married Paula's daughter Paolina. After her death, he devoted the rest of his life to works of charity. Together with Saint Fabiola, he built the first hospice in Rome, tending the sick and serving them personally. A gentle man, he tried to moderate Jerome's language when embroiled in one of his many controversies (as, for example, when Rufinus dared suggest that Jerome admired his translation of Origen).

Excavations of Pammachius's original home on the Coelian Hill – a popular area among wealthy Christians – revealed the title church or 'house-church' that he had built there, under which were discovered bodies believed to be those of the saints John and Paul, secretly executed in 362 AD by the Emperor Julian the Apostate in what was then their own home for refusing to renounce their Christian beliefs. The cult of the 'soldier saints' grew as ever more miracles were reported through their intercession. Today, the site is occupied by the Passionist Church of Saints John and Paul, in which there is a painting of Pammachius.

The feast day of Saint Pammachius is 30 August.

Paolina, born in Rome, date uncertain; died *c.* 395 AD, Rome. Second daughter of Paula and Toxotius, Paolina married the wealthy senator and friend of Jerome, Pammachius. Little is known about her, although Jerome speaks highly of her compassion for the underprivileged. Her life was clearly not devoid of suffering: her children were stillborn, and she herself died in childbirth while still young, prompting her husband to throw a banquet for the poor of the city in her honour.

Paul, Saint (or Paul the Apostle or Saul of Tarsus), born *c.* 5 BC, Tarsus, Cilicia, southern Turkey; died *c.* 67 AD, Rome. Born into a family of tentmakers and raised in Jerusalem among the Pharisees, as a young man Saul—as he was known—initially opposed Christianity and persecuted the disciples of Jesus. Following his famous conversion on the road to Damascus, Paul (as he was henceforth known) went on to become one of the most influential of the early Christians.

He travelled widely, covering Antioch, Jerusalem and Ephesus as well as Rome, and was particularly instrumental in forming communities across the Mediterranean. A large portion of the writings in the New Testament—fourteen Epistles—is attributed to him. According to tradition, Paul was beheaded in Rome during the Emperor Nero's reign, after spending two years under house arrest. Excavation of the sarcophagus inscribed with Paul's name at the Basilica of St Paul Outside the Walls in Rome suggest that the tomb is Paul's.

Paul is frequently depicted as seeing a vision of the resurrected Jesus while travelling to Damascus, or being temporarily blinded and having his sight restored by Ananias of Damascus—an experience which gave rise to the phrase 'the road to Damascus', meaning a turning point or defining moment.

Patron saint of authors, publishers and writers on account of his huge contribution to the New Testament, his feast day is celebrated together with that of Saint Peter on 29 June.

Paula, Saint (or St Paula of Rome), born 347 AD, Rome; died 404 AD, Bethlehem. Born into an illustrious Roman family descended from the Scipios and Gracchi on her father's side and from the kings of Sparta on her mother's, Paula married the nobleman Toxotius when she was fifteen. They had five children (Blesilla, Paolina, Eustochium, Rufina and Toxotius), enjoyed a lively social life, and were widely regarded as an exemplary family. Widowed unexpectedly at thirty-two, Paula sought increasing refuge in her religion and, inspired by the devout Marcella and her group of women, she gradually renounced her former luxuries and privileges in favour of a semi-monastic life. It was at this time that she began making the first of her many donations to the poor.

Paula's meeting with Jerome in 382 AD marked the beginning of a rich intellectual and spiritual association only temporarily rocked by her grief over the death of her daughter Blesilla, for which Jerome chided as well as consoled her. Emerging from her mourning with her faith strengthened, she continued assisting him with his translation of the Bible into Latin and editing his manuscripts.

In 385 AD, accompanied by her daughter Eustochium, Paula travelled to the Holy Land and settled in Bethlehem where, with the benefit of Jerome's spiritual guidance and her own sizeable fortune, she established two monasteries and a hospice. In charge of one of the monasteries, Paula worked tirelessly for the poor, leading her nuns in an ascetic life of prayer, penance and work. It was Paula who was responsible for the first recorded mention of the habit, introduced to ensure the poverty and simplicity of the sisters' clothing. In her eulogy, Jerome paid lavish tribute to her rigorous faith and boundless generosity. Paula was buried in the Church of the Nativity, close to where Jerome's body would later be laid to rest.

Patron saint of widows, her feast day is 26 January.

Pelagius, born c. 354 AD; died c. 420 AD. A British ascetic who moved to Rome in 380 AD and exploited his rhetorical powers to deny the doctrine of original sin and emphasise the role of free will. Arguing that humans are inherently good, he claimed that they could attain salvation through free will alone; that is, without divine intervention. This brought him into conflict with the Church, and in particular with Jerome, who declared him a heretic. Yet the effects of the 'Pelagian heresy' lingered on after he had fled Rome and even after his death, believed to be in Egypt where, with his followers, he had sought refuge.

Peter, Saint (or Simon Peter), born c. 1 BC, Bethsaida; died c. 64 AD, Rome. Originally a fisherman, he and his brother Andrew were called by Jesus to be 'fishers of men'. Peter is frequently depicted holding keys—a reference to Jesus's words to Peter: 'I will give you the keys of the Kingdom of Heaven'.

The first of the twelve apostles ordained by Jesus, Peter features more prominently than other disciple in the New Testament and, particularly in his advice on lifestyle, did much to shape early Christianity. He is venerated in many churches and considered by the Catholic Church to be the first pope. He was ultimately crucified by the Emperor Nero, allegedly upside down because he did not consider himself worthy to die in the same way as Jesus. His remains are in St Peter's Basilica in Rome.

Patron saint of popes, fishermen, net makers, cobblers and bridge builders among others, his feast day is celebrated together with that of Saint Paul on 29 June.

Petronius Probus (Sextus Claudius), born *c.* 328 AD, Verona; died *c.* 390 AD, Rome. Head of the noble Anicii family, he wielded immense power and amassed huge personal wealth. He was married to Anicia Faltonia Proba, by whom he had three sons and a daughter. He was Proconsul of Africa (358 AD) and Praetorian Prefect of Italy and Africa three times (368–375, 383–384, and 387 AD), and successfully defended Sirmium — a key town in the Roman Empire in what is now Serbia — against the barbarians. He also served under Emperor Valentian II, and worked alongside Emperor Gratian. His magnificent estates scattered throughout the Roman Empire drew admiration, despite the methods by which he acquired them and his reputation for being by turns obsequious and repressive.

Baptised a Christian shortly before his death, he is buried close to St Peter's, Rome.

Praetextata, born *c.* 340 AD, Rome; died *c.* 384 AD, Rome. Wife of Toxotius's brother Hymetius, she attempted, at her husband's bidding, to foil Paula's plans to dedicate her daughter Eustochium as a virgin. Dressing her niece up in fine clothing, making up her face and waving her hair, she presented her to society as an attractive, marriageable young woman with an eye to making her future matriarch of the family.

She was much affected by a dream she subsequently had in which an angel condemned her to die for putting her husband's demands above those of Christ for daring to touch the head of a virgin consecrated to God with her sacrilegious hand, doomed to wither. Interestingly, Praetextata's hand did become deformed, and she lost her family and died, as predicted.

Praetextatus (Vettius Agorius), born *c.* 315 AD, Rome; died 384 AD, Rome. Much in demand for his skills as an orator, the aristocratic Praetextatus was a Roman senator and Praetorian Prefect. One of the last of the well-known pagans, he restored many of the damaged statues in the Roman Forum, one of the most famous pagan sites.

His speeches are, unfortunately, mostly lost; much of what we know about him comes from surviving letters to and from his friend Symmachus, which remain one of the best sources on the pagan beliefs and practices of late antiquity. According to Jerome, when referring to the opulent lifestyle enjoyed by Damasus, Praetextatus jested, 'Make me Bishop of Rome and I will become a Christian!'

Propertius (Sextus), born *c.* 50 BC, Assisi; died *c.* 15 BC, Assisi. Roman poet whose elegiac couplets, although laden with mythological references, are highly imaginative and reveal a surprisingly modern psychological depth. Described by Ezra Pound (in his 'Homage to Sextus Propertius', 1919) as embodying 'the dance of the intellect among words', they were highly fashionable among the Roman nobility of the day. Propertius has also been credited with inspiring the modern ideal of romantic love.

Rufinus of Aquileia, born *c.* 345 AD, Concordia, in what is now northern Italy; died *c.* 410 AD, Sicily. A scholar held in high esteem for his translations into Latin of Greek theological writings, in particular Origen. His refusal to renounce Origen's more controversial theories—such as his questioning of the doctrine of eternal damnation—led to Rufinus's later condemnation by Jerome. He spent many years in Jerusalem, drawing to him a circle of distinguished intellectuals, and helping his friend and patron, Melania the Elder, found her monastery on the Mount of Olives.

Sallust (Gaius Sallustius Crispus), born 86 AD, Amiternum, central Italy; died *c.* 35 AD, Rome. Roman historian and statesman, whose *Conspiracy of Catiline* and *Jugurthine War* are the earliest known Roman historical monographs. Together with his *Histories*, of which fragments survive, these works exemplify the lively and epigrammatic depiction of historical facts and figures for which he was much admired.

Born into a provincial family, Sallust steadfastly opposed the old Roman aristocracy and supported Julius Caesar. As Proconsul of the Numidian territory in Africa, and protected by his patron Caesar, he amassed a fortune for himself through extortion, which he later used to create the famous Gardens of Sallust in Rome, and which later still became a resort favoured by Emperors.

Siricius, Saint, born *c.* 334 AD, Rome; died 399 AD, Rome. Successor to Damasus I, he was Bishop of Rome from 384 AD until his death. A strong defender of papal authority, he is remembered for his rigorous discipline and focus on the sacraments, as well as being the first to use the title 'pope' to denote the Bishop of Rome. In his famous decretal of 386 AD to Bishop Himerius of Tarragona, he insisted on the celibacy of priests—the first decree on the matter which has applied ever since. His tomb in the catacombs of St Priscilla became a popular pilgrim destination.

The feast day of Saint Siricius is 26 November.

Tertullian (Quintus Septimius Florens), born *c.* 160 AD, Carthage; died *c.* 225 AD, Carthage. A trained lawyer, he converted to Christianity and became one of the greatest of the early Christian apologists. Referred to as 'the father of Latin Christianity', he was responsible for creating the bulk of Latin Christian literature, and the first to use the term 'Trinity'. His most notable works were *To the Nations* and *Apologeticus*, both published in 197 AD.

Toxotius (Julius), baptised 385 AD, Rome; died *c.* 403 AD. The only son of Paula and her husband Toxotius, he was a ward of the Praetor for much of his childhood. It is recounted that, after her husband's death, when Paula was about to sail for the Holy Land, little Toxotius reached out to her from the shore, crying and begging her in vain to stay, to the consternation of all present.

Toxotius later married Laeta, the Christian daughter of the pagan priest, Albinus, in 389 AD. Their daughter, Paula the Younger, followed her grandmother to the Holy Land, where she lived with her aunt Eustochium and reputedly closed the eyes of Saint Jerome.

Toxotius (Julius Festus), born *c.* 323 AD, Rome; died *c.* 379 AD, Rome. The husband of Paula, Toxotius was a Roman nobleman and senator, said to trace his lineage back to Julius Caesar. They were married in 362 AD, and had five children (Blesilla, Paolina, Eustochium, Rufina and Toxotius). Although he adhered to the worship of the gods of ancient Rome, Toxotius gave his wife the freedom to practise her own religion and bring up their children as Christians.

Virgil (or Publius Vergilius Maro), born 70 BC, near Mantua, northern Italy; died 19 BC, Brindisi, southern Italy. Considered one of the finest Roman poets alongside Horace and Ovid, Virgil had a huge impact on Western literature.

His *Aeneid*, an epic poem in twelve books recounting Aeneas's journey from Troy to Italy and the founding of Rome, was a lasting testament to the glory of the Roman Empire and a must-have textbook for every educated Roman. It was embraced with equal fervour later by Christians too, many of whom conferred on Virgil the status of prophet (significantly, Dante, in his *Divine Comedy,* made Virgil his guide through Hell and Purgatory, although not through Paradise).

BIBLIOGRAPHY

Cain, A and Lössl, J (eds) 2009, *Jerome of Stridon: His Life, Writings and Legacy*, Ashgate Publishing Ltd, Farnham, UK.

Carcopino, Jerome 1956, trans. EO Lorimer, *Daily Life in Ancient Rome: The People and the City at the Height of the Empire*, Pelican Books, Harmondsworth (first published 1939).

Casson, L 1974, *Travel in the Ancient World*, Allen & Unwin, London.

Fox, RL 2006 (reissue), *Pagans and Christians in the Mediterranean World from the Second Century AD to the Conversion of Constantine*, Penguin, London (first published 1986).

Gibbon, E, 1999, ed. B Radice, *The History of the Decline and Fall of the Roman Empire*, Strahan & Cadell, London (first published 1776-8).

Jones, AHM 1964, *The Later Roman Empire*, vols I and II (284-602), Basil Blackwell Ltd, London.

Kelly, JND 1968, *Early Christian Doctrines*, 5th edn rev., A & C Black, London (first published 1958).

Kelly, JND 1975, *Jerome: His Life, Writings, and Controversies*, Gerald Duckworth & Co. Ltd, London.

Liebeschuetz, JHWG 1979, *Continuity and Change in Roman Religion*, Oxford University Press, Oxford.

Rawson, B (ed.) 1986, *The Family in Ancient Rome: New Perspectives*, Croom Helm Ltd, London & Sydney.

The Loeb Classical Library, *Select Letters of St Jerome*, trans. FA Wright, Harvard University Press & William Heinemann Ltd, London.

The Society for the Promotion of Roman Studies, *The Journal of Roman Studies*, Cambridge University Press, London.

Wiedemann, T 1989, *Adults and Children in the Roman Empire*, Routledge, London.

Wiseman, TP 1985, *Catullus and His World: A Reappraisal*, Cambridge University Press, Cambridge.

Acknowledgments

The following people are warmly acknowledged: JH Wolf G Liebeschuetz, Emeritus Professor at the Faculty of Arts, Nottingham University, UK for his expert advice on the nature of early Christian beliefs and paganism during the early drafts of the manuscript; Fred Mench, Professor of English and Latin at Middle Tennessee State University for his thorough reading of the manuscript and valuable advice on the precise nature of certain customs and their representation to the modern reader; Demetrios J Constantelos, Emeritus Professor of History and Religious Studies at Stockton University, New Jersey for his careful assessment of the manuscript from the historical and theological points of view; and Elizabeth Teller for her inspired teaching of Latin at City Lit, London.

Thanks are also due to Denise O'Hagan for her editorial support; Helen Gamble, Mary Keep, Jan Doolan and Jenny Bailey for their insightful comments; Fiona Sim for her careful proofreading of the final text; Bernard Devaux for creating the map of the city of Ancient Rome with which Jerome would have been familiar; Marlene Cases Zorn for her design support; and Xinling Jiang for her typesetting skills.

Printed in Australia
AUOC02n0811261015
271216AU00001B/1/P